"That's a Galactic Prime Security portal, Mark IV," Kith told the Terrans. "You'll not easily pry that open."

"I don't intend to try," Retief replied. "You'll open it for us."

"To have taken leave of your rudimentary Terry senses!" Kith hissed. "Never to admit vile interlopers to snoop in a sacred Groacian military reservation!"

"To change your mind in a hurry, I'll bet," Retief predicted, "when I start tying those wiggly oculars of yours in knots. Which ones shall I begin with?" So saying, he gripped two of the Groaci's wildly dodging eye-stalks and laid one across the other. "On the other hand, I might just pluck them out by the roots," he mused aloud.

"Retief! You wouldn't!" Kith and Magnan wailed in unison.

"I'd rather not," Retief conceded, "but I'd do it rather than let you Groaci steal an entire Galaxy unopposed."

KEITH LAUMER
RETIEF IN THE RUINS

BAEN BOOKS

RETIEF IN THE RUINS

Copyright © 1986 by Keith Laumer

A Baen Books Original

Baen Publishing Enterprises
260 Fifth Avenue
New York, N.Y. 10001

First printing, November 1986

ISBN: 0-671-65599-X

Cover art by Wayne Barlowe

Printed in the United States of America

Distributed by
SIMON & SCHUSTER
1230 Avenue of the Americas
New York, N.Y. 10020

CONTENTS

Retief in the Ruins

1

"Look at them!" Ambassador Gropedark ordered, stepping back from the wide double windows which commanded, through broken panes, a view of the Embassy compound, now densely packed with a yelling, jostling mob of enraged locals—tall, chitinous, green-hued fellows shaking agricultural implements and other sharp-edged tools at the Terran arms adorning the ancient facade before them. Gropedark shied as another missile came sailing through to impact on the deep-pile Azusian carpet among its fellows, scattering the huddle of Terran diplomats who had edged forward in response to the Chief of Mission's exhortation.

"They've already ruined the tourist trade," Gropedark grumped, "the mainstay of the Popurean economy." He broke off and ducked as yet another missile shattered the remaining glass.

"Geeze, another priceless relic rudely throwed at us like it was just another pebble!" Percy Ebbtide, the Cultural Attaché, mourned aloud as he retrieved the object, a fragment of deeply-carved purple stone.

"'Thrown,' Percy," the Ambassador corrected his subordinate's grammar.

"I don't see what the throne has got to do with this here rock," Percy returned defensively. "What I bet it is, it's a hunk of the cornice of the Embassy here, which I bet any muzeem in the Arm

3

would give a purty to have it in a glass case setting on a doily."

" 'Sitting,' Percy," Gropedark said wearily.

"I can't help it if I only got my Ph of D from a small cow-college on Moosejaw," Percy pointed out. "Name like Percy, I never had no time to study, fellers playing jokes on me and all. Oughta get special consideration, jest for sticking out grad school."

"I'm aware, Percy," the Ambassador Extraordinary and Minister Plenipotentiary conceded grandly, "that your expertise lies in the area of archeology and art history rather than in the realm of grammar and syntax."

"Sin tax?" Percy queried. "Never hearn tell they got a tax on *that*. Wonder how they keep track."

"Syntax, Percy, is a term employed in reference to the manner of arranging one's phonemes so as to form intelligible utterances."

"I flunked that part," Percy acknowledged. "All about diagramming sentences and such as that. But I was saying about this year art treasure and all—"

"It is precisely the art treasures of ancient Popu-Ri to the protection of which this Mission was dispatched here to see!" Gropedark snapped. "Meanwhile the place is disintegrating about our very ears!"

"You lost me on that one, Mr. Ambassador," Percy mourned.

"As for disintegration," Smedly Shortfall, of the Econ Section, spoke up, "my researches indicate that the town was built in what was once an area of peripheral tectonic activity, related to the underthrusting coastline some fifty miles to the east. In ancient times, spouts of sand issued from surface faults at various nodal points, building up circular mounds of debris, while at the same time an extensive system of subterranean caverns was formed as magma drained away in certain of the crustal readjustments. Doubtless the primitive forbears of the present population employed these handy caverns as shelter against the elements, in time elaborating their early village into a great city, seat of an interplanetary empire. Then their civilization collapsed, and now the decadent remnant of this once-great race lives on the falling ruins of its past glories."

"Sure, Smed," someone jeered. "Everybody knows that. It was a big Special on Art Fingerfink's show last year. And I heard that when the natives found this big mess—holes with sand and rock laying around 'em—they started to police the area and throw all the ejecta back in and pretty soon that turned into a like religious rite where they were 'sacrificing' stones and such to some earthquake god, and now they call it the Sacred Well— just an old volcanic vent, you understand?—and charge tourists to let 'em drop stuff down the hole for good luck, same time they dig down and excavate stuff thrown in there hundreds 'o years ago, and they sell *that* to the tourists. Get 'em coming and going. Only now, like Mr. Ambassador said, these riots has the place all stirred up, and the cruise ships don't come anymore. Tough E-pores."

"And another thing!" Gropedark barked. "It is what *I* was saying about that that is of importance, specifically the curious activity here on this out-of-the-trade-lanes world of an inordinate number of our Groacian colleagues, for whose presence there appears to be no readily apparent rationale."

"Art treasures," Percy supplied. "The sneaky little five-eyed sticky-fingers are tryna swipe the antiquities and all."

"Swipe, Percy?" his chief challenged. "On what basis do you make this seemingly baseless charge?

Only this morning I was having a friendly chat via tight screen with my esteemed colleague Ambassador Smoosh, and he assured me—"

"That knob-kneed little sapsucker will assure you of anything he thinks will get you off his back, Mr. Ambassador," the hard-pressed Cultural Officer interrupted.

"Let's not forget, Mr. Ambassador," Colonel Trenchfoot spoke up. "I am in possession of a firm rumor to the effect that the Groaci are amassing an attack force in this very subsector. Be quite a coop if we spotted it right here on Popu-Ri, eh, sir?"

"'Coo', Jim," the Ambassador corrected automatically. "And one can hardly evoke a hostile war fleet simply by wishing for it, Colonel," His Excellency reminded his Military Attaché wearily. "I remarked only that I have the impression of seeing more Groaci personnel in the bazaar and on the streets than can be readily explained by their modest cultural team which was authorized on-planet solely to carry out an inventory of recoverable antiquities. I imputed no fell motives to the Groaci."

"I ain't going to tell, even if you said them mothers was robbing the place blind," Percy reassured his chief.

"'Those mothers,'" Gropedark corrected automatically.

"How's come we're worrying about somebody swiping a bunch of junk?" young Marvin Lacklustre queried, "With an armed mob out there yelling for our heads?"

"The delegation of the local citizenry is hardly 'yelling for our heads', as you so inelegantly put it, Marvin," the Chief of Mission set the record straight. "I should imagine that they are in fact calling on me for a statement. Don't understand their barbarous dialect, of course: only caught something about 'the ruins', doubtless an appeal to me to confirm that their precious ancient capital will be protected against any attempted vandalism, and in due course restored to its original splendor."

"Percy," Colonel Trenchfoot addressed the Attaché in a crafty tone, "if the Groaci are looting the place, where's all the loot going? My watch-dogs at the port haven't cleared any tramp freight-ers off-planet, Groaci or otherwise."

"Beats the metabolic residues outa me," Percy acknowledged. At the window, the colonel was peering out, ready to dodge the next accurately thrown missile.

"Hey!" he blurted. "If it ain't Captain Kith of Groaci Central Intelligence, you can put me on pots and pans for the next month! And it's an open secret that 'Assistant Military Attaché' business is a double cover. He's the GIA's top dirty-work boy."

"Absurd, Jimmy," and "Impossible!" burst from the staff.

"Kith is a mere gofer," Gropedark declared with finality. "What possible reason would the Groaci High Command have for sending their number one sneak-killer to this peace-torn planet?"

"I guess I recognize Kith when I see him," Trenchfoot declared stubbornly. "He was on the Groaci delegation to the last Arms Summit, which I had the honor to head up internal security. Spent two weeks in the same room with the villain!"

"Very well, Jimmy, since you're so concerned, I'll send Ben along just to check on his movements—casually, of course, Ben."

"Why me?" Magnan yelped. "It's Jimmy's idea, I mean I wouldn't want to rob him of the glory—"

"Scant glory is to accrue from shadowing a code clerk on his daily trip to the bazaar for produce," Gropedark rebuked his Budget and Fiscal man. "Still, you may as well just keep an eye on the scamp. Better use the back way to avoid the crowd. Be back in an hour."

Magnan departed, muttering, "What for? It's just your fans, remember?" It was a remark His Excellency decided not to hear.

2

"You see," Ambassador Gropedark said contentedly an hour later, waving a plump hand to indicate the now-deserted courtyard, littered with dope-stick butts, empty gribble-grub bags and the usual assortment of priceless fragments of the lofty facades which looked down on it. "They've dispersed peacefully, just as I expected. Pity I didn't step out to say a few soothing words as they desired."

"If as you suggested," a timid Admin type spoke up, "the beggars were here to demand a full-scale restoration program to return this dump to its former glories and all, I don't see how jawing at 'em from a balcony is going to make 'em any happier."

"It is precisely that element of short-sightedness in your makeup, Ted, which has delayed your advancement in the Corps," Gropedark dismissed the cavil. "By the way, I distinctly told Ben Magnan to report back in an hour . . ." He paused to inspect his issue watch. "And it has been precisely one hour now." He barked the last word as if ordering the troops over the top. "Ben's inclined to be careless, of course—may have wandered into the tabu Inner City." He pointed. "You, fellow—you're Mr. Magnan's assistant, as I recall—perhaps you'd best run along and remind him he's keeping his Chief waiting."

3

The last of the crowd had dispersed when Retief reached the broad processional way, once paved with intricately carved and colored tiles but now showing large bare patches where the latter-day locals had removed them to sell to tourists, and littered with cut-stone fragments fallen from the formerly imposing facades which lined the street—some, such as the tomb of the legendary King Foop-Galoon, dating back across the full five millennia of the city's continuous occupation. Wedged between the great structures, or sometimes built within the capacious entryways, were shoddy boutiques, dubious pawn shops, and gaudy stalls, each with its shrill huckster who often ventured out into the street to hail passersby or even attempt bodily to haul them inside.

Today the street was silent except for the steady *car-rack!*ing sounds from the crumbling palaces and the steady pattering of debris falling therefrom. Retief noticed a scaly foot-long landfish as it wriggled sinuously away to disappear into what appeared to be a newly-opened crack in the ancient masonry of the looming structure before him, its broad stone stairway and cavernous, colonnaded entryway clogged with rude constructions of carved stone in incongruous juxtaposition with rough-hewn slabs of local oom-wood from the interstices in which curious eyes peered out, in silence for once.

"Hey, stranger," one bold fellow called. "You wantum one piecee fly-fly, him gottum feather, talkee talkee real good, same likee greenfella."

"No, thanks all samee," Retief replied absently. "No wantum parrot, wantum one piecee Terry diplomat, him get loose in street."

"Him big monster? Same like you?" the local demanded.

"No, him small monster, no gettum plenty too many eats when pickaninny."

"No seeum," the native merchant stated flatly, and slapped down the hinged board serving as a security shutter over the entry to his modest enterprise.

"Greenfella findum all same Terry, him gettum plenty too many green stamp," Retief pointed out.

"Long sundown, Terry come back one timee, maybe memory good one place, gettum one piecee hot dopee."

"When big kerosene blong Spood him finish, I come back bright day," Retief promised.

As he resumed his stroll along the chipped tiles, a wave of furtive movement ran ahead of him. He caught glimpses of green faces which appeared briefly at chinks and peepholes, then ducked back. Something caught his eye, lying on the sun-baked clay strip which had once been a floral border to the avenue. He paused to pick it up: half a crumpled Imperial-size tissue bearing the embossed arms of the Terran Embassy, carrying a faint aroma of bluemint. He scanned the adjacent cliff-face of eroded masonry, noted faint light gleaming from the dark opening just above ground level where the landfish had disappeared. Closer, he saw that it was a cramped passage leading some fifty feet through the ancient masonry to a dimly-sunlit patch beyond. Behind him, horny feet were approaching with no effort at stealth.

"Hey!" a coarse voice barked. Retief turned to confront a large Greenfella—an elongated, streamlined torso, scaly on the back and white beneath, standing on two thin legs, propped up by a large third leg, and a triangular-bladed knife in the knuckly hand of its single arm.

"Terry gettum lost! Go quick!" the fella snarled,

jabbing tentatively with the knife. "Run, or me killum!"

"With an invitation like that, who could resist?" Retief queried, and at the same moment took the knife away from the hostile fellow, thrust the blade into a crevice in the weathered stone, and snapped it off short, then offered it, hilt-first, to its owner, who leaned forward to take it but encountered Retief's knee, which knocked him onto his back.

"Terry sockum Greenfellow," the fallen alien said without emphasis. "Plenty too rough party."

Retief stooped down to look down the tunnel, saw a patch of white lodged halfway along the rough-hewn way. He thrust his head and shoulders inside. It was a tight fit, and the chipped stones which made up the floor of the tunnel dug painfully into his knees. He reached the white object: as he had expected, it was the other half of the tissue, with a large piece missing. He resumed the arduous crawl. As he neared the end of the tunnel, something—or someone—moved into position to block the egress, plunging the passage into darkness. He covered the last few feet, and at close range, saw that it was the posterior of a larger-than-average Greenfella which had plugged the way. Retief reached out and poked the alien sharply. It leapt up with a yell, restoring illumination to the cramped space and revealing a trash-lined nest containing half a dozen infant reptiles like the one which had fled at his approach. The little creatures crouched back with bared fangs, eyes riveted on the Terran. He picked one up carefully, not without receiving a painful nip on the thumb, and tossed it toward the opening. It righted itself and darted into the daylight.

"Hey! False alarm!" a hoarse voice shouted. "Only landfish takum one piece bitee on rump!" Then a broad green face came into view, peering into the

tunnel. Retief flattened himself against the floor
and the Greenfella's gaze swept over him, unsee-
ing. The local thrust a claw-like four-fingered hand
inside and was rewarded with a bite from one of
the infant landfish which Retief had placed before
him. The hand jerked back, and the hoarse voice
muttered aggrievedly, "Gottum bite on favorite
finger, needum one piece fire-shooter, clean out
vermin!"

Through the bright opening, Retief could see a
cramped, weed-grown courtyard, trash-littered,
where four of the perpetually tired-looking Greenfellas, all clad in grimy loinclothes, stood watching
with morose expressions something going on out
of Retief's view. He heard a metallic *click!*, then a
squeal of rusty hinges. The nearest Greenfellas
stirred restlessly.

Retief waited. Half a minute passed.

With a furious *bang!*, the unseen door was thrown
open violently, and a harsh yell brought every
Greenfella in sight to a position of rigid attention.
Then a taller-than-average representative of the
three-legged native species strode into view,
wrapped in a cloak of vivid chartreuse trimmed
with colored beads at wrist and collar. The nearest
Greenfella cringed as the newcomer approached,
then, at a sharp glance, straightened again into
rigidity. The cloaked VIP barked at him, and was
rewarded with a glum sound reminiscent of a boot
being pulled from the mud, which Retief recognized as the local term for "nossir." The imperious
local turned and Retief saw the three-eyed wedge-
shaped face set in an expression which, to Terran
eyes at least, reflected barely suppressed homici-
dal fury. As the grasshopper-like alien began to
rub its legs together, Retief switched on the field-
model translator woven into the fabric of the
stand-up collar of his mid-late afternoon hemi-

semi-formal cloak, short, middle three graders, for the use of.

". . . tole you bums a hunnert times!" the alien's thin voice shrilled. "Any o' them foreigners comes pokin around the Old Town, you lay low and inform me, pronto! Now Lee, here, tells me he started a like conversation with wonna 'em! He gets three in Level Six; as for the resta youse, I got to give it some thought. Wesley, you scoot down the tunnel where old Lee goofed up and take a look-see!"

One of the smaller Greenfellas scuttled toward Retief's place of concealment. He flattened himself against the rough-hewn wall of the passage, but Wesley halted six feet from him.

"Tunnel's clear, Sarge," the Greenfella fiddled awkwardly to his superior. "Seen a landfish come out, and she wouldn'ta left her nest if there was any monkey business goin' on."

"You got yer orders, Wesley!" the sergeant snapped. "Get in there! And don't be ascairt of a few landfish, all they can do is take jest a small bite outa ya!"

Reluctantly, Wesley came toward the tunnel-mouth. Reaching it, he stooped to peer inside and was looking directly into Retief's face. There he paused, his triangular facial plates set in an inscrutable expression, unmoving.

Then, behind him, Retief heard a scuttling sound, and three immature landfish raced past him and out into the watery sunshine, followed by the scaly foot-long mother. Retief heard pebbles falling somewhere behind him, then a deep-seated *craackk!* followed by the *thump!* of something heavy falling. At the sounds, Wesley recoiled, then dashed away, motioning excitedly to his fellows. Retief twisted to look back down the tunnel, saw that it was now half-blocked by debris apparently newly fallen from the roof, almost blotting out the ragged patch of daylight at the far end. As he watched, a major slab shifted, dropped down at one end as if hinged, then fell with a resounding *thud!* Sand and pebbles were dribbling down on his back. He looked out, saw that the courtyard was now cleared with the exception of one bedraggled Greenfella chained by both outer legs to the far wall. The prisoner jerked violently at the restraining shackles as Retief emerged fully from the crawlspace and rose to his feet; the Greenfella began to jabber excitedly in the shrill native dialect, producing the sound by rubbing his middle leg against the adjacent shin.

Retief went slowly across to the shackled Greenfella, which was clad only in a dirty rag and adorned with a Mexican-pink plastic disc on a string about his short neck; his vestigial wingcases bedraggled and askew, he crouched now against the stuccoed wall, straining the rusty leg-irons to their limit.

"You must be important Greenfella," Retief said quietly through his translator. "Got important job hold wall in place."

"You bettum plenty too much guck, palefella," the prisoner responded heartily. "Me Leroy; me plenty too big shot."

Retief nodded, coming close to examine the well-corroded chains. "That tallfella with the soothing voice," he commented, "must be plenty too swellfella."

"Him Boss Twill; him gottum plenty too many friend," Leroy remarked noncommitally, watching Retief warily as he took a firm grip on the left ankle-chain and jerked it sharply. The crumbling eye-bolt securing it to the wall snapped off short. Leroy tentatively moved his suddenly freed leg. "Boss Twill ream out zlotz orifice two fob oversize, him catchum palefella bugger up property b'long Morris," he predicted. "Morris him high priest chief god in Greenfella pantheon, Spood the Obtuse. Callum Obtuse because even though poor Greenfella tell plenty prayer, burn joss stick, Sacrifice old junk, tellum Spood wantum plenty guck, cozy den, snazzy Greengal, old Spood no gettum idea."

"So we'd better not linger here," Retief pointed out, shifting dialects to the Middle Obfuscese. Leroy seemed to understand, as he jumped to his feet and began yanking, not very effectively, at his other gyve. Retief lent a hand, and in a moment Leroy was free, hobbling painfully, dragging his chains.

"Maybe we'd better leave your chains-of-office here," Retief suggested. Leroy sat down on the hard clay and offered his right chain trustfully. Retief took the pitted chain, doubled it back on itself, and squeezed. A link snapped; he dropped the broken eighteen-inch length and attacked the other; it, too, yielded easily. Leroy hopped up and capered joyfully. In his enthusiasm, he came too near a beaten-brass gong suspended by the door. His flailing hand struck it, eliciting a penetrating *boinng!*

"Oh-oh, plenty too bad!" Leroy exclaimed. "Old pal Boss Twill him come plenty too quick, him listen Doom Gong!"

"Let's play a little trick on good old Twill," Retief suggested. "You wait beside the door, and stick out a foot and pretend to trip Boss. When he's down, I'll pretend to wrap up his ankles in his own chains. Better get in position."

They had but a moment to wait: the door *bang!*ed wide and the tall, ornamented Greenfella boss loomed, then dove face-first to the hard clay, his wing cases twitching in reflexive response. Retief stepped in, put a foot on the back of Twill's middle knee, and chained all three legs together at the knobbly ankles. Twill hunched and flopped impotently, screeching all the while. Retief slammed the door shut just in time to intercept the first of the closely following personal guards, who impacted the heavy panel with a force which drove dust from the crevices.

"Oh, boy," Leroy said glumly, to Retief, "Old Boss gonna be plenty too mad when him gettum act together."

"He's *already* mad," Retief pointed out. "He won't be any madder if we just frisk him for his keys and drag him back into some quiet spot where he won't be observed in such an undignified position."

"All right, Lee," the fallen boss chirped feebly in the Lesser Obfuscese, his diction somewhat marred by the chain around his hard green shins. "You better clobber this here palefella plenty too quick."

"Palefella plenty too right," Leroy concurred, and delivered a sharp kick to Twill's lower abdomen.

"Better let well enough alone," Retief suggested. Noticing yet another small scrap of white protruding from beneath an adjacent, closed door, he went over to it, put his shoulder to the age-worn spangwood panel, and heaved it open, eliciting a despairing shriek from the ancient hinges. Leroy dashed forward to interpose his person between Retief and the dark doorway. "Old Boss him send Greenfella kitchen do KP for year, then grate me up for put in soup, me lettum palefella desecrate Top Private area," he explained as Retief picked him up and tossed him aside.

"Groan," Retief directed. "Make it look good: you puttum up good fight, but overwhelm by palefella."

"Palefella plenty too big," Leroy commented as if to his biographer. Then, with a sudden leap, he hurled himself at Retief, delivering a ferocious snap-kick with his major leg to the space the Terran's head had occupied an instant before.

Retief caught the powerful member by the ankle, and Leroy lunged and surged like a carp hooked in the eye until Retief doubled the long limb at the knee and folded it behind its owner's back, at which point the lightweight, hard-shelled arthropod ceased struggling. "Boss see me give it old grade-school try," he announced. "OK, Terry palefella, you can lettum down nice and easy, and be careful no breakum knee-joint."

"No more showum boss zealous defense," Retief admonished. Leroy struggled briefly to rub his left leg against the trapped one, then subsided. Retief put him down and after a brief inspection of his middle knee, Lee got to his feet jauntily.

"Terry no stickum olfactory sensor in pot, no gettum blistered," he stated. "Nothing in there interest high-class Terry palefella, anyway."

"How is it that suddenly you know I'm a Terran?" Retief asked.

"Oh, just remember Special Order Number Six and a Half Billion and One," Leroy explained glibly, his injured member now as agile as ever. "Pain in crouch-pads not be able talk and walk at same time," he commented. "Old Spood make mistake not give Greenfella talk-box in eating department like palefella and five-eye fella, too."

"Where did you meet this five-eye fella?" Retief asked sternly. "And where's the other Terry who was here this morning?"

"*What* other Terry?" Leroy demanded. "Leroy never see other Terry, small like me, havum puce and magenta coat, stripe pants."

"Then where did you get that Order of the Perished Bladder you're wearing?" Retief challenged. "I'll bet you my second-best mess jacket against a plate of garg it's got 'First Secretary B.W. Magnan, III' engraved on the back."

"Terry too sharp for simple dweller in ruins of vanished glory," Leroy conceded. "Tell, me, pal, how did I give it away?"

"That fairly detailed description of him helped," Retief admitted.

"Drat!" Leroy rasped. "Should of thought of that. But to heck with it, we got plenty guck to earn before get too dark see way. Come on." He started through the open entry. Retief stopped him with a grip on a rudimentary wing-case.

"Not so fast, Lee," he counseled. "We still have things to talk over. And there's Twill to dispose of."

"You killum big-shot boss?" Leroy exclaimed with a rapid jittering of legs. "You force poor Greenfella serf manage without guidance of kindly counsellor and protector?"

"Could be," Retief allowed. "If you don't take me to Mr. Magnan double-quick and avoid troubling the Groaci Peacekeepers in the process."

"Last time see foreign five-eye fella, him kickum loyal Leroy; not want get kick plenty more; stay way five-eye fella. Him badfella."

"Whereas," Retief contributed, "Mr. Magnan is a goodfella; so let's find him and get him out of place him not gottum business be in first place."

"Too right!" Leroy agreed emphatically. "Loyal Leroy have job keep nosy goodfella out Headquarters; not my fault take little nap just when nosyfella poke aforesaid organ in Taboo Street. Wake up in time help Boss and boys draggum inside, then boss chain faithful Leroy to wall. Lousy treatment, got good mind form Local #728365 Brotherhood Dozing Doorkeeper, closed shop, gettum big pay, easy hour, plenty too much pension and other goodie."

"And supply luxury goods to your BDD boss in prison," Retief reminded the union organizer.

"Plenty too right!" Leroy agreed. "Otherwise greenfella gettum visit plenty too late in sacktime, collect few bruise."

"With such a realistic attitude," Retief commented, "I predict a great future for you as a social reformer."

"Not interest reform," Leroy corrected. "Interest in gettum high class consumer goodie."

"As I said, 'realistic,'" Retief repeated. "After you, Leroy." He indicated the closed door. Leroy used a key on it and it swung inward on darkness and silence.

"Oh, boy," the Unionfella said without eagerness. "Plenty too big penalty lowly Greenfella invade Inner Sanctum. Bring palefella, extra hundred lashes. But what the hell, me always curious about what go on in there." He advanced cautiously into the interior, waving his antennae dubiously, and paused just inside to listen to a profound silence. Retief went around him. Ahead, barely visible in the unlit passage, he saw yet another patch of white, this one lodged in a niche in the cut-stone wall. Leroy came up, muttering:

"Not good: smellum rare and valuable sacred foom-weed smoke, mean top-holy ceremony someplace close-by. Chamber of Doom, good place stay out of."

"What sort of ceremony?" Retief asked, keeping his voice low.

"Swell rite of Givvum More Goodie: make old gods do what we want—or what Top Medicine fella want. Not what sacrifice want. Him hard-luck case. Get to die painfully for good of tribe. Big honor."

"Where does this passage lead?" Retief inquired.

"Lead to john, broom closet," Leroy said in the tone of One Who Has the Answers.

In the darkness Retief studied the wall beside the scrap of paper, saw in the gloomy recess a wide crack from which a faint glow and a pungent odor emanated. He pushed; it yielded and a panel pivoted inward, admitting feeble light. Leroy grabbed at Retief's arm.

"Chamber of Doom," he reported. "Plenty too dangerous stick antennae in here," he whispered hoarsely, sticking his antennae through the opening. "Oh, boy," he chirred awkwardly. "Dread chamber worse than rumor tell."

Retief moved him aside and took a look for himself. He saw a low-ceilinged chamber with a layer of yellowish smoke just below head-height. Half a dozen Greenfella heads projected above it, and one half-bald Terran cranium. A wisp of smoke was curling out through the open port. It had an odor like smoked sausage, which Leroy was sucking in eagerly through his central respirator-orifice. Apparently unconsciously, he began rasping his vestigal wing-cases together rhythmically, and swaying like a strand of kelp in turbulent waters. Retief pushed him away from the spicy aroma.

"This isn't the time or place to get spaced out, Lee," he reprimanded the ecstatic Greenfella. He took another look through the haze below the dense smoke-layer, then turned to Leroy.

"I'm going in," he told the astonished Greenfella. "Stand by here, and if any of Boss Twill's friends come along, pitch them in behind me."

Leroy agreed, though puzzled. "Palefella him volunteer for Death of Ten Terrible Anecdote?" he asked, sounding skeptical.

"Not until Staff Meeting, Tuesday at ten AM," Retief corrected, and eased through the narrow opening, keeping below the opaque deck of aromatic smoke. At this level he could see that Magnan was shackled to a three-legged stool and surrounded by armed Greenfellas. Keeping well below the smoke layer, he went quickly to Magnan. A glance showed him that the shackles holding the slightly-built diplomat to the stool were a common Groaci

VIP model. He tapped Magnan's thin ankle in Under-the-Table code: "Play it cool. Get ready to drop to the floor." It was the work of a moment to pick the simple lock and remove the light-weight eka-bronze gyve. Then he grasped one of the stool's three legs and jerked sharply. Magnan uttered a yelp and collapsed on his back, staring up at Retief. A shrill buzz of startled conversation broke out above.

"Heavens!" Magnan gasped. "You could have been a bit more explicit; I was expecting something a trifle more dignified!"

Retief ignored his supervisor's plaint and moved on to the spindle-shanks of a lone Groaci wearing plain greaves with the dun-colored jellybeans of a reserve paper-pusher, medium grade, standing firm among the agitated rod-like shins of the chattering Greenfellas, and used the ankle-cuffs to clamp them carefully together. Just as he finished, the Groaci attempted to take a step, but instead fell full-length. Retief grasped his ankle and dragged him along to the opening. When the Groaci began to expostulate in his feeble voice, Retief shushed him with a vigorous prod in his sensitive zatz-patch, then passed him out through the narrow orifice to the waiting Leroy, whose voice was at once raised in shrill Popurese. Ignoring the noisy fellow, Retief assisted Magnan through, heard him utter a sharp shriek followed by excited jabber in three dialects. Retief followed, saw Magnan backed against the wall, while before him an excited Leroy fiddled a shin in frantic expostulation. The Groaci was standing by, all five eyes adroop, his skinny ankles firmly linked by the shackles. One eye twitched at Retief's arrival, then snapped erect.

"To recognize the infamous Retief, bane of saintly Groacian bureaucrats!" he hissed. Retief ignored him, stepped between Leroy and Magnan.

"Take it easy, Leroy," Retief advised the Green-fella. "It's only Mr. Magnan, my esteemed associ-ate: I think you startled him. This other one is Captain Kith; he doesn't appear to have experi-enced much in the way of intellectual develop-ment since he was pulling four on and eight off as an Embassy guard back on Fust."

"To err, vile Soft One!" Kith snapped as harshly as his feeble voice would allow. "I now handle the rank of First Secretary of Embassy of Groac and Vice Consul of Career, assigned as liaison to the underdeveloped Guiding Council of unfortunate Popu-Ri! You may escort me at once to the Chief of Council, my conference with whom you so rudely terminated but now!"

"Me plenty scare," Leroy complained. "Strange palefella jump out, utter savage war-cry—look mad, too; and five-eye fella, him say plenty too many bad thing me, me no lettum loose. But I foolum: I pretend no kapoosh bad-accent Obfuscese."

"Ingenious, Leroy," Retief acknowledged. "Now he's demanding an audience with the Chief of Council. But I think he's bluffing: he's only a reservist, probably an Assistant Military Attache; he doesn't rate a tete-a-tete with a Chief of State."

"Here, Retief!" Magnan barked. "Do you intend to natter of trivialities while this horrid local men-aces me?" As he spoke, he continued to shred bits from the crumpled paper napkin clutched in his hand.

"That's just Leroy," Retief soothed the excited Second Secretary. "He's helping me find you. That was very clever, Mr. Magnan, to leave a trail for me to follow. But you can stop now. We're here."

Magnan blinked at the shredded paper in his hand, quickly stuffed it into a pocket. "Didn't mean to be littering," he said apologetically. "Ner-vous habit. 'We're here,' you say, but where is 'here'? Insofar as I can judge, we're lost in the bowels of a collapsing ruin, surrounded by hostile aliens and vicious landfish, to say nothing of Kith! Retief, I feel there's something irregular going on here!"

"Actually," Retief said soothingly, "we're not lost. We're only trapped. The route to the street is near at hand, but it collapsed. In any case, I think we'd better snoop around a little so as to be able to report more than that something's irregular."

"To be sure," Magnan agreed. "But *do* tell this noisyfella to go away. I find I'm allergic to him." As if to prove it, he sneezed into the tattered remnant of his paper hanky.

"To escort me at once to the street," Kith demanded. "To overlook the irregularities of which Ben Magnan speaks, if you make amends promptly."

"Suppose I just chuck you back through the hole in the wall," Retief suggested, taking a grip on the Groaci's thin neck. "Or perhaps I'll shackle you to one of those." He indicated one of a number of well-rusted staples set in the wall, from which the wooden slats they had once supported had long since rotted away.

"To dare not so to handle a diplomatic member of the staff of the Embassy of great Groac!" Kith challenged in his faint voice.

In reply, Retief lifted him and thrust him feet-first toward the open fissure.

"Stay, Terry miscreant!" the Groaci rasped. "Chair-being Morris would order me dismembered!"

"Before I say goodbye," Retief said to the struggling fellow, "You'd better tell me a few things, such as why you're here, the details of the plot, what Groac gets out of it, and so on."

"Never, vile Terry!" Kith hissed. "To suffer living dismemberment gladly ere I disclose state secrets."

"Better hold him and grill him thoroughly," Magnan suggested. "It seems we've stumbled upon something Big."

"By the way, Mr. Magnan," Retief said. "What brought you here? I understand you were simply out for an innocent stroll to spy out the activities of our friend Kith, here."

"To be sure," Magnan acknowledged. "I was but meandering along the avenue when of a sudden, a brace of fierce Greenfellas leapt from concealment and raped me away through a dark tunnel; then, in a gloomy cell full of nauseous fumes, chained me to a hard stool. They crowded about me, demanding that I disclose unspecified secrets, when abruptly you arrived; the rest you know."

Retief turned to Leroy, still holding the now quiescent Kith by the neck. "Do you have any idea why they grabbed Mr. Magnan?" he asked the Greenfella.

"Me plenty dumb," Leroy confessed. "Not know Boss Twill and five-eyes fella cookum big scheme make all big shot happy, get plenty too many green stamp, gold, guck, all good stuff like VIP-model Chevy ragtop go undersea, on surface, over land, fly in air, go in space, whole nine yard! Also catchum condo on beach at Fatworld, snazzy greengal, plenty other loot, too. Me chain up when me sneakum round try get in on goodies. Wantum Ben for sacrifice to gods."

"A gross injustice, Mr. Leroy," Magnan put in. "But just like the Groaci: to despoil a virgin world and deny the autocthones any share in the loot!"

"Ben," Kith cut in coldly, "I deeply resent, on behalf of His Excellency, this 'apporth o cor'elpme's excessively crass assessment of enlightened Groacian policy on this pest-world."

"Five-eye fella bad-leg home slum," Leroy fiddled indignantly. "Me know 'pest,' plenty too bad word. *Him* pest, come excite Boss Twill, start diggum hole, makeum whole town fall down."

"Ben!" Kith protested. "Are you going to stand by without protest while this sweeper-caste local abuses a fellow diplomatic officer?"

"While Mr. Leroy's remarks *did* rather emphasize the material aspects of Groacian aspirations," Magnan responded sternly, "his allegation of the disruption of the even tenor of the ancient Popu-Ri lifestyle by Groaci underlings has undeniable merit."

"Me never get ceph-tape on Super Obfuscese," Leroy protested to Retief. "What skinny palefella him tell?"

"Never mind, Leroy," Retief counseled the local. "It's just standard diplomatic terminology for 'I'm firmly astride the fence, fellows. *You* work it out.' "

"No need to look smug, Ben Magnan," Kith hissed. "Though this shabby structure *is* indeed in process of collapsing, no tribunal in the Arm would cry Groac culpable. It is, after all, twenty-seven thousand years old!" Then to Retief: "Why not be reasonable? After all, these grasshoppers have been dumping their treasure down that damn Sacred Well of theirs for millennia: there's enough for everybody, even Leroy here, if not that greedyguts Boss Twill."

"Leroy says you Groaci are responsible for the accelerated collapse of the town," Retief replied. "Anything in it?"

"A base canard!" Kith dismissed the charge. "Our skilled engineers have, of course, taken sonar traces of the underground configurations, the vent system of a defunct volcano, so as more effectively to conduct those excavations necessary to promote ready access to the archeological deposits."

"And what happens to these deposits once you've dug them out?" Magnan pressed the Groaci.

"They are stored in a secure place, pending cleaning, evaluation, classification, and dispatch to those institutions of higher learning most qualified to assist scholars desiring to elucidate the rise and fall of the ancient civilization whose chief monument this ruin and its contents constitute," Kith stated tartly.

"Speak plain Groai," Magnan urged. "Your Pidgin Obfuscese, while doubtless fluent, is a trifle ponderous for ready interpretation."

"Ha!" Kith sneered. "You Terries need to spend more time on your ceph-tapes, picking up at least the basic languages known to all sophisticates. Any low-grade Groaci assistant strawboss could tell you I said 'Go stuff lint up your nose.'"

"How about it, Lee?" Retief inquired of the local, who was standing sullenly by, shifting nervously from foot to foot.

"Greenfella long time drop stuff down Sacred Well," Leroy acknowledged. "Fool gods, think garbage sacrifice. Lately Greenfella fall on hard time; after few get squash when old spaceport fall down, no more tourist come make point with gods drop few guck down old hole in ground, so honest Greenfella can wait foreigner go, then retrieve cash. Five-eyes fella come, take all guck, dig through old trash, grab plenty burnt-out TV chassis, spare tire, stone axe, *baton de commandement*, Greenfella bone, dead landfish, gold statue, diamond big as floom egg, get in hurry, dig wall, well fall in, cover up more good stuff, foundation old dump all around start shift, wall crack, whole place go to Hell in handbasket. Pretty soon, greenfella have no place get in out rainwater and stuff. Last week pal b'long me, him gettum brain knock out by hunk rock big like moobyfruit, right in front own burrow. Palefella make all five-eye fella go away quick, Greenfella give plenty gratitude and few green stamp too."

"That's a stirring appeal, Leroy," Retief conceded. "But Ambassador Gropedark takes the position that it's not up to us to meddle with the status quo."

"No talk statue," Leroy objected. "Not know this fella Quo anyways. Just get rid five-eye fella, and grateful populace fix big feast national delicacy one piecee Landfish, now you fly him, now mooby fruit."

"Doesn't sound any worse than Furthuronian garg," Retief conceded. "Let's go take a look at this Sacred Well, and maybe we can devise a viable strategy."

"No needum strategy," Leroy demurred. "Needum plan. Anyway, palefella no allow defile sacred precincts, Chamber of Doom, or holy well, either, unless have honor select for sacrifice, like Ben."

"Tell you what," Retief suggested. "We'll overlook it just this once if you lead us there by the shortest route."

"Extra-short route open up just last week," Leroy offered enthusiastically. "Reason big foog-ceremony, sacrifice old Ben here to demon, make crack stop, dear old hometown not fall down too much."

"Why Mr. Magnan in particular?" Retief inquired.

"No particular; any old palefella OK," Leroy replied off-handedly.

"Then why lose a noble palefella and not a scoundrelly five-eyes fella, for example?" Magnan demanded. Kith began to sputter indignantly, then in plain Obfuscese stated: "Clearly it is the privilege of you Terries to placate the gods whom you yourselves have angered!"

"Curious logic," Magnan sniffed, "since it is none

other than the Groaci who have violated the Inner City and profaned the Sacred Well. We Terrans knew nothing of the matter until the sudden acceleration of the civic collapse about our ears." Magnan shifted his aim to Leroy.

"Can you in conscience, Mr. Leroy," he demanded, "lay the guilt for this unpardonable blasphemy, to say nothing of unrestricted looting, at the threshold of benign Terra, in the face of the open activities of the insidious Groaci?"

"Conscience expensive luxury," Leroy declared sadly. "Anyway, Boss Twill, him tell poor backward Greenfella him need help five-eye fella stop greedy palefella want steal whole planet."

"What possible motivation could mighty Terra have for purloining, as you suggest, this crumbling remnant of a world?" Magnan inquired, seemingly of a grandstand full of newsgatherers.

"No talk 'pearl-on,'" Leroy objected. "No catchum too many school-piece, no learn big word. Say 'Lousy Terry swipe Popu-Ri.'"

"'Lousy!'" Magnan echoed. "That's a rude word you doubtless learned from Kith, here!"

"No learnum word 'Kithere'," Leroy contradicted. "Who him? Big-shot five-eyes fella teachum. His name Ambluster Smoosh."

"Ambassador Smoosh is far too polished a beaureaucrat to stoop to imparting terms of abuse to one of your stripe!" Magnan declared.

"No stoop. Me taller than old Mr. Ambluster. Me no stripes; me solid turnbuckle dun, prove me real Untouchable caste full-juice, all way back to primordial *urschliem*, all sides family!"

"Spikking pedigrees," Kith said in his Groaci-accented Terran, "I myself am of imperial blood—due to a well-attested incident involving the legendary beauty, Princess Sish, a blundering janitor and a tub of hot sand—all this being back in the reign of His Imperial Majesty Emperor Fish-Withering, ruler of Groac and viceroy of numerous outlying district, some tens of centuries agone."

"Impressive credentials indeed, Kith," Magnan acknowledged. "Why then are you still struggling to attain medium-exalted rank in your Foreign Service?"

"Jealousy," Kith explained succinctly. "My cadet branch got all the looks in the family. Besides, there's still a few hardliners who deny the authenticity of the legend."

"Let's concede that we're all descended from the original living cell of one's respective world," Magnan suggested.

"Fine," Retief agreed. "Now let's see what we can do about getting out of this pile before it collapses the rest of the way."

"What?" Magnan responded as if astonished. "And leave unanswered the burning questions that confront us here, to say nothing of the confrontation with His Excellency the Ambluster—or Ambassador—I mean, of course—should I return without the aforesaid data!"

"You have, Ben," Kith seconded promptly, "enunciated a position with which I have the honor to be in complete agreement. There's just one catch: precisely what *are* these burning questions? Shall we begin with a query as to by just what authority a pair of notorious Terry spoilsports have trespassed here in the Popu-Ri Holy of Holies?"

"Hardly appropriate, Kith," Magnan objected, "when the puzzle of the Groacian presence here is itself yet unresolved."

"What's to resolve, Ben?" Kith inquired airily, reverting to his flawed Terran. "I guess Groac got a few rights. We came along and established diplomatic relation with this dump just like Terra. You tryna tell me that ain't OK?"

"Exchanging Ambassadors is all very well," Magnan stated coldly, "but that is hardly to legitimize the looting of national treasures."

"You heard old Leroy hisself," Kith countered. "All we're doing is tryna tidy up the place a little. One can hardly expect His Excellency the Groacian AE & MP to hack his way through the stench of an open garbage pit each morning—then conduct foreign affairs immersed in that heady aroma."

"I believe you'll find," Magnan said glacially, "that His Terran Ex endures precisely the same hardship, all in the name of harmonious relations."

"Sure, but us Groaci got no hangup where we got to put up with a lot of crap from these benighted natives so they'll think we're sweet."

"Pity," Magnan countered. "A trifle of humility would do wonders for your image."

"Image, shimage," Kith rejected the criticism offhandedly. "What kind image you think you get when you let Ralph the janitor come busting inta yer staff meeting and shoo all your top boys outa the room so *he* can sit in the old hip-u-matic and smoke one of Clarence Gropedark's Ropa del Manuras? Hah?" He aimed all five eyes directly at Magnan, an effect like an armed ack-ack battery tracking a bandit.

"Why, how did you—that's ridiculous, I mean!" Magnan gobbled. "Where ever did you acquire such a notion?"

"From the tapes," Kith told the agitated Magnan. "We set the whole thing up last week, just to see how far you'd carry your 'inferiors are superior' policy. Had a camera rigged through the john to follow the action. And when Clarence came back to get his comic book, he sees the crudbum sitting there, and he says, 'Ah, sir, I do hope you're enjoying your smoke.' And Old Ralphie comes back, "Not much, with all the disturbances; besides, this stogie'd choke a mud-pig.' With that, the rogue deposited the cheroot in His Ex's favorite potted jelly-flower and ups to Clarence and says, 'Get outa the way, chum; I wanta walk where you're standing.' " As Kith recalled the scene, he waggled his eye-stalks in expression of hilarity. "Then Clarence done everything but polish the slob's shoes while he's holding the door for him and stuffing another half dozen 'o them firecrackers in the sweeper's overalls pocket!"

"A bit of courtesy is surely not amiss," Magnan sniffed. "Despite its contrast with Groaci arrogance."

"Courtesy is OK in its place," Kith conceded, "but giving big ideas to insolent upstarts ain't the place. Right, Leroy?" The cheeky Groaci prodded the greenfella in solicitation of confirmation, which Leroy withheld.

"Problem with your policy, Ben," Kith mused on, "is when a guy is like in a middle position, so he don't quite rate as a big shot, and he ain't quite low enough to qualify as a superior inferior. Like you, Ben. Tough barfnodes, eh? When you get that next promo, about the time the Big Sandy glaciates, you got no way to know if you're going up, or down."

"You exaggerate, Kith," Magnan commented sadly. "Though one must concede that one is sometimes called upon to employ all of one's subtlety in establishing correct relations with those of ambiguous position, as at disarmament talks and the like. Who is to outrank whom, thereby conferring superiority upon the inferior, is a question even more Gordian than, for example, table-shape, a once-burning issue hardly visible in recent centuries."

"Sure," Kith jeered. "I seen your veteran, most-decorated Lieutenant-Generals falling-in to the left and slightly to the rear of some jumped-up ex-corporal decided to call hisself 'General Foo,' or whatever. Kinda takes the edge off the old military courtesy."

As they chatted, dust and pebbles continued to dribble down from the darkness above, accompanied by the occasional golfball-sized fragment, one of which elicited a sharp yelp from Magnan.

"Retief!" he snapped. "I've been telling you, we must depart this disaster scene *before* the disaster! What have you done to implement my instructions?"

"I've been considering them in depth, Mr. Magnan," Retief reassured his supervisor, "and I can find no egregious flaw in them. I have only one reservation: you forgot to mention what the instructions are."

"Retief!" Magnan protested. "I hardly expected whining from you in this emergency. My instructions were clarity personified: 'Get us out of this fix.'" As he concluded his spirited rebuttal, a long section of the stone-slab floor just ahead dropped from view, and only after a breathless minute did a resounding impact echo from the black pit thus exposed.

"No good orders, skinny palefella tell," Leroy observed critically. "No detail tell *how* gettum out fix!"

"One is hardly interested in any critique of one's techniques of leadership emanating from one such as yourself," Magnan sniffed. "I dislike to burden subordinates with an excess of detail," he amplified glibly. "After all, one does expect some ability to improvise even from non-medium-exalted ranks. Retief usually performs adequately, if unconventionally," he concluded. "The proof of the validity of my policy."

" 'Methinks he doth protest plenty too much,' " Leroy misquoted.

"Whilst you natter of these trifles," Kith put in

sharply, "the venerable structure you have so rashly violated, even to laying hands on my person, continues to crumble about our auditory membranes."

"That's ridiculous!" Magnan snapped in reply. "You suggest that it is the Terran presence which has precipitated the dissolution of the town, while in actuality it is precisely your *own* depradations which have undermined the foundations!"

"To what end the allocation of responsibility?" Kith demanded, "when none will survive to expiate his guilt?" As if to punctuate the panicky Groaci's peroration, a block of stone dropped from the side wall of the lightless passage with a dull-toned *thunk!*

Retief went to the newly-opened space and looked into an only slightly better illuminated space, crowded with intricately carved stone slabs fallen from the ceiling. He secured a grip on a stone gargoyle and pulled himself up into a narrow space between blocks of jumbled debris, then reached back to lend a hand to Magnan, whom he pulled up, protesting.

"But, Retief—it's too crowded! We'll be crushed if these horrid great stone slabs shift position!"

"Still, it's our only way past the pit," Retief pointed out quietly and reached again to hand up Leroy, who in turn lifted Kith, hissing in indignation at being hauled up unceremoniously by his tattered cloak. "This area seems pretty stable," Retief added. "And obviously, someone's cleared it out recently."

"We're doomed!" Magnan wailed. "Buried alive!"

"Nonsense, Ben," Kith cut him off curtly. "Don't allow your arboreal genes to deprive you of your cool. I, as a scion of a ground-dwelling form, am quite at home here. Most soothing, in fact. I note a flow of air from *that* direction," he added, pointing, after readjusting his hip-cloak as well as its bent ribs would allow. "Clearly we've but to trace the draft upstream or down, and we shall win free of this crumbling pile in good fashion."

"Not a bad idea," Retief commented. "On the other hand, we're now next door to the Chamber of Doom. Maybe we can do a little eavesdropping."

"Plenty bad idea, Retief!" Leroy objected. "Time now tunnel up through loose slab, get back out in alley behind boarded-up warehouse."

"You go ahead, Leroy," Retief urged. "Escort Mr. Magnan and his captive outside; I'll be along in a few moments."

"Plenty too bad," Leroy commented to Retief, while urging Magnan toward a talus slope. "You pretty good fella, for palefella. Sorry no see again take to little grog shop and demonstrate local firewater."

"Perhaps I'll see you there later," Retief said, and turned to the heaped debris on the far side of which lay the Chamber of Doom. Among the stones he saw fragments of a bamboo-like wood, apparently an interior partition crushed by the collapse. From just beyond came the low scrape of Greenfella voices. Leroy crept cautiously up beside Retief.

"Plenty too spooky," he commented. "How palefella know dread chamber here? Me plenty lost."

"Actually, Leroy, it's quite simple," Retief explained. "Since we had gone only a short distance along the corridor, it follows that when the wall fell in, since we were outside the room adjacent to the Chamber; when we entered the space thus rendered accessible, we had to be next door to the chamber."

"Too complicate for simple Greenfella," Leroy objected. "Anyway, good place get away from, plenty too quick, before Boss Twill notice eaves-drippers violate security." He started away. Retief returned to his scrutiny of the collapsed stick-and-paper wall, and found a rent affording a view of the chamber beyond. He studied the half-dozen Greenfellas crouched uncomfortably on their low stools, heads ducked below the smoke layer. Abruptly, all rose, thus placing their sense-organ clusters squarely in the dense fumes. Then a new figure appeared, having apparently entered by a door across the room.

"To give you greeting, fellow communicants," the newcomer said in Groaci.

"Plenty greets you, too, Litter-boss Zilth," a Greenfella responded in his native dialect.

"No, no, the correct style is 'Colonel Broodmaster Zilth,'" the alien corrected sharply. Retief recognized him as Colonel Zilth, the Groacian Military Attaché. "Now, down to cases," Zilth went on briskly, unstrapping a bulky briefcase of worn tumphide to extract a gaudily-wrapped packet which he placed on the table before his hosts. "This is, of course, only a token, representative of the truly munificent gift of the Groacian people to Spood the Obtuse," the spindly diplomat announced grandly, now speaking flawless Business Obfuscese.

"Hey, already give plenty too many goodie old Spood," one local dignitary objected. "How about little baksheesh for faithful priest? We gottum eat too, you know." The others shushed him unenthusiastically.

"As you know," Zilth continued, ignoring the interruption, "it has already been my honor to deposit a major Groacian gift in the Sacred Well."

"If we know, hows come five-eye fella tellum again?" someone inquired, not without a trace of asperity in his tone. "You thinkum Greenfella dumb?"

"Merely to place matters in the proper frame of reference," the Groaci said smoothly, but incomprehensibly, in his own tongue.

"Plenty bigshot five-eye fella," Leroy explained to Retief. "Come few weeks ago, givum plenty gift. Tell how him big pal all downtrodden Greenfella. High priest tellum, 'Never mind scum; what kind goodies you got for high class priest?' Then five-eye wave all eye, make dizzy, tell get something special for High Priest Morris. So five-eye and Greenfella big pal now. Tell Terry palefella plenty too bad fella. But palefella untie me from moaning wall, make pal me."

"That gift package," Retief said. "I'd like to get a better look at it."

"Plenty too easy," Leroy assured the Terran. "Me slip through crack—you too big get through—stay under sacred incense layer, grab and get out before old Morris know." He clambered up, twisted sideways, and slid through to disappear in the murk. He was back a moment later with the prize, a brick-sized object in gaudy wrappings.

"Old Morris catchum now he fly me, no moobie-fruit," Leroy observed, handing over the heavy packet. "Him no gottum sense of humor."

"He'd make a capital ambassador," Retief commented, and moved back to where a shaft of daylight from above provided illumination. He opened the gift-wrapped parcel and sniffed it, detecting a sharp odor resembling crushed almonds.

"Leroy, how do we get to the excavation in the Sacred Well?" he asked quickly.

"Could go top, jump, but spoil when hit bottom," the local advised. "Better use tunnel five-eye fella dig."

"Lead on," Retief directed his guide. "Better hurry."

"First put gift back, old Morris needum, make big juju," Leroy countered.

Retief shook his head. "That wouldn't be a good idea," he told the anxious Greenfella.

"Old Morris notice prezzy him gone-gone, him blow stack," Leroy predicted.

"How long before he plans to make big juju?" the Terran asked.

"Climax of whole ceremony," Leroy supplied. "Wait five-eye bigshot come first. Now him here, maybe half hour to finish up ritual."

"Good," Retief said. "That ought to give us time."

"Better put back plenty too quick," Leroy insisted, grabbing for the small package. Retief blocked him off.

"That won't be convenient," he told Leroy. "Let's get going. Twenty-nine and a half minutes left."

"Better tell Mr. Magnan get move on," Leroy advised. "Morris drop palefella down well first, on top bigshot five-eye fella special gift, then fancy prezzy last, top off impressive offering make old Spood get on ball, but prolly no use: him plenty Obtuse."

They found Magnan awaiting them anxiously where they had left him.

"Candidly, Leroy," Retief told his voluble companion, "I doubt that Mr. Magnan intends to participate in the festivities."

"Him spoilsport?" Leroy inquired in a shocked tone. "Morris already tell big honor, him go direct to fancy hotel underground, get shine up Spood shoe, givvum manicure, supervise feast, organize celebration, keep blind eye on harem."

"But I hardly qualify," Magnan pointed out. "I don't have a blind eye."

"Oh, no sweat, Ben," the greenfella reassured the putative sacrifice. "Use special blind-eye tool, belong old Morris, fix right up."

"One could hardly debase oneself by participating in such barbarous rites," Magnan's reedy voice spoke up loftily. "Accordingly, while sensible of the honor proffered, I must decline."

"Too bad," Leroy commented. "Old Morris not take disappoint too good. Him love use eye-tool, not get practice in long time. Prolly do *both* eye, time him catchum."

"That being the case," Magnan muttered, "I shall take steps to defer that occasion so long as possible. By the way, Retief, I found the way above quite blocked, though that scamp Kith did manage it. That means you'll have to devise another means of egress—and speedily."

"Plenty too right!" Leroy seconded. "Old Kith spill bean, pretty soon have all cop in Forbidden City beat out, poke stick in all hole, find palefella, and me, too! So which way we go, Retief?"

"I didn't realize I'd signed on as town guide," Retief commented. "But there's only one way to go, so we may as well be about it."

"Palefella overestimate escape route by one," Leroy stated gloomily. "Sum total way out secret passage equal big goose-egg. So better compose self, die quietly, save strength for fight with devils in Underworld." He folded his talking-leg and lay down on the stone floor.

"Bye-bye," Retief said and turned toward the fallen paper partition.

Magnan dithered, then followed. "But as I reckon it, you're heading straight for the Chamber of Doom," he protested.

"We wanted to find the way to the entry to the Sacred Well, didn't we?" Retief reminded his supervisor. "Where would it be except here?"

"But—if I go back, they'll throw me down the horrid pit," Magnan quavered. "And they'll be doubly vindictive since I once cleverly eluded their grasp. They'll take measures to insure I don't outwit them again!"

"We'll just take a few measures ourselves," Retief told the agitated bureaucrat soothingly. He paused and handed Magnan the gift-package Leroy had filched from the High Priest.

"What does that look like, Mr. Magnan?" he asked. "Or, more to the point, smell like?"

Magnan fingered the heavy polygon, sniffed it gingerly, then passed it back to Retief, recoiling.

"Why," he exclaimed. "That's Verbot Seven! Wherever did you get it? Be careful, it's touchy stuff."

"Leroy found it in there," Retief replied, indicating the dim-lit Chamber visible through the shattered parchment panel.

"But—Verbot Seven's even more potent an explosive than Verbot Six," Magnan objected. "And that's been compared with a primitive fission bomb. Still," he mused, "one wonders what they hoped to accomplish with only a pound or so of the devilish stuff."

"Don't worry, Mr. Magnan," Retief reassured the senior officer. "They dumped a ton or so of it down the Sacred Well; this is only the detonator, and it seems Zilth has the firing button."

"What?" Magnan yelped. "A senior Groacian attaché is actively participating in this diabolical scheme? His own Foreign Office will disown him for this!"

"Not unless we find a way out of old ruin to tell on him," Leroy pointed out.

Retief moved forward to the thin partition, just as Assistant High Priest Irving approached the paper screen, through which Retief could see him as he leaned casually against the flimsy partition. Leroy, who had crept forward, jabbed at the taut paper with a talon-like digit. The flimsy material split and Irving crashed through it and directly into the embrace of Leroy, who used a complicated throw to propel his former tormentor into a cramped space between fallen roof-slabs, where

he threshed and fiddled frantically until Leroy
nudged a precariously balanced stone new-fallen
from the wall, causing it to rock alarmingly toward
the discomfited churchman's unprotected head.

"No!" Irving protested almost unintelligibly. "No
squashum saintly gourd, help out instead, give
former sweeper-caste nobody plenty green stamp,
title, personal executioner, all prerogative bigshot!
Don't waste only chance be important Sir Leroy!"
Irving flinched as Leroy set the balanced stone to
rocking again.

"Leave in hands Spood," he told the fallen priest
indifferently. "Me givum little nudge, even chance
it fall on gourd, not squash; squash, better give
prayer wheel extra spin."

"Give plenty promise, spin wheel till bearing
over-heat," Irving vowed, meanwhile attempting
to edge sideways in the confined space.

"Old Spood not need promise, got plenty already," Leroy dismissed the suggestion curtly.

As Leroy and his captive held their whispered
conversation, Retief observed the Greenfellas in
the chamber through the now wide-open rent in
the partition.

"Where assistant High Priest go?" someone demanded. "First palefella sacrifice split, now Number Two hocus-pocus artist him go without say
'Ciao.' Not much in way of ceremony left; Old
Spood be in bad mood!"

"Not makum difference," another returned. "Old
Spood in good mood when city fall down; can't be
plenty too worse him gripe; maybe better. Maybe
him not only obtuse, but mix-up in head, too."

"Not *too* mix-up in head," the other demurred.
"Him con Greenfella into keep supplied with old
tire, defunct picture-tube and all kind good stuff
five thousand, six hundred and five year. All time,

him no givum answer one prayer. Him shrewd operator."

"Where you catchum precise age Sacred Well?" someone challenged.

"Easy," the malcontent replied. "In college, prof tell five thousand, six hundred year old; that five year ago."

There was a sudden stir at the far side of the smoky room, and Retief saw Kith clamber down into view through a gaping hole in the ceiling. The Groaci went at once to Zilth, made the ritual obeisance due a Broodmaster, and began scooping up dust and dribbling it over his head.

"To have clemency on this dutiful one," Kith keened before pausing to sneeze. "To have hot dope to report, so take it easy on the head-lopping for a sec, OK?"

Zilth spurned his underling with his foot, nearly losing his balance in the process. Hastily reassuming his dignity, he hissed: "To report at once, base reject of the spawning-racks! To have expected to find you in attendance upon our arrival here at this barbaric ceremony in this desolate trash-dump! Instead I was obliged to wing it, hoping the while to avoid giving lethal offense to these three-legged bucolics, thereby lousing up my mission! Give me the hot dope first, then pour out your excuses at leisure!"

"Some leisure," Kith responded cheekily. "The dump is about to collapse, and you talk about leisure!" As if suddenly realizing what he was saying, Kith reversed himself with commendable verbal agility: "What I'm tryna say," he said, "is how cool your greatness is in the face of imminent demise, even taking thought to plan this lowly one's leisure-time activities, which if I ever had any, I got a few ideas my ownself. Anyway," he amended lamely, "I just now managed to wrest myself from the clutches of Ben Magnan, the well-known enemy of the Groacian people, which he—"

"To have ordered you to lay this same Ben Magnan by the heels," Zilth cut in imperiously. He made a show of looking around the murky chamber. "So where is he? I was given to understand he'd be the chief sacrifice today."

"I'm tryna tell you, sir," Kith protested. "He was right here, setting on that stool, but Retief come along and cut him loose!"

"Retief!" Zilth cut in. "The arch-criminal of all time! Are you saying he's here, in the tabu quarter, violating not only solemn interplanetary accord and the local sanctum sanctorum, but Groacian claim-territory as well?"

"I guess so, Colonel," Kith agreed confusedly. "But mainly he's sneaking around spying on you and the local bigshots here—"

Zilth cut him off with a commanding gesture. "And whilst the miscreant roams at large, you babble of leisure time?" He turned to the High Priest, who had been standing by gaping at the exchange between the aliens in their breathy tongue.

"Visiting bigshot tellum what give!" he fiddled as he caught Zilth's middle eye, the other four being occupied in scrutinizing all four corners of the murky chamber, "What bad news five-eye coolie tell?"

"We were merely nattering of administrative trifles," the Groaci diplomat replied smoothly. "Captain Kith is a devoted servant of Groac, but he needs a little smoothing up about the edges before he truly fits in as a Groacian diplomat." With that he returned his attention to the prostrate Kith.

"Now palefella sneak out," Morris explained to Zilth, "needum new sacrifice, purely honorary, so you nominate and elect by acclamation. No worry, not real sacrifice, just play like sacrifice, fool old Spood." The High Priest proffered the ceremonial noose. Zilth brushed it aside, not having understood Morris's hasty Obfuscese. He aimed four eyes accusingly at Kith, still groveling at his feet.

"To rise, lowly one!" he hissed. "To venture forth and confront the Terry evil-doer, truss him, and bring him here in the instant!"

"To not know where the scoundrel is by now, Great One," Kith moaned. "He was trapped with his hench-beings in the rubble yonder—" the Groaci paused to wave vaguely "—and was actively seeking a route of escape. If he found it—alas, I fear he's gone! Besides, to not have no truss in my pocket."

"To abstain from assuming the worst!" Zilth commanded. "To know well that I have arranged a secure route from the Well to the street! To make use of it to reconnoiter!"

"Not like listen foreigner tell stuff in whispers Greenfella no kapoosh," Morris fiddled impatiently. "To use the Obfuscese, as previously agreed!" As he finished his speech, one of his underlings came close and spoke softly to him. Morris nodded and his mouth-parts writhed in the expression that Retief recognized as a sinister smile, the equivalent of a Corps 921-m (Just Wait'll I Lay This on Him.)

"By the way, Broodmaster," Morris fiddled as if casually, "Chester here just remind me: me fallum behind with big juju, old Spood might be out to lunch. So better get on with formality. Time now generous worshipper have ceremonial rope arrange around neck." Morris turned to a morose-looking sub-priest who had come forward with a length of stout hemp, which he carefully arranged in a hangman's noose. "Be careful, Henry," Morris cautioned. "Broodmaster gottum plenty skinny neck.

No want break accidentally." He nudged Henry and nictated an ocular membrane in a grotesque parody of a conspiratorial wink.

"To be sensible of the honor," Zilth said carefully, recoiling from the noose. "But to be forced to decline."

"Five-eyes bigshot insult great Spood?" Morris scraped in a shocked tone.

"Whom, I?" the Groaci queried. "You forget, fellow, that it is even I who have made the munificent contribution to this same Spood's material welfare! Such ingratitude is not to be borne. I'll take my goodies and go home!"

"Too late be Indian-giver," Morris pointed out glumly. "Dump all goodies down hole, no way fetch out again. Spood obtuse, but no dummy; him protect all goodie belong him!"

"Very well, let it go!" Zilth urged in a more conciliatory tone, allowing Morris to drape the ceremonial rope about his neck. "Come along, Kith," he added in the manner of One Who has Tired of Disputation with his Intellectual Inferiors (73-f).

"Bad tactics, that 73-f," Magnan whispered to Retief. "There's a limit to the amount of sass these yahoos will absorb. We'd best follow him," he added as the two Groaci swept from the dread chamber as grandly as was possible with their triangular crania precisely in the smoke layer, above which the locals towered.

"This way, sir," Retief suggested, and led the way along the paper wall to a sliding panel he had noticed in the corner, behind a fallen slab of the porous local rock. There was a scuttling sound as a large landfish wriggled away ahead of him. The door, though warped, moved aside silently.

"Hey, you-fella on ball," Leroy squeaked in a muffled tone as he attempted, awkwardly, to speak and simultaneously squeeze past Retief. "You findum special exit for official use only, priest get bore long ceremony, sneak out for quick one. Assistant High Priest Irving decide want see last of us. Him tellum. Me leave in safe place."

Keeping below the smoke-layer, Retief, Magnan, and Leroy moved silently across to the inconspicuous exit through which the Groaci delegation had departed. It stood ajar; beyond it a narrow passage, seemingly reinforced recently and cleared of debris, led off into darkness, trending slightly downward. A landfish scuttled past Retief's feet, eliciting a startled yelp from Magnan and "Pesky bugger!" from Leroy, who slapped futilely at the creature with a worn sandal.

"Shocking!" Magnan exclaimed. "Simply because it startled you, to attempt to take the life of an innocent creature!"

"No take life, landfish plenty too tough," Leroy demurred as he awkwardly replaced the sandal on his left foot. "No startle; no likum pest because all time find eat while honest Greenfella hungry!"

"On the other hand," Retief mused aloud, "the landfish spend their time looking for food, while the honest Greenfellas catch up on their rest."

"Right!" Leroy agreed. "What good be dominant lifeform if force by circumstance work like landfish?"

"Really," Magnan put in, "that seems a quite unreasonable basis for such hostility."

"*Au contraire*, Mr. Magnan," Retief demurred. "It's the traditional basis for all social unrest."

"Plenty too many politic," Leroy muttered, nearly tripping in the process. "Oh-oh," he added. "Got to watch step along here: five-eye dig passage in big hurry, get finish before Terry delegation arrive, leave plenty rough spot."

"Oh, the unprincipled treachers!" Magnan groaned. "They took advantage of our courtesy in making a prior appointment to prepare this scheme, whatever it is."

"No schemes," Leroy objected, "just quick escape route in case need in hurry."

"And all the while that plausible Deputy Assistant Foreign Minister Shiss pretended to be negotiating in good faith for an equitable division of spheres of influence here on Popu-Ri," Magnan registered his indignation with the order of things, "they were actually preparing positions beneath the sacrosanct ruins of the ancient capitol."

"Sure," Leroy agreed. "Pretty sneaky, five-eye fella have good idea before palefella."

"Are you implying, Mr. Leroy," Magnan demanded with asperity, "that high-principled Terran diplomats would stoop to the level of double-dealing chicanery exemplified by the very passageway we traverse at the moment?"

"Plenty too many big word, Ben," Leroy objected. "Mean pretty good plan get in on ground floor, build escape route so come and go while palefella hold meeting. Old Kith got careless, tip off palefella, him in for hot time when litter-boss find out."

"To be sure," Magnan murmured. "And the scamp deserves all he shall receive; imagine his darting off, after pledging his word he'd make no move to escape if only I'd remove his chain. Disgraceful!"

"You plenty gullible, Ben," Leroy commented in the helpful tone of one explaining arithmetic to a six-year-old.

The two Groaci were invisible in the darkness ahead, but the clatter of their sandals was clearly audible, until it abruptly ceased.

"Hold on," Leroy counselled. "This where get chance make big mistake. Passage branch out, could go either way. One way lead to Sacred Well, other way go straight to street—anyway, what older boy say."

"And how, pray tell, are we to know which is which?" Magnan inquired coldly.

"Try one, fall in Sacred Well, not right way," Leroy explained solemnly.

"Are you saying," Magnan demanded, "that you have led us into this Stygian maze with no knowledge of how to extricate us?"

"Not know about stagy part," Leroy demurred. "No time now for extrications. Better concentrate on get out of here before desiccate like all mummy find here in sub-popurean passage."

As Magnan continued his quarrel with the local, Retief pressed on, arriving ahead of the others at a side passage apparently recently hacked in the ancient stonework. He stepped inside and paused to listen. From not far ahead he heard the stealthy tread of floppy Groaci sandals and the breathy whisper of muted voices. Behind him, Magnan and Leroy stumbled past the entry, still wrangling.

"Just keep go, Ben," Leroy was urging the nervous Terran diplomat. "Figure out which way lead to surface, sunlight, and safety—"

"This is no time for alliteration," Magnan rebuked the frivolous Greenfella.

"Not have stick juicyfruit unwrap so can litter," Leroy protested. "Some other slob guilty party. Anyways, no seeum litter."

"I said *nothing* about litter," Magnan declared in an indignant (3-c) tone. "One can hardly be expected to be concerned about keeping Popu-Ri beautiful where one is faced with mummification here in this uncharted warren!"

Retief, flat against the wall of the side passage, heard the sudden cessation of whispers, then, in Kith's sibilant tone: "To flee instanter, great one, to hear the vile Terries beating the brush close at hand!"

"To be beating their gums, not the non-existent brush, genetically deficient litter-mate of drones," his superior corrected. "To have nothing to fear from the feckless Soft Ones, whom you yourself quite properly led into the maze to be lost. Now to return to our task in haste, ere Morris and his three-legged nitwits come along to finish off the silly ceremony prematurely."

"Great One," Kith's feeble voice came hesitantly, "to be absolutely *certain* our escape route is clear? To have no desire to be in the vicinity when the ceremony reaches its dramatic climax."

"To fear not, feckless one! To have no more desire than your lowly self to experience self-immolation!"

As the two conspirators fell silent, Retief picked up a golf-ball-sized stone and tossed it toward them, then faded back around the corner and flattened himself against the rough-hewn wall of the main passage. A moment later Kith thrust his triangular head out, all five oculars erect and moving hypnotically in the reflexive basic search pattern. Retief quickly grasped his skinny neck in a firm grip, his thumb carefully against the Groaci's vulnerable throat sac to discourage any effort to utter a bleat of alarm. After the briefest of scuffles, Kith went limp.

"To report instanter, drooling defective!" Zilth's breathy command came as he hurried up to investigate. Retief tripped him and put a foot on his horny chest, holding him prone, then stooped to remove from his captive's hip-pouch a small cylindrical object which was instantly recognizable as a Bogan Mark LVI all-application detonator.

"To remove your clumsy pedal extremity and to

assist me to my feet at once, vile Terry!" Zilth hissed. "Where's that sorting-bin reject Kith?"

"Here, sir," Kith reported from his supine position near at hand. "To have rescued me too precipitately, sir," he went on, "to better have played it with a trifle of subtlety, creeping up on the miscreant."

"To presume to criticize your immeasurable superior in performance of his solemn duty to undo the mischief an inferior has done the mission by his stupidity?"

"To not quite see, Elevated One, what use your stupidity might be in undoing disaster," Kith came back cheekily.

"It was not *my* stupidity to which I alluded!" Zilth snapped.

"While on the subject," Kith put in, "might one point out that we wouldn't have been pelting through these perilous passages in the first place—"

"By no means!" Zilth cut him off. "And no more of your abrasive alliterations!"

"You just alliterated your ownself," Kith muttered rebelliously.

"As is my privilege," Zilth reminded his underling. "Now, Retief," he continued smoothly. "You forget to help me up, after which you may assist poor Kith here."

Retief stooped to grasp one of Zilth's elaborate shoulder-boards and lift the excited officer to eye-level.

"To continue on your way, Colonel," he told the struggling Groaci. "Kith and I will trail along behind, just so you don't get lonely." He thrust the disheveled Colonel back into the side passage; Zilth at once scuttled away. Retief grabbed Kith's thin arm and followed, dragging the protesting fellow. Some twenty feet along the passage, Zilth halted and stepped from view. Kith made a lunge and ran ahead, disappearing just as Retief came up. Feeling over the wall, he discovered a narrow vertical crevice through which he squeezed with difficulty, finding himself in yet another rudely-hacked tunnel. Bright light glared briefly up ahead and Retief advanced to a heavy metal door, clearly salvaged from a spacecraft, and fitted with an elaborate electrolock. Just as the mechanism was about to close the heavy panel the last inch, he thrust into the narrow opening the massive gold-braided shoulder-board from Colonel Zilth's uniform, wedging it open. Through the crack he could see heaped crates and long shelves filled with smaller cartons. The Groaci were nowhere to be seen.

"Gracious!" Magnan exclaimed, arriving out of breath. "Did he . . .? Are we . . .?"

"Almost," Retief replied. "It seems to be a warehouse. Shall we take a look?"

"Goodness, no!" Magnan responded quickly. "We're already hopelessly lost in this crumbling pile; let's get out before it all falls in!" Even as he spoke, bits of perished masonry were dribbling down around the group.

Leroy had squeezed close to peer through the aperture into the bright-lit chamber.

"No use get in too big hurry, Retief," he fiddled. "Playum right, plenty goodie here makum Greenfella bigshot and some left over give palefella tip, too."

"You'd loot your own temple precincts?" Magnan asked in a shocked tone (421-B).

"No point waste masterful 421 on poor native him no understand diplomatic subtlety," Leroy pointed out. "Also, no point waste good loot just happen find near Sacred Well. Look like old five-eyes stockpiling plenty too many death-ray, rubber-band gun, other heavy armament, maybe plan take over Popu-Ri, but not reasonable: what good old, wore-out planet to five-eyes fella, got nice desert world back home?"

"The urge to expand is an insidious one," Magnan informed the naive fellow. "Once started on a planet-grabbing kick, the Groaci almost reflexively seize whatever real estate they can get their sticky fingers on."

"Sound like racial prejudice remark," Leroy commented without heat. "Me hear tell that big no-no for all Terry."

"Not *pre*judice, Leroy, *post*judice," Magnan corrected sharply. "After all we've suffered in our enlightened campaign to prevent the Groaci from invading half the underdeveloped worlds in the Arm, we're entitled to draw conclusions from their demonstrated behavior."

"Plenty too many big word," Leroy sighed. "But even unsophisticated native Greenfella see givum five-eyes fella inch, him takum couple country mile. Pretty dumb not face fact. Honest Greenfella got plenty wholesome prejudice, only Terry pamphlet give idea Terry think bad thing learn from experience."

"You have a flawed grasp of Terran policy anent proper treatment of inferiors," Magnan sniffed, jostling for better position. "I don't know about the rubber-band guns," he announced after a prolonged study of the lettering on the nearest crates, "but there does appear to be the better part of the authorized bench stock of a Class Three arsenal here, including dismounted infinite repeaters and even a hellbore designed for a ship of the line, all of Terran manufacture. So," he concluded, "I suppose that clears up the mystery of the raid on our depot at Stringbean last fall."

"Five-eyes steal plenty too many weapon," Leroy stared heavily. "Gottum big caper up figurative sleeve."

"Retief," Magnan said, plucking at his subordinate's arm, "you don't suppose we've by any chance stumbled upon the secret Groaci Prime Depot postulated by Colonel Trenchfoot, do you?"

"Not by chance," Retief corrected, "by following Colonel Zilth."

"To be sure," Magnan agreed. "I shall be sure too make clear in my report that I came here for the very purpose—speaking of which, where do you suppose the scamp has gotten to? I don't see him, or his toady, Kith, anywhere in there."

"Palefella too tall," Leroy said from his position in a low crouch, whence his talking member jabbed like a fiddler's elbow. "See five-eyes fella crawl under bench over on left side, not come out. Prolly door belong tunnel hide in there."

"Try to get this thing open, Retief," Magnan ordered nervously, the while tugging ineffectually at the unlocked but unmoving panel. Retief gripped the edge, put a foot against the jamb, and heaved. A sharp tinkle of breaking metal came from the interior of the close-and-lock mechanism, and the door yielded grudgingly, with a protesting squeal.

"Quietly!" Magnan cautioned. "We don't want the beggars to know I'm here!" He leapt and uttered a yelp as a scaly landfish scuttled between his feet and through the opening.

"Watchum landfish," Leroy counselled. "Him know way to surface—and bettum him go straight to five-eyes tunnel."

"You're right!" Magnan declared. "The nasty thing is headed straight across to the spot where they disappeared!"

"Rather than chasing Zilth," Retief suggested. "I think we'd better go back and look a little further into the nature of the Groaci's gracious gift to the local populace."

"Now *you're* doing it!" Magnan charged. "These

dreadful alliterations: you picked that up from Kith! But I suppose you're right. We really ought to be specific when we prepare our report."

"Bad medicine poke snoot in priest business," Leroy stated. "No need swipe old Groaci's prezzie anyway; gottum plenty old tire already, sell tourist."

"I assure you, Mr. Leroy," Magnan declared idly, "that to purloin pretties dedicated to the deity—" he broke off, said "Excuse it, fellas," and resumed, "was the farthest thing from my mind."

"Spood pretty obtuse," Leroy pointed out glumly, "but even him notice five-eyes foreigner foraging—" he checked himself, made the greenfella gesture of abject apology, and finished lamely: "—and palefella poking around, him vent all kinds wrath on humble Greenfella happen to be along."

"You keep to the rear," Magnan proposed.

"No foolum Spood," Leroy predicted. "Him see everywhere, even around corner."

It was an uneventful ten minutes of groping along the dark passages back to the point where they had turned aside to follow the Groaci.

"Sacred Well straight ahead," Leroy announced, reverting to his brisk tour-guide manner. "Big hole in ground plenty legend tell where Spood chase devil straight up through solid rock long time passing, then him go in business number one deity in Greenfella pantheon. Not far, but watchum step, fall in crack take three-week climb out again."

They moved on, finding the way dim-lit now by barely glowing chemical lamps of Groaci manufacture placed at wide intervals.

"The vandals have hacked unheeding through the ancient masonry," Magnan mourned. "There's no telling what priceless antiquities they've destroyed in the process—look there at that fragment of a mosaic they exposed, doubtless destroying the rest."

" 'Restroom,' palefella mean," Leroy corrected. "Five-eye, him smashum genuine prehistoric flush-john, no respect achievement of ancestor. Reach ramp just ahead, now," he added.

"You nearly did it again," Magnan snapped. "It's an insidious disease. We must be careful not to bring it back and infect our colleagues. Can you imagine Staff Meeting, Retief, if everyone were attempting to one-up everyone else with the most ingenious example of the device?"

"It's too dreadful to contemplate, Mr. Magnan," Retief agreed solemnly.

"Take slow, now," Leroy cautioned, edging out ahead of Retief. "See edge Well pretty soon—look out!" he scraped the warning and jumped back as a number of small objects *whoosh!*ed past, falling from above, where a dim disc of pale daylight was rimmed with the silhouetted heads of Morris and his sacredotal assistants.

"Over here," Leroy suggested, indicating one of the multitude of inconspicuous narrow openings in the wall. The Terrans followed and traversed a curved passage terminating in a cloudy panel of translucent plastic affording a view of packed trash.

"All priest come down, look over take, maybe find good sneaker, not too many hole, almost fit," Leroy explained. "Old Spood not know difference. Open up access door here," he paused to indicate a metal plate resembling an incinerator door, "Take out what like, use, sell to tourist. Well, priest got to eat, too. Old Spood got plenty stuff spare for hard-working priest. Plenty secret this, you wager hat, posterior, and athletic supporter," he concluded proudly.

"Are there other such peepholes?" Magnan asked anxiously. "One can't see a thing here except all this rubbish that's probably been here since your last ice age. We really must get a look at the Groaci gift. It's up at a higher level, one supposes."

"Right again, Ben," Leroy congratulated his attentive audience. "Long haul ahead, got climb couple geologic era get up to Holocene."

It was a toilsome hour's ascent up crumbling steps inside the massive wall to the top level, as evidenced by the wan sunlight striking down through various chinks in the rock-slab ceiling. Magnan approached the murky window and at once exclaimed:

"There it is, in one-pound packets, just as stolen from the armory; there must be tons of it!" He stepped back to afford the others a view of a jumbled heap of brick-sized olive-drab objects, pressed down by the weight of more of the same above.

Retief tried the access panel; it popped open easily, pressed by the waxed packages inside. Retief picked one up, sniffed it, read the notice printed on the top in bold black letters:

WARNING: THE CONTENTS OF THIS PACKET ARE HAZARDOUS TO ALL KNOWN LIFE-FORMS. IN ADDITION THE PACKET WILL DETONATE IF DESTABILIZED BY ENERGY INPUT EXCEEDING THAT SPECIFIED IN CWM16-23 (62c).

"Kills on contact, and blows up too," Magnan translated. "It's a wonder it didn't blow when those ignorami dropped it down the well. Actually," he added, eyeing the solid wall of tight-squeezed bricks nervously, "it could blow at any moment from the pressure alone."

"It's safe until the date on the carton," Retief

pointed out. "After that, it's touchier than a crooked politician."

"And the date . . . ?" Magnan prodded.

"Last July," Retief supplied. "So be sure you don't drop it." He handed Magnan the explosive. Magnan shied, but gripped the polyhedron firmly.

"Whatever am I to do with it?" he quavered. "If I should relax for so much as a moment . . ." he trailed off. "We'd better put it in a safe place," he amended.

"How about the warehouse?" Retief suggested.

"You mean we have to transport these infernal packets, one at a time, all the way back there?" Magnan protested. "We'd never finish!"

"Hey, Ben," Leroy interrupted. "Me fixum—"

"Silence!" Magnan ordered. "This is no time for your tortured syntax. This is an emergency of the first order! If that charge should blow, the entire city will be leveled, including the Terran Mission!"

"Go ahead, Leroy," Retief put in. "How you fixum?"

"No shush loyal guide, Ben," Leroy demanded resentfully. "Make mad; but Retief tell nice, so me remind you boy, gottum tight union, give secret cry, all Greenfella roustabout come help load gift in Groaci godown."

"Oh," Magnan breathed, "in that case, Mr. Leroy, I must apologize for my intemperate remarks but now; I'd no idea—"

"No temperature-regulatory exudation," Leroy soothed. "Hold tight!" Immediately after the warning, he drew his sound-producing member across the rutch-pads on both outer limbs, eliciting a screech which seemed to penetrate to the bone marrow.

"Sorry," he said quietly, "but need plenty gain boost signal through solid rock and garbage, reach all loyal Greenfella within one mile. Outside range five-eyes-fella auditory membranes, so no tippum off. Get ready: eager helper come now."

A lanky Greenfella arrived at a run, jostled by those behind, and in a moment the passage was packed solid with excited volunteers. Leroy quieted them with a second whistle almost as piercing as the one that had called them. As the clamor subsided he briefed them tersely:

"Got plenty bomb five-eyes fella sneak in here, need move fast! Cedric—" he paused to administer a sharp rap to a still-excited colleague. "Cedric, you takum one piecee bomb, takum to five-eyes godown plenty too quick. Let him through, you bums, or maybe palefella get impatient, clear passage with bomb!"

At this, the agitated locals fell into a column of twos, flat against the walls, affording passage to a steady stream of porters, each supplied with a two-pound packet of Verbot Seven. In an hour, the Sacred Well was clear of explosives and only an innocent layer of household garbage was visible, adorned with a scattering of shattered plastic joss-figurines of Groaci provenance.

"Five-eyes fella sell plenty sacrificial statue ignorant Greenfella, tellum high-class original art by master five-eyes sculptor, say plenty too cheap, make point Old Spood, not wreck budget, too," Leroy explained. "Me sacrifice couple hundred self, only last week. Another two guck shot to hell," he fiddled disgustedly.

"A pity," Magnan commiserated. "But this time the infamous Groaci greed has undone the rascals. Clearly, they'd hoped to blow the Forbidden Precinct wide open, thereby giving them free access to the archaeological treasures. Speak of killing the goose that laid the golden egg . . ."

"Oh, Ben," Leroy offered breezily. "You givum goose me, me see Old Spood get plenty golden egg, you gettum credit, with reasonable percentage of credit to me, for set up deal, OK?"

Retief preceded the others through the files of porters coming and going. At the warehouse he supervised the stacking of the explosive in a heap one hundred feet square. When the pyramid was half complete, he inserted the detonator block in the center of a layer where it was soon covered.

When Leroy and Magnan arrived, Retief took a Greenfella aside to counsel him solemnly.

"Spread the word to everybody to clear the area," he instructed the puzzled local. "You'll have to get at least half a mile from the Sacred Well to be on the safe side. Tell the boys to spread the word."

"No point now," Leroy demurred. "Sacred Well no blow up, all blow-up stuff gone. So why worry!"

"There still might be an accident," Retief suggested. "So get busy. Mr. Magnan and I have another errand to attend to, so be sure everybody gets the word."

Leroy reluctantly agreed, and began at once to harangue the nearest of the volunteers still loitering in the area, all of whom objected vociferously to the sudden dislocation.

"Really, Retief," Magnan sniffed. "One fails to see the need for such a draconian measure, now that the contraband is safely back where it belongs."

"Verbot Seven is tricky stuff," Retief reminded his supervisor, "You can't be too careful with it."

Magnan shied from the towering stack so near at hand. "It's true," he murmured, "the slightest jar has been known to set it off. Let's go, I have some paperwork back at the office."

"First, let's round up Kith and the colonel," Retief countered. "I still have a few questions to ask them."

"But—that might be dangerous," Magnan objected, edging farther away from the explosives.

"Is that what you intend to tell His Excellency the AE & MP when he presses you for details?" Retief inquired in a tone of honest inquiry.

"Good lord, no!" Magnan objected. "I shall merely point out that as intruders in the sacrosanct Holy of Holies of Popu-Ri, I was hardly free to roam at will, interrogating their honored guests, members of the Groacian Mission to the planet."

"Certainly a valid point, Mr. Magnan," Retief conceded. "No point in confusing his Ex with an excess of detail."

"Precisely," Magnan concurred in a more confident tone. "Now if we can but extricate ourselves from this maze, we can be about the proper business of bureaucrats, which is to say, the preparation in quadruplicate of reports clearly reflecting credit on my egregious competence in uncovering, ah, whatever it is I've uncovered, while at the same time exonerating myself of any culpability for any possible shortcomings in our handling of the matter."

"I notice you said 'our,' Mr. Magnan," Retief commented. "It's generous of you to share the credit."

"*And* the culpability," Magnan amended sharply. "Hark! I heard a sound but now—from there . . ." He pointed an unsteady finger toward a dark aisle between ranks of well-stocked shelves. Retief nodded, motioned Magnan off-side, and advanced quietly in the lee of a lower stack to skirt the dark passage; he came around its far end just as Kith darted forth. Retief caught him by one skinny arm, at which the Groaci uttered a breathy shriek.

"There!" Magnan yelped from the middle distance. "I heard it again!"

"That was just Kith greeting me," Retief explained as he dragged the protesting fellow out to the spot where Magnan was hunkered down behind the inadequate shelter of a small tarp-covered object. Retief lifted the cover to reveal a squat, compact field-model droonge projector.

Magnan leapt back with a shrill cry. "Why, it's a squat, compact field-model droonge-projector!" he exclaimed. "How *could* they? This is escalating into a full plot of hemi-galactic proportions! Whatever they intend to do with that infernal device is quite contrary to solemn interplanetary accord!"

"Solemn interplanetary horsefeathers, Ben," Kith riposted coolly. "The so-called Yllian Accord to which you doubtless have reference is a scrap of paper. Do you seriously imagine that Great Groac would permit such yivshish to interfere with the orderly unfolding of her manifest Galactic destiny?"

"Oh, your scheme embraces the entire Galaxy, eh?" Magnan pounced verbally. "Candidly, I'd hoped you'd limit your visionary plans for aggrandizement to the Arm."

"A great power is not to be suppressed forever by a few squiggles on a sheet of foolscap," Kith came back firmly.

"Kith," Magnan said cautiously. "You may as well know that I'm aware your persona as a low-caste gofer is but a ruse and that you are, in fact, a communicant in high Groacian Councils."

"At a policy-making level, Ben, you may be assured," Kith confirmed smugly. "And now that I have observed your meddlesome Terry policies in action at first hand, you may be assured that Groacian policy will reflect that enormity."

"It's a little too early to be going on the offensive, Mr. Undersecretary," Retief admonished the suddenly haughty alien. "We still have to get to the bottom of just what you have in mind for Popu-Ri and the Greenfellas."

"To be assured we have made due provisions for these trash in the New Order," Kith responded without apparent embarrassment.

"Such charming, trusting beings, the locals," Magnan gushed. "How could you take advantage of their naiveté to undo them? Why, this cavern alone, which you've stealthly excavated in the foundations of their most hallowed shrine, represents the destruction of a vast treasure of ancient artifacts, to say nothing of the obfuscation of orderly archaeological research into the early history of the site and of Popu-Ri prehistory!"

"So?" Kith whispered in the tone of one who earnestly seeks enlightenment as to the pertinence of an apparently irrelevant comment (261-g).

"Don't attempt to shrug this off with that inept 261 of yours," Magnan rebuked sharply.

"By the way, Mr. Undersecretary," Retief put in, "what were you doing back there in the stacks?"

"I? Doing?" Kith exclaimed in a tone of Utter Amazement at a Wild Implication (41-G). "I had but retired to meditate."

"Yes, your 41 *is* a bit more polished then your 261," Magnan commented judiciously, "but now that we've seen it, let's get on with the answers, eh?"

"To have been but innocently taking inventory, as is my duty as Acting Foreign Service Inspector," Kith hissed sullenly. Retief at once patted him down and came up with a pale purple document printed in green Groaci pot-hooks.

"Looks like a list of equipment for invading a Galactic cluster," he commented, after scanning it. "Listen to this: 'Cars, ground-effect, scout (armored, class three) in local national colors, three squadrons, 999 each,' and, 'Self-propelled energy cannon (space-capability) remote controlled, Category Ultimate, spec G-925831. 21 each.' And there's lots more." Retief turned to the second page, then riffled through to the back of the thick document.

"Battle cruisers, torpedo boats, infinite-range bombers," he read aloud. "You seem to have a fully equipped strike force HQ here." Then, to Magnan: "There must be more than just this one warehouse. Let's take a closer look at that dark alley where Kith was skulking." He led the way to a massive, vault-like door, closed tight.

"That's a Galactic Prime security portal, Mark IV," Kith told the Terrans. "You'll not easily pry that open."

"I don't intend to try," Retief pointed out. "You'll open it for us."

"To have taken leave of your rudimentary Terry senses!" Kith hissed. "Never to admit vile interlopers to snoop in a sacred Groacian military reservation!"

"To change your mind in a hurry, I'll bet," Retief predicted, "when I start tying those wiggly oculars of yours in knots. Which ones shall I begin with?" So saying, he gripped two of the Groaci's wildly dodging eye-stalks and laid one across the other. "On the other hand, I might just pluck them out by the roots," he mused aloud.

"Retief! You wouldn't!" Kith and Magnan wailed in unison.

"I'd rather not," Retief conceded, "but I'd do it rather than let you Groaci steal an entire Galaxy unopposed." He gave the stemmed organ a gentle tug. "So why not save time and a mess by just saying the magic word to open the thing?"

"Never!" Kith declared. "To be forced, Vile Terry, to acknowledge that Groacian might is not to be brought to naught at the mere whim of a buck Second Secretary and Consul!"

"Don't count on it, Mr. Undersecretary," Magnan counseled. "Retief has a whim of case-hardened duralloy." He winced as he watched Retief knot the two stalked oculars loosely together, but interrupted Kith's continued protest.

"How could you, Mr. Undersecretary?" he demanded, "possibly attempt to justify your brutal takeover of a peaceful, backward world such as Popu-Ri?"

"The possession of the means confers a right to employ those means!" Kith declared heatedly. "Or, 'Might is right!' as our great philosopher Slooth once said in an unguarded moment."

"I'm glad you brought that up," Retief told the unhappy diplomat. "It will save Mr. Magnan and yourself all sorts of moral dilemmas about my right to use my unquestionable opportunity to extract your obscenely agile optical members."

"To be undone!" Kith sighed, going limp. "To be hoist on my own petard! His Excellency Ambassador Ith once warned me about glibly enunciating large principles of ethics, lest they come back to roost on the fan that heeds them, or however the saying goes."

"Yes," Retief commiserated. "That's the trouble with the enlightened policies so often announced by scoundrels: some cynic will demand that they live up to them, and that's inconvenient."

"Still," Kith countered. "Once the gambit has served its purpose, what do I care for the whining of losers?"

"There you go again," Retief admonished, and gave Kith's eyeballs a tweak that elicited a distinct whine from their owner.

"Unless you want to report in tomorrow with these in your hip pocket," Retief pointed out mildly, "you'd better get that open—now." He released the broken Groaci, who at once lunged for the complex locking mechanism, placed his oral orifice close to an inconspicuous microphone and whispered "Yivshish!" Tumblers chattered inside the foot-thick slab; it trembled and began its slow swing inward.

"Yivshish!" Magnan yelped. "He said 'Yivshish'!" The vault-like door halted and swung briskly shut; an intricate sequence of mechanical sounds came from the lock, concluding with a hearty *clack!*

"I didn't like the sound of that last '*clack*,'" Magnan commented glumly. "All I did was repeat 'yivshish.'"

"It seems the lock responds to the same cue for both operations," Retief commented as the locking sequence sounded in reverse and the door opened a second time.

"Enough!" Kith screeched. "You'll wear out the mechanism! It cost as much as a gunboat, which is to say more than I'll earn in a century, standard— but that won't keep that tyrant Ambassador Ith from hitting me with a Statement of Charges that will keep my descendants strapped for the next four generations."

"Too right, Kith, you miserable incompetent," Zilth's voice came from just behind the door, now standing ajar. Retief gave the heavy panel a hearty shove and stepped through to be confronted by Colonel Zilth, just rising from where the sudden movement had pitched him.

"Oh, it's you, Retief," he said aggrievedly, rubbing a bruised elbow. "Rather shabby tactics, toying with Kith's oculars in that fashion—but effective, I'll grant you that. Of course I shall have to court-martial the scamp for divulging military secrets to the putative enemy."

"What he said is nothing to what *you're* going to confide in me," Retief commented.

"To be insane, rash Terry?" the colonel hissed. "My mandibles are sealed! You'll get nothing from me!"

"Wanna bet?" Retief inquired. With a swift move he knocked aside a power gun the colonel had extracted from beneath his warped GI hip-cloak. Then he took a firm grip on three of Zilth's stemmed eyes, eliciting a sharp yelp of protest.

"But you only twisted two of Kith's oculars!" he complained. "Three is dirty pool! Not even a general officer could be expected to resist in the face of such enormity!" The discomfited saboteur attempted to edge away, but halted at the resultant torque applied to his sensitive oculars.

"You go right ahead, Colonel," Retief urged. "I'll be here with your eye-stalks when you get back."

"Barbaric Terry!" Zilth charged. "Now, as to the data you require . . ." he broke off and edged closer to Retief to ease the strain. "This installation, constructed in total secrecy in a period of only three standard months under my personal supervision, is no mere staging depot; it's a full-scale field HQ, ready to launch Operation Gotcha at a moment's notice!"

"Let's get on to details," Retief prompted his suddenly voluble captive.

"Your tactics, Retief," Colonel Zilth complained, "are quite contrary to solemn interplanetary horse-feather; that is, I'd not anticipated such crudeness from a civilized Terran diplomat."

"The course of empire is full of these little surprises," Retief reminded the colonel. "You should have taken better notes in your Galactic History course at the Academy."

"History knows no infamy to equal your meddling in, nay, aborting the orderly unfolding of the Groacian destiny!" Zilth grumped. "Besides that, I'd have had the old promo cinched, but for you!" he twisted abruptly and Retief released him rather than permit the frantic plotter to sacrifice his vision. Zilth dashed off into a dark aisle with a wild cry. "All is not yet lost, vile Terry miscreant! To but reach my field office!"

Retief remained where he was until the colonel attempted a sudden dash back out the way he had gone; as Retief stepped into his path the startled Groaci shied violently and darted off into the warehouse area, where he concealed himself in full view behind a packing case marked, in spidery Groaci pot-hooks: VICTORY BANNERS AND CETERA. Retief, miming stealth, crossed to a point a few feet from Zilth and motioned Magnan over.

"Now, if we can just cut him off and prevent his getting to his command center," Retief told his supervisor in a stage whisper, "we'll have him." He motioned Magnan to take the far side of the aisle, while he himself moved casually closer to the colonel's crate, at which the Groaci darted out, encountering Magnan squarely in his path, skittered aside and made a dash for an inconspicuous door in the near wall, darted through and slammed it resoundingly.

"Pity," Magnan commented. "The beggar eluded me. In fact, Retief, you practically shooed him along to his hidey-hole."

"Correction, Mr. Magnan," Retief said quickly. "*You* cleverly herded him into his hutch—" he paused to shove a heavy crate in place to block the door "—where we could pen him up for safekeeping."

"Safe?" Magnan queried, eyeing the pyramid of Verbot Seven dominating the room. "But of course; clever of you to follow my lead so nicely. Now, I think it's time to go back and report to His Ex."

"Just as soon as we explore the rest of the facility, you mean, of course," Retief amplified.

"To be sure," Magnan agreed glibly. "I heard Zilth bragging about having everything but a Class

Nine Planet-wrecker here, so it actually wouldn't hurt to just glance about a bit." He followed Retief down the passage along which the colonel had been fleeing before his interception.

4

Leroy returned as the two Terran diplomats were inspecting the fourth and apparently last in the series of oversized caverns in the underground complex. The curious local noticed the packet of Verbot Seven which Magnan had placed on a shelf to free his hands to riffle through bound inventory sheets.

Leroy took the waxed packet, looked it over, held it near his lateral olfactory orifice to smell it, shook it gently, and commented: "Retief tellum five-eyes prezzie big excite; look pretty plain. Me unwrap take look-see—"

"Better not," Retief cautioned. "It could be rigged—" his voice was blanketed by a vast, echoing *Boom!* as Leroy, bored, tossed aside the two-pound carton of Verbot Seven into a crack in the wall. The blast dislodged a slab of recently applied concrete, which dropped down to reveal a yawning cavity beyond, into which most of the blast had been discharged. Retief helped Magnan to his feet, by which time Leroy was already through the opening; brilliant light sprang up, and automatic alarms yelped.

Under the actinic light of banked polyarcs set high on the curving walls of the great cave, rank on rank of armored vehicles were revealed, their rigidly-aligned rows stretching off into the distance, where the immense cavern narrowed, then widened again into yet another vast chamber where rows of air-cars could be seen.

"It's another whole series of volcanic magma

chambers," Magnan croaked. "All stuffed full of war materiel! The Groaci have assembled an entire invasion fleet here, the sneaky things, all the while chattering of art surveys!"

The intruders strolled the length of the warehouse, noting shelves and bins full of neatly tagged hand-guns, computer parts, mess-kits, ammunition, and office supplies. After the third hundred-yard-long cache of military supplies, the looted art works began: load after load of unsorted stonework, ceramics, corroded and uncorroded metal objects, dumped in heaps along the long axis of the cavern.

"Doubtless awaiting sorting and cataloging at their leisure," Magnan grumped. "It's shocking that they show so little reverence for the ancient treasures of a world."

"Show more reverence for all gold item," Leroy noted, scouting ahead. "Also take time sort out all old rubber boot, busted household appliance, back issue *Playbeing*, Interplanetary Geographic in big bundle." He hurried on. "Oh boy," he called back, "Hit pay-dirt, findum relic one-time fad for Detroit iron: 1923 Apperson Jackrabbit, Mercer Raceabout, Kissel Kar, even couple '27 Nash four-door, with original water in bud-vase! Maybe find Chevy ragtop yet."

"We need a full-scale survey team to sort and classify the loot," Magnan mourned. "No wonder we couldn't catch the smarties shipping anything off-world! Still, in spite of their irreverent handling, I suppose we should be glad they preserved all this."

"Dirty trick, seal all old junk underground," Leroy commented. "Long time Greenfella use old stone build hut, old pot cook up one piece fly-fly, not need work plenty too much, find everything need in old stuff. Five-eyes take away all goodie and don't even use. Look, here nice brass ceremonial chafing dish, make good spitoon."

"Your crassness is beneath comment," Magnan snapped. "Left to you locals, ancient Popu-Ri would have been stripped to bare lava."

As Leroy expressed his disillusionment, Retief strolled over to a former double door now blocked with fresh masonry. He used a handy cargo-hook to scratch away mortar joints until the stonework shifted and, at a hearty heave, collapsed. Beyond the opening he saw still more Groaci government-issue stacks, these not loaded with neatly packaged munitions but rather with row on row of tagged and numbered artifacts clearly dug out of the ancient city.

"Good lord!" Magnan exclaimed behind him. "No wonder no cargoes of looted treasures have been intercepted! It's all here, sealed in the cavern!" He stepped inside, went to the nearest shelf and fingered a squatting demon-god carved from a single crystal of the local green corundum.

"An emerald as big as a moobie-fruit!" he cried. "And look! There's an archaeologist's dream stored here! Objay d'ar of precious metal and stone, old tires—there's a perfectly preserved Michelen 250-16 whitewall—and an emperor's ransom in lesser treasures!"

"Handy," Retief commented. "It will save a lot of grubbing in the dirt when the official Commission arrives to catalog everything."

"To say the least," Magnan agreed smoothly, then addressed Leroy: "One assumes that in light of these disclosures your government will not be averse to assisting Terra in ridding Popu-Ri of these vile opportunists."

As Leroy considered, Kith appeared from a hidey-hole between crates.

"How did you hope," Magnan demanded of the

crestfallen captain, "to export all this under the very noses of our alert patrols?"

"Simplicity itself, Ben," Kith bragged. "When, in due course, the old dump finally and unfortunately collapsed, with a trifle of assistance from Groaci's gift to the Popurean deity, this reinforced chamber would have survived intact, to be stumbled upon by clever Groacian scientists assisting in the rubble clearance; then, of course, EGO would be forced to acknowledge our claim to the find."

"Diabolical!" Magnan breathed in a tone of Profound Admiration for Consummate Strategy, (1095-x).

"Just between us beings-of-the-galaxy, Ben," Kith said cheekily, "The scheme rates your z, eh? Even Enlightened Galactic Opinion couldn't fault it, umm? Umm?"

Impatiently Leroy broke in. "Not know plenty too many big word," he pointed out. "Greenfella glad throw out nosey five-eyes plenty chop-chop! Sue for few billion guck in reparation, too, plus civil suit recompense Greenfella for louse up tourist trade. You think Galactic Court sit still for fix jury vote ten megaguck?"

"Quite a lively possibility, Leroy," Magnan reassured the greedy local, "provided there are no atrocities, of course. That would lose you the sympathy of Enlightened Galactic Opinion."

"Problem area, Ben," Leroy pointed out unworriedly. "Simple Greenfella me, no know big word 'acortisy' . . ."

" 'Atrocity,' " Magnan corrected. "It means beating, torturing, or killing unarmed Groaci, stealing their fingering-stone collections, and so on."

"Oh," Leroy replied. "Sure thing, Ben. Idea catch and kill five-eyes popular enough not need special big word mean beat, torture, kill nosey five-eyes, takum all pretty, and other good stuff undisclose. OK?"

"Exactly," Magnan corroborated. "Spread the word, just to be sure no one accidentally does it."

As Leroy left at a lope, Kith spoke up.

"Ben," he said anxiously, as evidenced by the rapid fluttering of his outermost eyestalks, "to be quite sure these dumb locals won't misinterpret your admonition as a mandate to commit precisely those atrocities against which you so properly warned?"

"Surely, Kith, it hardly matters," Magnan replied airily, "inasmuch as I have both your and Colonel Zilth's solemn assurance that no Groacian personnel have in fact been illegally imported here in violation of solemn interplanetary horse-feathers—"

"To be once again hoist by my own petard," Kith cut in gloomily. "To wish now the colonel had been somewhat less all-encompassing in his denials."

"Still, why take the gloomy view?" Magnan jollied the crestfallen fellow. "A few of your troops—even perhaps yourself—may survive to testify at the trial to Groacian misconduct."

"Ben—to suggest—to hint that my own personal epidermis could be at hazard here?" Kith shrilled. "To flee instanter to a place of refuge, ere the insidious Leroy returns with a legion of his creatures to flay alive a faithful toiler in the vineyard of interbeing amity!" Kith tugged at Magnan's sleeve frantically. "The colonel would never let me take refuge with him inside his private nefarious-stuff parlor over there, so let's get moving, fast!"

"First," Retief suggested, "I'd like to give the colonel a chance to clear up a few more points Ambassador Gropedark will be curious about."

"To have no need to wait," Kith assured the

Terran. "I myself am not uninformed. What first, Retief? Name, rank, and organization of all crack troops on standby on the farside of the local moon? Schedule of propaganda incidents to be precipitated to put the locals in a mood to dismember all Terries on sight? Initial attack points to secure all tactically significant positions? Identities of major commanders, with classified service records? Allocation of funding to the various areas of the service? Victualing arrangements? Rendezvous points for massing of ostensibly peaceful mercantile vessels now deployed throughout the Sector?"

"To speak not one more word, vile treacher!" the badly-amplified voice of Colonel Zilth racketed across the cavernous room. "This place has, due to my providential arrangements, more bugs than a waterfront hostelry on Raunch Seven! I've recorded your pusillanimous tender of cooperation with the vile enemy, and you may be assured your betrayal will avail you naught! You'll never leave this installation alive, Kith! To have prepared even for this contretemps!"

"To do your worst, feckless Zilth!" Kith yelled breathily in response. "To go ahead, pull the chain! You forget, *sir*, that I am as well-informed as to your measures for betraying your faithful aides as I am of your schemes for Terran undoing!" As Kith's wheezy speech ended, a distinct tremor vibrated the stone floor, accompanied by a deep-toned rumble.

"This way, gentlemen," Kith urged, edging along into one of the many pitch-dark aisles. "The escape route lies here." Retief restrained Magnan with one hand as with the other he lit a permatch which he wedged in a convenient crevice in the steel shelving, to shed a wan glow on the narrow ledge along which Kith was moving cautiously.

The rest of the narrow strip of floor between stacks was gone.

"To make haste!" Kith hissed. "Phase two of the colonel's booby-trap will eliminate even this frail path."

"He's right, for once," Magnan quavered. "Only I fear I shall be unable to negotiate that tiny ledge; my vertigo, you know." He stared gloomily down into the yawning emptiness at his feet. "You'd best go ahead, Retief," he urged, "and get help." He squeezed his eyes shut.

"Just think about strolling down the Rue de la Pay on a spring afternoon," Retief suggested. "Relaxation is the secret. Come on." He urged the unwilling Magnan ahead.

"N-never," Magnan objected, balking after a few steps. "Were I on the broad avenue you invoke, I'd sit down at once at a convenient sidewalk cafe and order onion soup and a flask of Chateau d'Yquem."

"Shocking, Ben," Kith commented. "A sweet dessert wine with soup in the mid-afternoon? Barbaric!"

"Keep going, Mr. Magnan," Retief encouraged. "You're doing fine." He urged his rigid chief along a few inches more.

"Fine?" Magnan squawked, "I'm about to fall to my death or worse and you speak of fine? Why, I haven't even had my soup yet!" His eyes still shut tight, Magnan spread his arms and flattened himself tighter against the wall.

"Just edge sideways a few more inches," Retief suggested.

"Never!" Magnan declared. "I shall take up my position here, not to be budged by wild Caucasian ponies, until the rescue squad arrives." Retief give him a gentle shove. "Just a few inches more," he reassured his terrified chief.

"Don't!" Magnan yelped. "My equilibrium is in a fragile state. The slightest eccentric thrust will send me plummeting to the depths!" He shied, and Kith caught his sleeve and tugged.

"Unseal those flat eyes of yours, Ben," the Groaci urged. "You're betraying us all to our dooms."

Magnan opened his eyes slowly and looked down to discover that he was on solid floor, the narrow bridge behind him. "How—what . . ." he stammered.

"You waltzed across there like a high-wire artist, without even looking!" Kith congratulated the astonished Magnan. "Now to get it in gear! We've got ground to cover!"

"You know," Magnan said aggrievedly, "that confounded waiter never did bring me my soup."

"We'll make it up to you, Mr. Magnan," Retief soothed his rattled superior, as Kith hurried ahead across another perilous span. Magnan followed uncomplaining, as if half-dazed. Wan daylight appeared ahead, falling through a cleft in the masonry wall which on closer inspection was revealed to be a narrow ramp like a coal-chute. They climbed it like a rock chimney, arriving at the surface in a small courtyard curiously clear of debris. A group of armed Greenfellas awaited them there, Leroy in the van.

"Byemby me tellum all local big shot you Terry not like greedy five-eyes fella," the latter assured Retief. "Me tellum old Morris you findum plenty bang-stuff in Sacred Well, all priest grateful, help Terry get back to office before quitting time, sign treaty, make point with old Ambluster, get plenty promo, pat on head, nice vacation over nearest R & R planet."

"Leroy is becoming too sophisticated by half," Magnan muttered to Retief. "Still, his proposal is not without merit. So—shall we be off?"

"First, better lock five-eyes coolie up, in handy dumpster, come back bright day punish." Leroy proposed.

"Good notion," Magnan agreed and assisted Leroy in stuffing the protesting Kith into the capacious steel rubbish bin, where he pounded and yelled faintly.

"You'll be safe here," Magnan advised the noisy fellow.

"Better keep five-eyes one piecee, maybe make trade," Leroy told Morris. "No use waste trade good, eh?"

As the Terrans, with Leroy in the van, started toward the arched opening leading to the deserted street, Morris began fiddling excitedly. "Palefella no go away big hurry, leave mess belong Greenfella clean up! Old Ambluster Dopegark tell Terry fix all socio-economic problem area plenty chop-chop!" He leapt back as an oversized landfish scuttled across his foot. Retief blocked it off and picked up the wriggling scaled creature, which went limp in his grasp as he studied it carefully.

"Ingenious," he commented and carefully replaced it on the dusty ground; it at once dashed for a dark crevice and was gone.

"Indeed, Retief, ingenious are the ways of Spood," Leroy commented piously.

"Spood had less to do with that critter than the Ministry of Gadgets back at Groac," Retief told him.

Magnan gasped. "Retief! You don't mean those supposed vermin are in actuality electronic spy devices? I suspected it all along, of course."

"Not all of them," Retief corrected. "And not strictly spy-eyes."

"You may elaborate on that later," Magnan said graciously, "so that I may fully brief His Ex and Colonel Trenchfoot."

"Me gottum long trail to go, get sophisticate like Ben," Leroy observed morosely to himself just as he was negotiating a fallen lintel deeply carved with old Popurean Linear X script, occasioning a heavy fall. "'Wise Greenfella keep olfactory membranes out of other fella pidgin,'" he read aloud as he rose. "No gettum nostril pack full of lint.' Plenty good advice get from ancestor," he observed brightly as he regained his feet. "Old ancestor plenty smart, build fancy town in old volcano crater, sucker plenty tourist throw coin, hotdog, diamond pin down hole in ground, but then Spood get careless, let city fall down. Look like can't win old ballgame. Now, Greenfella descendant plenty dumb native, live in ruin, get cheat by five-eye fella, maybe start over. But to what end? *'Haec olim meminisse juvabis,'* as old Vergil say."

"You've read the Latin poets?" Magnan gasped.

"No, Vergil old snarf-node buddy, finger plenty kiki stone together, raise hell, get pinch, sing it off in jail. Him talk plenty too much, tell wisdom all time, big bore."

Back in the wan twilit avenue, they turned toward the sound of a high-revving vehicle engine, saw the Groaci Legation's car, ground-effect, Deputy Chief of Mission, for the use of, round a corner in a full slide, then skid to a halt as Counselor Ush of the Legation dashed toward the car from a half-collapsed doorway, followed closely by a mob of excited Greenfellas.

"I fear my admonition to moderation was indeed misinterpreted," Magnan mourned briefly, then dashed up to signal frantically to the Groaci driver, who ignored him to dismount and open a door for his hard-pressed chief, who dived into the capacious machine, slamming the vault-like door in the faces of the on-coming crowd—led, Magnan noticed, by Morris himself. Magnan went up to the irate priest, thrusting his way through the clamoring rank and file.

"Here, Reverend Morris," Magnan accosted the cleric, "kindly call off your chaps and I'll see to it that Terra steps in to right your wrongs."

"No givum gnawed moobie-fruit rind for so-called right and wrong," Morris demurred. "Leave all moral issue old Spood handle. What in deal for hard-working priest?"

"Carloads of pretties, under our Goodies for Undesirables program," Magnan soothed the agitated fellow, then rapped sharply on the limousine's window. It slid down a cautious inch and Ush poked an eyestalk tentatively out.

"Oh, it's you, Ben," the Groaci diplomat greeted his Terran colleague. "The streets aren't safe. Something's stirred up the confounded locals; to have barely escaped a horrid demise at the manipulatory members of the ungrateful swine! What do you want? I must be off to my Legation at once. The Minister will be furious!"

"He'll be furious anyway," Magnan reminded the Groaci. "As it happens, my party and I require a lift."

"What, I to pull you Terries' fat out of the fire? Scant likelihood, Ben. Ta." Ush leaned forward to tap on the divider glass.

"Not so fast, Ush!" Magnan objected, bounding alongside the car as it moved off. "But for my intervention, the locals will yet disassemble your transport as well as yourself! Open up, or I'll loose the wrath of outraged Popu-Rihood upon you, unimpeded!"

"What 'swine'?" Morris inquired loudly. "Nice compliment five-eyes give noble priest, or what?"

"More of a what," Magnan panted. "But stay your hand, Mr. Morris. Remember the GFU program." The car doors popped open at that point and Leroy and Retief slid in beside the driver, while Magnan took a position on the jump seat adjacent to Ush's special tump-leather throne.

"Drink, Ben?" Ush offered urbanely, poking a button to deploy the elaborately silver-fitted bar. "Spot of Baccus black wouldn't be amiss, I suggest." He helped himself to a shot of aged Pepsi.

"Good thinking, Ush," Magnan sighed. "Goodness, I can hardly wait to get to the Embassy and tell Ambassador Gropedark all about my day's adventure."

"Damned frustrating day I've had," Ush grumped. "Colonel Zilth failed to make our rendezvous to report on the Groacian Cultural Program. Imagine! Keeping a Deputy Chief of Mission hanging about for half an hour in a drafty warehouse!"

"Don't blame the colonel," Magnan admonished. "He was delayed by circumstances quite beyond his control."

"Impossible!" Ush spat. "Nothing is beyond the control of a Groacian field grade officer!"

"No doubt authority carries with it a commensurate responsibility," Magnan conceded. "So—whatever eventuates here, we may be sure that it is indeed the colonel's doing."

"*With* the advice and consent of his superiors, of course," Ush confirmed complacently. "Here, Ben," he added irritably. "Do I hear the subtle *whirr* of one of your sneaky CDT sound-recording devices?"

"Just rewinding after the colonel's fascinating disclosures," Magnan reassured his host. "Kith, too; gabby little devil."

"Pay no heed to the gossip of underlings," the Groaci whispered hoarsely. "What do *they* know?"

"It's not so much what they know," Magnan corrected. "It's more what all that video footage we got of a full Imperial War Fleet stashed under the Forbidden Precinct will tell for itself. Not to mention the immense trove of looted art treasures you and your toadies have stashed away, under cover of conducting a survey."

"You said you weren't going to mention that, Ben," Ush protested. "Then you went ahead and mentioned it anyway. Inconsistent at best, I'd call that."

"Inconsistent?" Magnan yelped. "A benign inconsistency is to be preferred to your own consistent avarice and guile, eh?"

"Maybe better croak noisy five-eyes now," Leroy suggested cheerfully, "before badleg nice palefella and noble Greenfella pal."

"Good thinking, Mr. Leroy," Magnan purred, fingering the edge of a slim cheese knife included in the bar-fittings, while eyeing the Groaci's slender neck. He made a move toward the arrogant diplomat, who squeaked and leapt into Retief's lap.

"To be kidding, Ben!" Ush hissed. "To not badleg you! To feel only gratitude for rescuing me from that gang of troglodytes back there!"

" 'Trod light' badleg, Ben?" Leroy inquired, taking the knife from the Terran's limp grip. He edged along to a position closer to the Groaci diplomat. "Me scientific type," he commented. "Me wonder what color juice run out when stick pointy thing in skiny neck blong diplomat."

"Pale greenish-brown," Magnan supplied. "Not at all spectacular, Mr. Leroy. And as for 'troglodyte,' it's quite a neutral term, merely referring to those whose chosen abode is below the ground's surface."

"Chosen, heck!" Leroy fiddled, his enunciation somewhat muffled by the close confines of the crowded limousine. "Greenfella like live in open, plenty tall grass, jump with joy. Not like force live in old ruin, no electric, no run water except when drip from roof! Long for return old day before ancestor get big idea, build town so priest collect more offering for Spood, live fat, have snazziest Greengal, fine eat, vintage booze, all hardship endure to serve old Spood, but him so obtuse not notice priest get all goodie, only old tire and moobie-fruit rind and few gold statue too heavy for steps stay in Sacred Well. But better dim-witted chief deity of pantheon than no deity at all, as old Clarence say, in recent historical time, three weeks ago. Amen. Me takum nap now, after cut diplomat neck, all tucker out, tell big speech."

"Why not snooze first and commit murder later?" Magnan suggested.

"To do your worst, Ben," Ush urged sadly. "To bet you a Yalkan humidor full of hyacinth-scented dope-sticks that you wouldn't allow this primitive to soil his Ex's carpeting with the vital juices of his very own Special Aide for Nefarious Affairs." He broke off with a sharp *yip!* as Leroy jabbed lazily in his direction.

"Quite true," Magnan agreed, waving Leroy back. "I have too much respect for diplomatic privilege to sully Smoosh's personal conveyance in the fashion you so luridly describe. Oh, driver, pull over, please, beside the vacant lot just there."

"Ben! You wouldn't!" Ush groaned in passable Terran, averting all five eyes from the lonely weed-patch. "Are all our halcyon days of mutually respectful rivalry to end on this dismal note?"

"To be correct, Mr. Counsellor," Magnan replied in flawless Groaci Court Dialect. "Actually, I wouldn't. Just playing with your ventral, ladder-type nervous system."

"To have a care, Magnan!" Ush wheezed breathily. "You meddle in matters you wot not of! There are certain arrangements designed to deny to Terry spoilsports any profit from their meddling!"

"What?" Magnan gasped. "You *boast* of having mined the Holy of Holies?"

"Hardly, Ben," Ush fell back and regrouped. "A mere figure of speech."

"In any case," Retief pointed out, "since you Groaci conveniently used the old volcanic vents to enlarge for their storage areas, I rather think that any unfortunate accident is likely to be channeled directly along the path of least resistance, venting via the nearest bore, and will just give the old row a good dusting."

"Path of Least Resistance main street in old city," Leroy spoke up. "How palefella know?"

"Just a lucky guess," Retief reassured the Greenfella.

"In any event," Magnan sniffed, "It's hardly *our* responsibility. Now, let's get our story ready; collate data, that is, so as to—"

"So as to record a new page in the history of infamy!" Ush hissed. "To have a care, Ben Magnan! When word leaks out . . ."

"Not if I change my mind," Magnan purred, while Leroy angled the knifeblade so as to glint in the Groaci's primary eye, which instantly retracted, thereby reducing the alien's effective IQ to a basal, non-aware level. As the diplomat began to babble and play with his toes, the car pulled up before the once-ornate facade of the Embassy of Terra, housed in the former palace of an ancient beer baron. Just before the heavy car had come to a full stop, a larger-than-average landfish came wriggling across the tiled walk and under the car—to be precise, under the right front traction-disk, which elicited from it a meaty *crunch!* Magnan leapt out with a yelp; Retief followed and Leroy scrambled past him to grab up the flattened thing, smell it, and toss it aside.

"No good eatum polystyrene," he commented

in an awkward little dance. Retief looked down at the remains and saw, inside the burst cover, color-coded conductors and micro-chips, plus the remains of a Groaci Model L general utility electron motor. At his shoulder, Magnan uttered a sharp cry.

"Mr. Counselor!" he moaned. "Right in the Terran Embassy, too! You wouldn't! You couldn't! Sending out your infamous spy-eyes all over town! Why, I even saw them in the environs of the Sacred Well!"

"To underestimate Groacian abilities as usual, Ben," Ush remarked blandly. "But to point out, not all the landfish are ours; the ruins swarm with their natural prototypes. Still, I fancy we deployed an adequate number, and quite in keeping with the pertinent provisions of intra-galactic law, I assure you. Now, if you'll excuse me——" He started away, but checked abruptly at sight of a number of disreputable-looking Greenfellas quietly emerging from concealment behind weathered stones, shrubbery clumps, and a lone chowsicle-and-dopestick wagon which had deployed its awning squarely in the center of the entry walk.

"Here, Ben," Ush stammered, "to claim asylum; let's get inside, there's a good fellow, before these dacoits turn to savage me."

" 'Dacoit' nice word call Greenfella, Ben?" Leroy inquired, coming around behind the agitated Groaci. He signalled to one of the menacing mob, which had begun to disperse, fiddling shrilly.

"Oh, quite the best," Ush babbled. "It's a term the vile Terries often apply even to my own exalted kind, right, Ben?"

"To be sure," Magnan agreed. "Let him alone, Leroy," he added. "What Ambassador Smoosh will tell this chap, once I've briefed him, will make him rue the day he left his brooding nest."

"To protest!" the indignant Groaci hissed. "To have but performed my duty!"

"Oh, you admit it," Magnan spoke up eagerly. "To strip Popu-Ri bare of her antiquities and then blow up the Holy Precinct was no mere impulse of an over-zealous underling, but was in fact official Groaci policy, eh? Most interesting," Magnan made a ceremony of whispering a note into the field recorder in his left lapel identifying the foregoing as a free and voluntary confession.

"To 'confess' nothing!" Ush shrilled at top volume for the record. "To proclaim the coup!"

Retief ushered the frantic Groaci back inside the cavernous limo. "Better clam up, Ush," he advised, "before you get in so deep that even bureaucratic inefficiency can't save you."

"Ben, do advise his Terran Excellency to expect a courtesy call from Minister Plenipotentiary Smoosh. As you know, my chief is keen to cement Terran-Groacian relations, this little lift being a sample."

"Terry-Groaci relations are already encased in concrete and dropped off the end of a deepwater pier," Retief told the talkative official. "But thanks for the ride."

"Me givum plenty thank too," Leroy fiddled. "Too bad me missum spectacle see five-eyes big shot disassemble by piss-off crowd back in town. Still, get plenty too much time correct omission."

"On that cheery note we'll bid you good day, sir," Magnan commented as he carefully closed the heavy car door on Ush's worried expression, evinced by the droop of his four outer eyes while the center ocular stood erect, quivering.

The Groaci snorted as the big car dug off with a squeal of air-bladders against embossed paving tiles. The last few local agitators began to drift off. Retief made a shooing motion to the lone reluctant malcontent.

"Show's over, fella," he advised the disappointed vandal. "Phase One, anyway. Better tell everybody to head for the hills before Phase Two happens." The Greenfella bounded away awkwardly down the dirty avenue.

"Tail-end Charlie not get word," Leroy commented. "Me tellum all Greenfella get out of town before five-eyes fella make big juju, but better remind. Ta, palefellas, me hope seeum again sometimes."

"Stange fella, that Leroy," Magnan whispered to Retief. "At times he appears so sophisticated, then again he talks of 'big juju.' So inconsistent. Incidentally, Retief, you still have that little gadget you took away from the good colonel, I trust?"

"Nope," he told his chief cheerfully. "I planted it back on him where he'll find it as soon as he reaches for a dopestick."

"But—but—" Magnan stammered. "If he should make use of it, imagining that his blasting charge is still securely in the Sacred Well . . ."

"Five-eyes colonel pushum button," Leroy spoke up from directly behind Magnan, "all flat-sides bokkis gift turn into thunder and lightning, right?"

"So to speak," Magnan conceded.

"I'd call that heap big juju, Ben, wouldn't you?" Leroy fiddled triumphantly. "Ta." He hurried off.

"Didn't even wait around," Magnan grumped, "to receive his official expression of Terran gratitude for his assistance, and public acknowledgement of his part in what is about to eventuate."

"I think he's in a hurry to get back and help divide up the supplies old Morris had stashed in Cavern Number Two," Retief suggested. " 'Snazzy ragtop in hand worth plenty too much bronze testimonial,' as Leroy himself put it."

"He'd loot the Groaci loot?" Magnan yelped. "He wouldn't! His very own national treasures! Why, that Chevy must have been exported here centuries ago as a gift of the Terran people to the newly-discovered Popurean nation! Too bad the Greenfella anatomy wouldn't fit it unmodified!"

"I suspect, Mr. Magnan," Retief suggested, "that the Popurean in the street has less reverence for the past than has our own Cultural Attaché."

"Speaking of Perce Ebbtide," Magnan blurted, "I'll wager the dilettante is up there at the moment, cheek by jowl with his Ex, watching our every move. Come, Retief, let us proceed. Fear not: I shall give you, as my assistant, full credit for the manner in which you carried out my instructions."

"So if it comes to a Corps trial," Retief clarified, "you're prepared to take all the blame?"

"Trial?" Magnan yelped. "Whatever do you mean? Why, I've but done my duty as I saw it, selflessly implementing Corps policy while at the same time safeguarding hallowed Popurean tradition! Surely the Ambassador will see that!"

"Just kidding," Retief comforted his chief. "Now to see what our Chief of Mission thinks of his esteemed Groaci colleague now."

"Don't remind him of that unfortunate remark," Magnan cautioned. "He was only getting in a modest plug for approval by Enlightened Galactic Opinion."

"How did he expect EGO to hear him, secure in the privacy of his own chancery?" Retief inquired rhetorically.

"One would almost think he knew about the Groaci landfish-cum-bugs with which this infernal ruin is infested," Magnan said testily. "But at least his liberal position will indeed have been conveyed to EGO. That's enough smalltalk, Retief," he concluded. "We're out of sight of the Chancery wing now, so he can't read our lips."

"There goes another landfish," Retief pointed out. "But maybe it's a live one."

Magnan paused to peg an orange-sized and colored chunk of fallen stone at the creature, missing by a wide margin. "Pesky vermin," he commented. "Be it organic or otherwise. Infernally cheeky of Ush to plant them even here, on sacred figurative Terran soil."

"Still, since he doesn't know we hay-wired his com center," Retief reminded Magnan, "we may pick up a few tidbits of our own from his bugs."

"Retief! You scamp!" Magnan exclaimed, grinning. "You wouldn't! You didn't!"

"All at your command, if you recall, Mr. Magnan," Retief pointed out modestly. They went in past the Marine guards and took the lift to the Chancery wing, encountering Herb Lunchwell in the passage. The portly Admin Officer greeted them shortly.

"If, as seems apparent, you've been summoned to the Presence," he tipped them, "play it pianissimo. He's in a towering pet since his favorite local art treasure, that dreadful ithyphallic ashtray, has disappeared, probably pilfered by one of the sweeper staff."

"Thank you, Herb," Magnan acknowledged the warning. "But there's plenty more knicknacks where that came from. Ta."

"I heard that, Ben Magnan!" the Ambassador's reedy voice, amplified, boomed from the squawk box in the lift's roof.

"Don't worry," Magnan reassured his colleagues. "Corps regs preclude the use of clandestinely recorded utterances as evidence in court." The lift jolted to a stop.

Lunchwell dashed for cover as Retief and Magnan

proceeded calmly along to the glass door marked CHANCERY—AUTH PERS ONLY.

"I *do* think that 'auth purse' is terribly tacky," Magnan commented as they passed through into the air-conditioned hush of the Great Man's sanctum. "For a few cents more in issue decals it could read: 'Access limited to those persons conducting official Embassy business requiring the personal attention of His Excellency.'"

"Long-winded, but undeniably classic," Retief agreed. Then they were in the Presence.

"Well, Ben," the great man breezily greeted his First Secretary for Trifling Affairs, "why are you still fooling around here at the office, when I sent you out to do a job of work?"

"If Your Excellency would glance out the window," Magnan suggested, "it would see—I mean you'd see that the mob has dissipated."

"What do I care about the drinking habits of these grasshoppers?" Gropedark yelled. "There, Ben, don't be alarmed," he amended as Magnan seemed about to turn and flee. "Just been having a most unsettling chat with Perce Ebbtide," he amplified. "The rascal informs me that the market for Popurean antiquities has recently been flooded with exceedingly clever fakes in carload lots; blown prices all to hell, which didn't prevent some scoundrel from lifting my very own treasured masterpiece of the Early Classic period. You remember the nifty little sacrificial offering dish, or ashtray, with the handy stubber sticking out. Gone! Ben! Gone! right from under my very nose!"

"Forget it, sir," Magnan advised cheerfully. "I can get a better one by lunch time tomorrow."

"But not hung like my precious Rudy, as I used to call the little rascal," the bereaved Ambassador mourned. "Reminded me of Valentino, you know, only more candid."

"I respect Your Excellency's grief," Magnan reassured his superior, "but I quite assure, sir, that an abundance of suitable replacements for the little fellow are at hand."

" '*Is*' at hand, Ben," Gropedark snapped. " 'An abundance *is* . . .' "

"I interpret 'abundance' as a plural," Magnan returned stubbornly. "Thus, 'are' is required."

"Logic has nothing to do with it," Gropedark dismissed the objection. "The Manual covers it. Check Part Ten, Section A, paragraphs one and two, as amended, of course."

"Sure, sir, I know my Manual," Magnan cried. "It's just that, after all, the Corps can't really lay down policy on a matter still disputed by the most imminent grammarians."

"It is precisely to put an end to such disputes, Ben, that the framers of the Manual issued the referenced fiat. Now you'd better get busy attending to some of the urgent substantive problems confronting this mission."

"Before I go, Mr. Ambassador," Magnan put in quickly, "I just wanted to mention I've dealt with the matters to which you refer."

"What?" Gropedark yelled. "You, Ben Magnan, a mere PSO-two, First Secretary and Consul and my Acting Counselor of Embassy of Terra, have the effrontery to stand there and tell me that you have single-handedly, in a matter of hours, eliminated *all* of the intractable difficulties over which Departmental Deep Think Teams have racked their brains in vain for over a century, plus the newer disasters specially arranged for my tenure as Chief of Mission here?"

"Precisely, sir," Magnan purred. "Only not *quite* single-handedly: Retief was along."

"Good job you've a witness," Gropedark barked. "Now as to the rumored leakage of fake Popurean artifacts into the Galactic black market: you say you've halted the illicit traffic?"

"There has been no traffic in fakes, Mr. Ambassador," Magnan intoned solemnly. "The flood is of real artifacts, though the bulk of the artifacts in question are safe here in the city, awaiting collection. Technically, Ambassador Smoosh wasn't lying when he assured Your Excellency that no such treasures had departed the planet in Groaci bottoms."

The Ambassador snorted. " 'The bulk *is*,' Ben! But pass that; now, as to Groaci violation of this open planet—I suppose you're now going to tell me they've not infiltrated the city, in spite of my having seen that sneak Captain Kith with my very own eyes peregrinating in perilous proximity to the tabu Precinct itself!"

"No, indeed, sir," Magnan diffidently contradicted his superior. "The scamps are here, along with an entire Grand Battle Armada with abundant stores for a long campaign. But they've lost interest in their scheme for planet-napping."

"Just like that, eh, Ben?" the Ambassador retorted. "Smoosh is hardly the bureaucrat to allow his great opportunity for promotion to slip away, willy-nilly!"

"Not just like that, sir," Magnan amended. "Smoosh is powerless to act: he's pinned down in his Embassy by the same mob which menaced your own Mission earlier. As for Kith and his boss Colonel Zilth: they're safely tucked away, awaiting formal arrest; caught the sticky-fingered treachers red-handed. And by the way," he added, "Once the dust clears, the Greenfellas will find that the Groaci have unintentionally supplied them with a battle fleet, ready for action, safely stored in reinforced caverns."

"Nonsense, Magnan!" Gropedark snapped. "The

Groaci have no more love for these flighty locals than *I* have—than is warranted by their fondness for mob action, that is."

"Oh, it was quite unintentional, sir," Magnan caroled. "Colonel Zilth had every intention of deploying his forces *against* poor, bleeding Popu-Ri—only I came along and turned the tables on the scamp!"

"Magnan—you can't mean—" Gropedark started, then strode to his desk, delivered a savage kick to his hip-u-matic swivel chair before sitting in it, and grabbed his hotline talker. "Put me through to His Groacian Excellency, Minister Plenipotentiary Smoosh at the Legation, Willy," he snapped. Then to Magnan: "You're saying the Groaci *had* in fact violated the Precinct for their own fell purposes as rumored?"

"All that was rumored, and more," Magnan confirmed smugly. "Still, I fancy I've stonewalled the entire plot."

"Hallo, Smoosh!" Gropedark boomed jovially. "How's every little thing?" He recoiled as a stream of sibillant vituperation issued from the talker:

". . . to have kidnapped my Military Attaché, Colonel Zilth! And—"

"Nonsense!" Gropedark cut through the sputtering torrent of abuse. "What would Ben Magnan want with an ill-tempered martinet like Zilth? Here, I'll let you talk to him—he's right here." He handed the scarlet instrument to Magnan, who took it gingerly and cooed:

"Why, hi there, Mr. Minister. What's this about dear Colonel Zilth? On his field-phone, you say . . ." Magnan was nodding sagely, holding the noisy talker a foot from his ear.

"Just put him on, Mr. Min—" he attempted to cut in, "on the open screen, if you please. Yes, I'm sure there's an explanation . . ." He covered the screen with his hand momentarily for an aside: "I'll say there's an explanation," he advised his chief. "One that will live in infamy for centuries to come."

"I have no ambition to live in infamy, Ben," Gropedark pointed out. "You'd better hand me back that phone before you set Terran-Groaci relations back to the Stone Age!" Magnan dutifully handed over the sputtering talker.

Meanwhile, a second dim picture had appeared on the split screen beside Smoosh's nine-foot iridium desk, executive, Chief of Mission, for the use of. It showed Zilth's furtive-looking Groaci visage with all five eyes waving hypnotically against a background of battle-area charts and decoding machines.

"—got 'em by the sneakers!" Zilth was assuring his boss. He held up the Mark V detonating device with a triumphant gesture. "The notorious wrecker and enemy of the Groacian people," he ranted on, "to wit one Retief, of infamous reputation, this Retief, I say attempted to steal this, my ace-in-the-hole," he shrilled. "But I, by superior guile, recovered it, to the lasting sorrow of haughty Terra. Now, unless this same Retief at once releases my presence, takes the vow of silence, and surrenders himself to my personal vengeance, I shall dispatch to perdition the entire store of sacrificial objects now waiting collection in the noisome pit so-called the Sacred Well. So—what about it, vile Terries? Am I to rid the Galaxy of this rubbish, along with most of the local population, or do you agree to bend the knee and bow the neck to Great Groac? Which is it to be? I give you thirty seconds. Mark, twenty-nine . . ."

As the infuriated colonel's breathy voice droned the fatal count, Gropedark gibbered into his talker.

"Smoosh! You can't let him! Irreplacable objay d'arc, innocent civilians—"

"Innocent, Clarence?" Smoosh cut him off. "These same 'innocent' savages threatened to overwhelm your own Embassy but this morning, and all but dismembered my Counsellor this afternoon. As for your so-called art treasures, what's so valuable about an Atwater Kent TV chassis with a busted picture tube? And an inner tube to fit a 750-16 tire? Punctured, at that; can't even use it to go tubing in the river, even if it wasn't full of the garbage these innocents of yours have been throwing in it for thousands of years. Eh, how about it, Clarence?"

Gropedark jumped as his beeper uttered an extended burst.

"Yes, Prunella, what is it?" he yelled in response. "I'm busy. Can't it wait?"

"It's a delegation of grasshopper big shots," the receptionist returned shortly. "Say they gotta see you pronto. They're carrying some kinda big knives."

"Tell them I'm on vacation in the highlands, Prunie, there's a good girl," Gropedark temporized. He cast a bloodshot eye appealing at Magnan. "What's a Chief of Mission to do?" he inquired of History. "Surely I can't let Zilth vent his Groaci spleen on this ancient city, the preservation and excavation of which are the prime concern of my mission here. But equally I can't throw a diplomatic member of the Embassy staff to the mob!"

"Tell him to do his worst, Mr. Ambassador," Magnan replied crisply. "He's bluffing. Well, not exactly bluffing, but there are circumstances he wots not of."

"You mean when he activates that Mark V, nothing will happen?" Gropedark quavered hopefully, as a fist pounded heavily on his door.

"Well, no, sir, just not what he expects," Magnan explained.

"No explosion?" the Chief of Mission pursued the point, though relaxing a trifle.

"Oh, there'll be a jim-dandy explosion, sir," Magnan gabbled in a reassuring tone.

"In that case, what—" Gropedark broke off as the door burst inward and a seven-foot-tall Greenfella with a scythe gripped in his fist came halfway across the deep-pile carpet and halted to allow three other heavily-armed and scarcely smaller locals to crowd up beside him.

"Boss palefella tell problem solve," the angry autocthone charged. "But Ben Magnan not lettum jolly throng Greenfella tear arm and leg and eyeball off five-eye bigshot. We wantum action: Now! Palefella tell long Friday, all civic improvement accomplish, and already Wednesday! Me cuttum Terry gourd, show crowd, maybeso crowd not cut off gourd me. OK, boys, let's do it!" he added over his shoulder.

"Stop!" Gropedark commanded, retreating behind Magnan. "You must have misunderstood me. I didn't mean to give you the impression I'd restore the entire city in a day!"

"Who wantum restore old dump?" the Greenfella leader demanded. "Wantum plenty high-tech pogo stick, other goodie!"

"Tough barf-nodes, Zilth," Retief told the Groaci officer, still gaping from the screen. "We're not buying. So go ahead and use your play-pretty."

"To imagine a Groacian officer to stoop to bluffing?" Zilth hissed. "You'll rue the day, Retief!"

"A word of advice," Retief put in. "Get under your desk first."

"Just in case the shock should dislodge a roof-slab, eh?" Zilth mused. "Good thinking, Retief. I shall remember your thoughtfulness at the mass funeral." He brandished the Mark V and ducked out of sight; a moment later the screen went blank. The next instant a sharp shock drove dust from every crevice in the ornate room. Then a dull and long-drawn *BARROOM!* rumbled like distant thunder. Beyond the window, tall facades trembled, cracked, split apart and fell into the street. Dust came boiling along the avenue.

"Good lord!" the Ambassador gasped. "He did it! However am I to explain to the Undersecretary? Or more to the point, what am I to say to these dacoits?" He backed away from the scythe-wielder. A smaller local came forward from the rear rank.

"Leroy!" Magnan burst out. "Are you associated with these brigands?"

The leader turned to Leroy. "You takum correspondence course: 'Brigand' nice name tell honest Greenfella?"

"Sure. Me lookum up in Webber electronary," Leroy reassured his leader. "Tell same like 'dacoit.' Mr. Ambluster," he nodded courteously toward Gropedark, "you big dacoit, too! See, simple native know how be gracious: you fix all Greenfella problem. Much gratitude."

"But . . . but . . . the city is leveled," Gropedark sputtered. "It's most generous of you to take this enlightened view of the contretemps, but I must say, I hardly understand— "

"No enlighten," Leroy corrected. "Greenfella all same wantum slum clearance! Clear away all old junk, makum nice vacant lot, grow tall grass, Greenfella jump around, have fun, like in old day before ancestor get big idea!"

5

"And, Ben, you say all the antiquities are safe in an underground cavern?" Gropedark demanded for the tenth time. "I can scarce comprehend it: the natives, ah, indigenous people, that is, pacified, the Groaci halted in their treachery, and the art treasures safe, along with my promotion—all accomplished with a simple mighty blast! Magnan, you're a genius. I shouldn't wonder if you should be bumped to the exalted rank of Career Minister on the strength of what you've done here—but be sure you give me a chance to look over your report before it's beamed to Sector—just in case there are any trifling irregularities, not to say atrocities, to cover up—ah, interpret, I meant to say."

"Nothing minor, I assure Your Excellency," Magnan told his Chief. "Now I really must away. I promised Mr. Leroy I'd assist him in the selection of a group of representative artifacts from the trove for dispatch to the Terran Museum on Deadfall."

"Save snappy Chevy ragtop for Mr. Ambluster," Leroy offered. "Air and music, too."

"Whatever you feel appropriate sir," Gropedark said faintly. "Unless there just happens to be a '31 Model A cabriolet."

"If not find in Spood offering, make deal swap old junk with planet call Grub, not half a light in-Arm; findum classy A with twin sidemounts, trunk rack and quail mascot," Leroy assured the euphoric bureaucrat. "Bye, now," He hopped away, keening a little tune. "Come, Ben, Retief," he called. "Go findum grog shop no fall down yet."

Outside, Retief and Magnan paused with Leroy to survey the broad expanse of newly cleared ground, from which crews of Greenfellas were even now toiling to clear away the heaps of rubble.

"Sell all rubble so many guck per fragment,"

Leroy commented, pausing to break in two a fallen gargoyle. "Now, you boy excuse me, look like nice pub all gone, but what the hell? Me go plant grass-seed, get in shape for jump around, have fun, like Morris tell. Ta."

"If I should live to be a thousand," Magnan sighed, "I shall never understand the alien mind."

"Amen," Retief agreed.

There is a Tide

As Second Secretary and Consul Jame Retief approached the dowdy facade of the Embassy of Terra, a cluster of Slubbese locals who had been closely grouped around the Embassy limosine, a replica 1931 Bugatti *Royale*, abruptly dispersed and assumed casual saunters, a ploy rendered nugatory by the cloud of dense purplish smoke issuing from beneath the classic vehicle. Retief went to it, stooped, reached under to detach a small smog-bomb of Groaci manufacture which he tossed into the nearest refuse bin. Then he went quickly up the steps in time to intercept a smallish alien in tight tan khakis and engineer's boots as he attempted to exit the building via the narrow window-well lighting the spare vault.

"To unhand me instanter, Retief!" the Groaci yelped. "I was just rushing to put out the fire!"

"It's under control, Whish," Retief told his struggling captive. "But what were you doing in the vault?" He glanced through the barred slit and saw heaped cartons marked with curlicue Groaci script: *SECRET—SPY EQUIPMENT AND TOUCH AT YOUR PERIL!*

"To have but delivered a token of His Groacian Excellency's esteem to his colleague, Ambassador Hairshirt!" Whish declared vehemently. "But to what avail these gestures of civilized regard between diplomats, in the face of such brutality?"

"Oh, we haven't gotten to the brutality yet," Retief corrected the Groaci. "Let's go see His Terran Ex and find out how he feels about messengers of civilization who pay a crowd of loafers to booby-trap his precious Bugatti."

"Have a care, rash Terry," Whish keened in an attempt at self-assertiveness which Retief dispelled by shaking him as if to dislodge foreign particles. Inside, he left the Groaci in the charge of the Marine guard and went upstairs.

In the conference room, Ambassador Clarence Hairshirt looked coldly along the conference table at his assembled staff.

"What General Faintheart has to tell us, gentlemen," he began as soon as he had accorded a chill glance to Herb Lunchwell, the plump Econ Officer and last to arrive, "is nothing less than a Class A breach of solemn interplanetary accord . . ."

"Yeah," the general took up the account, "which that sneaky Groacian Admiral, Thinth, under the guise of outfitting an aid station, has went and fortified Big Moon into a regular Fortress Luna. And right under your noses, too," he added. "So now we're looking down the muzzles of about nineteen batteries of Thunder-guns while we try to negotiate with Groac on the trade-lanes question and all. Kind of gives 'em a like psychological advantage, know what I mean?" The sour-faced general looked defiantly at the civilians. "Which, if I would of been shipped in here a couple of years sooner," he declared, "it wouldn't of happened."

"Aside from the question of rearranging history, Fred," Hairshirt responded mildly, after a strained silence broken only by throat-clearing along the table, "We have the *de facto* situation with which to deal. Now, in view of Groac's preemption of the major satellite, what can we do to normalize the balance of power? I am open, gentlemen, for suggestions. What about you, Sid?" He impaled the luckless Assistant Political Officer with a glance half amused, half challenging. "What action would you, in my position, take?"

"Would I in your position take?" Sid gibbered, taken off guard. "Well, sir, first I guess I'd get off those gold-embossed invites to the reception—just to show that everything's cool—and then, ah . . ."

"Your proposed strategy will be duly noted, Sid," Hairshirt stated in a tone which encouraged no fantasies of early promotion. "Now," he went on, as one Getting Down to Business, "I summoned you here to consider a more immediate matter which has come to my attention, to wit: a firm rumor that the Groaci Deep Sea Drilling Project is more than it appears. I have been informed by a Usually Reliable Source . . ."

"Oh, you mean George, the janitor," Sid put in, eager to remind his chief that he, too, was In the Know. "Sure, Georgie and I had a nice chat last night, which he heard from the local sweeper staff they had it on good authority that the word in the street is, the Groaci sneaked a Class One hell-bomb in here to Slub under cloak of diplomatic privilege and all. Heck, sir, that's nothing new."

"New or old, Sid, a contraband hell-bomb on this virgin world is not to be lightly disregarded," Hairshirt reminded his victim.

"Sure, sir, I only meant, heck, it's easy to believe Yer Ex has got the straight dope, seeing it happens all the time. I mean, why start a dumb rumor like that if there's nothing in it, eh fellows?" Sid looked brightly along the table for signs of support, encountered only stony looks plus a stifled yawn from Hy Felix.

"In the interest of getting on with the solution of the substantive problems confronting this Mission," Hairshirt stated glacially, "I shall for the nonce overlook the mainfold deficiencies in your attitude toward Ambassadorial Infallibility, Sid. Now," he changed the subject abruptly, directing a swift glance along the table to note the reactions of his staff, "What about this Hell-bomb, eh?"

Brigadier General Freddy Faintheart, the Military Attaché, rose to his feet. "That can wait," he dismissed his Chief's query. "The Number One priority is Big Moon," he declared. "I'm quite convinced," he went on, "that the rascally Groaci, under the cloak of providing an emergency aid station, have installed a full-fledged combat operations facility on the satellite."

He glared along the conference table as if daring anyone to contradict him. "The evidence is incapable of misinterpretation," he grumped. "Not only that," he went on, "I have spy-satellite data indicating that a full field force of the Groacian Navy is emplaced there as well, fully manned and equipped! This, gentlemen, means *war!*" the general subsided, looking triumphant, but was rebutted by the Ambassador.

"Provided, that is, Freddy, that I do not simply decide to give Slub up as a bad job and recommend breaking off relations in time to avoid direct Terran involvement in the coming holocaust."

"But, sir," a youthful Third Secretary objected. "That would be pusillanimous in the extreme, to simply run away and leave poor, backward Slub to her fate. After all, we *do* have a Most Favored Planet relationship with her."

"What Wilbur means," a portly Econ type put in quickly, "is that certain irresponsible elements of the yellow press, inspired by traitorous motives and paid by Entrenched Interests, might misinterpret Your Excellency's noble motives."

"Sure, I know all that stuff," Ambassador Hairshirt cut off the rescue attempt. "But it's time you learned, Wilbur," he fixed a flinty gaze on the lad, "that in most 'relationships,' as you so naively term Terra's solemn diplomatic understanding with this benighted pest-hole, somebody gets, ah, is recipient of an act of copulation, shall I say, and I don't want it to be me—Terra, that is."

"Sure, sir," Wilbur acceded brokenly. "I only meant about the yellow press and all, like Mr. Lunchwell said."

Hairshirt shifted his eye to a slender, narrow-faced chap half concealed behind Retief, a tall, broad-shouldered Second Secretary and Consul assigned as Assistant Political Officer, and said, "Magnan, I'm taking a chance on you. I'm assigning to you, and your assistant, of course, the little task of dealing with this arrogant violation of solemn treaty by the scurvy Groaci. In spite of a number of unflattering comments in your record by your former Chiefs of Mission, I want to give you this chance to redeem yourself."

"Gosh," Magnan, the Political Officer, said, "that's big of you, sir. I'm sure Retief appreciates the honor as much as I do."

"That's good, Ben," Hairshirt said in a tone as kindly as that of an executioner inviting his victim to utter his last words. "Because if you didn't, I have the Help Wanted pages of the Slubbese *Morning Dagblad* handy."

"Oh, I see, sir," Magnan quavered. "It's a little joke, ha ha."

"This is hardly the time for japes, Ben," Hairshirt rejected the attempt at levity. "By the way, Retief," he went on, changing sights, "had you been a millisecond later, you'd have been late to Staff Meeting."

"Curious, isn't it, Mr. Ambassador," Retief replied easily, "that one can be later, or even latest, without being late."

"Your apology is accepted," Hairshirt snapped. "What delayed you?"

"I noticed a local citizen planting a smoke-bomb under the official limousine," Retief explained. "I stopped to recover it."

"Cheeky locals!" His Excellency snapped, mottling. "Another of their confounded Booch Day pranks, I suppose, designed to panic me, since they know how I treasure my Bugatti. Good show you nipped the gambit in the bud."

"But worse is to be expected, Mr. Ambassador," Wilberforce, the cultural Attaché cried, rising. "It's traditional that the finest Boochers always conceal a jape within a jape; that is, one practical joke distracts attention from the arranging of another, larger jest. So we'd better be prepared, sir, is what *I* say, Mr. Ambassador."

"Nonsense, Willy," Hairshirt boomed jovially. "They love me far too well to plan any such chicanery directed against the dignity of my Mission. Still, Retief, it wouldn't hurt for you to go check once more on the Bugatti, just in case."

As Retief left the room, a clerk from the Message Center hurried in with a grubby envelope which he handed to the Ambassador, who slit it open, extracted a sheet of re-used paper and scanned it quickly.

"Well, what's it say?" Hy Felix demanded.

" 'The bomb' " Ambassador Hairshirt began portentiously, "will detonate in approximately . . ." he paused to examine the genuine Minnie Mouse watch strapped to the underside of his plump wrist, ". . . .twenty-three—no, make that twenty-two seconds from. . . .*now!*"

"You never said anything about any bomb, sir," Hy Felix charged.

"And might one ask, Mr. Ambassador," the Budget and Fiscal man inquired diffidently, "just how it is your Excellency knows precisely when the thing is due to go bang?"

"Certainly, Hector," Hairshirt replied kindly. "The note said so."

"Maybe it was lying," someone suggested.

"But why impute a diminished capacity for veracity to someone you haven't so much as met, Clarence?" His Excellency reproved mildly. "Hardly the diplomatic way, eh?"

"Twenty two—or one, now, I guess, seconds. That hardly affords one time to evolve a rational evacuation plan," Ben Magnan pointed out, "to say nothing of finding and disarming the infernal device. . . ."

"Yes, as to that, Ben," Hairshirt cut in impatiently. "It hardly encourages one even to begin any long sentences. Action is what we need now, gentlemen, not words."

"Still, sir," a pudgy Second Secretary from the Economic Section put in doggedly. "One *does* hope that a trifle of rational verbal analysis will assist us in determining the correct action. Like finding the bomb, for openers."

"Yeah," Hy Felix, the Information Agency man put in. "do you have any idear where it's at, Mr. Ambassadore?"

"Hy," Hairshirt began in the melancholy tones of an indulgent parent rebuking an errant offspring. "I am not an avenue of entry or egress. The word is Ambassa*dor*. And have you not yet learned," he bored on, "that I, as your Chief of Mission, make it my business to be aware of matters within the sphere of my responsibilities? 'Any idea?', you ask. I assure you that I know precisely where the bomb is."

"That's just what *I* was saying," Magnan interjected urgently, not directly addressing His Excellency, precisely, but setting the record straight for posterity, so to speak. "I said 'finding and disarming' it, remember? So if your Excellency knows where it's at, why don't we *do* something, instead of standing around jawing?"

"*Do* something, you say, Ben?" the Ambassador Extraordinary and Minister Plenipotentiary echoed in a tone which did little to elaborate on the thesis. "Would you expect me to abandon time-honored diplomatic procedures at the first hint of danger, sir?"

"Not exactly, Mr. Ambassador," Magnan explained. "Just sort of suspend them, or at least compress the conversational phase in the interest of getting rid of the bomb before it goes off in. . . ."

"What Ben means," Felix interjected, "is let's cut the chin music and ditch the bomb."

"Twelve seconds, precisely," Hairshirt supplied smoothly. "I am saddened, Ben," he went on, "to find that a Foreign Service Officer of Class One, whom I had been personally grooming for assignment as my Counselor of Embassy, would so lightly propose dispensing with chin-music, as you so colorfully characterize your Chief's briefing—a measure calculated, Ben, directly to attack the role of diplomacy in the postponement of the inevitable Galactic holocaust."

"I never said 'chin-music'!" Magnan blurted. "That was Hy."

"So it was," Hairshirt acknowledged. "But surely the matter of attribution is of less importance than my principle thesis, to wit. . . ."

"OK, if you know where it's at," Colonel Underknuckle, the Assistant Military Attaché, overrode his Principle Officer's comments, "tell us! Show me where to find it, and. . . ."

"And what, Teddy?" Hairshirt cut in encouragingly. "Are you volunteering to smother the blast with your body?"

"Heck, no!" Ted denied emphatically. "But we can at least. . . ."

All heads turned as the door to the conference room opened and Retief reentered the room, gripping in one hand, by his slender neck, a spindly Groaci wearing a replica of an antique Western Union uniform embellished with plain olive-drab shinguards and plastic dime store eyeshields. As half a dozen questions rang out simultaneously, the newcomer went directly to the head of the table, picked up the Ambassador's briefcase, and took out a square package in colorful gift wrappings, jostling the AE and MP slightly in the process; he handed the packet to his prisoner, who threshed to avoid it, until Retief tucked it under the alien's Sam Browne belt.

"Three seconds left, Whish," the big man told the reluctant Groaci. "Better not waste any more time."

"To see a just and dispassionate revenge taken on your dying corpse, Retief!" the alien hissed. "To tell Uncle Shish how you Groaci-handled me right in the lobby of the Terran Mission to Slub!"

"Not unless you make the correct decision right now," Retief countered.

Whish moaned piteously, and without further resistance, ripped open the gaudy paper wrappihgs of the parcel and probed with a bony finger through the opening while all eyes watched in fascination. There was a crisp *click!* from within the box, causing three of the observers to dive for shelter beneath the table, the Ambassador securing the most favorable position as his underlings yielded pride of place to their Chief.

". . . and dunk it in a bucket of water," Ted Underknuckle's voice rang out clearly. He stepped in briskly to reach for the package, then changed his mind and stepped behind Nat Sitzfleisch, the portly Admin Officer.

"Thank you, Whish," Retief said, and dropped the undersized fellow, who at once lunged in the direction of the door, only to rebound from Ted Underknuckle's foot.

"One moment, fellow-me-lad!" the colonel said sternly, as he recaptured the Groaci. "This bears looking into. Now, just what do you know about all this, eh? Tell all, there's a good fellow, and I shall attempt to do what I can for you at the trial. Go ahead, Retief, tell us about him."

"When I went downstairs just now," Retief told the colonel, "I noticed Whish sneaking out by a side door. Since I'd left him under guard earlier, I grabbed him."

"And how did you deduce. . . ." Ted started.

"I didn't have to deduce, Ted," Retief replied. "I asked him, and after a few seconds he told me."

"Seconds," Whish put in in his shrill whisper, "which will live in infamy, once I tell Uncle Shish about how you repeatedly tossed me up and barely caught me before I impacted the floor!"

"And?" the colonel prompted.

"He mentioned delivering a bomb addressed to Ambassador Hairshirt," Retief explained. "So it seemed well to bring him along to disarm the gadget."

"Time's up," Hairshirt said with finality from his position under the table. He put his head out, twisting awkwardly to look up at Magnan. "Ben," he asked quietly. "Did you hear anything? After the final *click!* as the fuse tripped, I mean."

"That was Whish disarming the bomb, sir," Magnan explained, attempting to assist the Great Man to his feet, and simultaneously avert his eyes from his chief's undignified situation, and as a result causing Hairshirt to trip over Ted Underknuckle's foot, retaining his balance by executing a clumsy *plié*.

"Ben, will you kindly stop babbling about wishing someone would disarm the bomb?" Hairshirt demanded excitedly. "And precisely what explanation have you for this attack on my person? Gone mad with terror, have you, Ben? Pity. Won't look at all good in your ER."

"Hardly an attack, Mr. Ambassador," Magnan disputed hastily. "I was just assisting Your Excellency to his feet, ah, your feet, that is, and you tripped over Ted's size fourteens."

"Size twelve, double E, Ben," Ted corrected coldly. "And had you not thrust His Excellency so vigorously, doubtless he would have retained his balance."

"We'll work all that out later," Hairshirt cut short the dispute. "Right now I want an explanation for the fact that we're still alive—or dead and dreaming I'm alive," he amended. His eye fell on Retief.

"You, sir! I dispatched you on an errand! Why are you standing there?"

"But it was Retief who brought Whish up here to disarm the bomb, sir!" Magnan advised the Ambassador hastily.

"Ben—stop babbling about what you wish," Hairshirt commanded. "As for the alleged bomb, clearly it was a hoax." With a dismissing forefinger, he prodded the torn paper-wrapped carton now lying neglected on the table. "Otherwise, it would have gone off five seconds ago, or more." He fixed Retief with a steely, though slightly bloodshot eye. "Have you any possible explanation for this lapse, sir?" He demanded.

"Sure, Mr. Ambassador," Whish volunteered breathily, but clearly, in his heavily-accented Terran. "He was late because he was busy using excessive force on a Groacian national enjoying diplomatic immunity here on Slub! Darn near squashed my bope-nodes, too," the alien finished, fingering his stringy neck tenderly. "And him three times bigger'n me, and me the favorite nephew of your very own colleague, His Excellency Ambassador Shish!" With that he darted under the table, eluding the colonel's grab.

"Have you some explanation, Retief, for this breach of decorum?" Hairshirt demanded in a deceptively lazy tone, jotting a note as he spoke.

"Probably just racial prejudice," Retief conceded unconcernedly. "I'm inclined to be suspicious of any Groaci I see lurking around the Chancery."

"Lurking, indeed!" Whish sneered, poking three of his five stalked oculars above the edge of the table. "I waltzed in like I owned the joint, and the dumb guards on the gate never even looked at me! I rode the lift up with Oscar Tunrbuckle from the Political Section, and all he done was say 'To have a nice day,' in lousy Groacian, too."

"It occurs to me, gentlemen," Colonel Underknuckle spoke up from a kneeling position as he dragged Whish from his retreat, "that these Groaci explosive devices usually have a back-up detonator, in case the primary fuse is somehow disarmed—it would be set to go any time in the next six hours. Let me see that thing: if there's an electric hum at about twelve thousand cycles, it means she's still hot." The others scattered from his path as he rose and went to the suspect parcel and held it to his ear for a moment. "Yep," he replied in a satisfied tone. "She's alive, all right."

"Then whatever shall we do?" Magnan dithered. "Before, we at least knew when to expect the blast, but now—all is uncertainty again."

"Let's throw it out the window," Sitzfleisch suggested, reaching for the package.

"And blow half the façade off the Terrestrial Embassy?" Hairshirt demanded, interposing his bulk. "To say nothing of the slaughter of some dozens of innocent passers-by. Very poor for Slubbese-Terran relations, Nat."

Retief went to the closet beside the washroom door and returned with a bent coat hanger. He took a turn of the wire around the bomb and secured the other end to the frantically struggling Whish's neck. "I think he'll want to tell us something," Retief commented. "Let's lock him in the spare vault until he's ready."

Whish twisted in vain to free his neck of the wire.

"Vile miscreants!" he hissed. "Have you no compassion for youth and beauty?"

"As soon as you tell us about the back-up, or neutralize it yourself," Hairshirt told the disturbed fellow, "I shall see to it that steps are taken with all deliberate haste to defuse you, remove your person to a more comfortable situation, and notify your uncle of your whereabouts."

"Yeah," Nat added. "Shackled to the wall in our detention tank, eh, Mr. Ambassador?"

"To release me at once!" Whish hissed, more confidently now. "To temper my report to Uncle Shish, if you make amends instanter!"

"Looks like it's not going up right away," the scholarly-looking Cultural Attaché suggested. "He's not in a big enough hurry."

"To lack completely the spirit of the occasion!" Whish demanded. "To fail utterly to conform to local custom! To predict harsh treatment of the contretemps in the local press!"

"I should think the local press would rejoice that they didn't have a bomb crater where their best street used to be," Colonel Underknuckle put in. "To say nothing of a flotilla of Terran Peace

Enforcers inquiring into the slaughter of an Embassyful of harmless Terry bureaucrats."

"But it's Booch Day here on Slub!" Whish keened. "A festival honored by every Slubbese, regardless of caste, age, or political alignment! Big shots, too. Even school kids. It's the day when the usually suppressed Slubbese love of fun is released for full, free expression!"

"I wondered why those fellows were setting the Embassy limousine on fire as I came in," Herb Lunchwell, the plump little Econ Officer commented tonelessly.

"What!" the Ambassador yelled and rushed to the nearest window. "Blowing up a building of no particular distinction is one thing," he muttered. "But putting the torch to a work of art . . ." he broke off with a whimper. "But that's right—Retief removed the device, Herb," he added. "There she sits as lovely as ever! Gosh, it's almost worth the scare, to feel such relief!" He turned to embrace the portly clerk.

"How did it happen you failed to correct the situation yourself, my boy?" he cooed in tones implyiny Advance Forgiveness of Human Error (42-d).

"Gee, sir!" Herb burbled. "Never thought I'd rate your 421-g, Mr. Ambassador!"

"That was my 'd', Herb," the Great Man said kindly. "Now you'd best get back to your semi-annual requisition, eh?"

"And not get to see what you **do** with the bomb, sir?" Herb protested. "Heck, **the** old requisition can wait another few minutes, I guess. Anyway, my mind wouldn't really be on my work with that thing still ticking away."

"More of a hum, Herb," the Military Attaché put in.

"Hum, schumum," Nat commented in a stage

whisper. "In maybe a couple minutes or so, we'll all be corpses, the messy kind, from all kinds explosion. And these schmendricks want to stage a debate it's a tick or a hum, already."

"You still here, Herb?" Hairshirt inquired in a tone of Mild Surprise (166-d).

"Sure, sir," Lunchwell confirmed readily. "I said about how the bomb makes me a little nervous and all, you know."

"Your gambit seems not to have been successful, Mr. Retief," the Ambassador commented, transfering his attention to the latter. "The bomb remains to be neutralized."

"If we stuck him in the spare vault, wired to the bomb, like I said," Ted Underknuckle put in, "I bet he'd get busy on it."

"To do your worst, vile Terries," Whish suggested calmly. "To await my fate with equanamity, knowing I am to take a roomful of the enemies of the Groacian state with me."

"Only you're not going anywhere, eh, Whish?" Retief addressed the wizened Groaci. He removed the parcel from the alien's neck and stripped away the colorful paper to reveal a dun-painted box. He handed it back to Whish. As soon as the messenger touched it, the lid snapped open, deploying a grotesque head at the end of a long spring, causing the Groaci to stumble back with a yelp, dropping the box, which at once began to play *Tenting On the Old Campground* slightly off-key.

Quickly regaining his composure, Whish hissed, "Do you hope thus to unnerve a reserve lance-corporal of the twelfth Zouaves? Fie! Enough of this zorchplay and on to matters of substance!" With his foot he spurned the fallen box, even as it wheezed its final melancholy notes.

"You're too modest by far," Retief commented. "We're aware you're a major in Intelligence." Then, turning to His Excellency, "Mr. Ambassador, I suspect that all this nonsense is a diversion designed to keep our attention from something more important."

"Good thinking, Retief," Ted Underknuckle said. "My idea exactly. And it's the Groaci machinations on Big Moon our attention is being diverted from."

"One wonders," a frail Secretary from the Political Section murmured, "if there could be any significance in the smoke issuing from beneath the table."

"Just a wastebasket fire Whish started while he was there," Retief pointed out, as he doused the flames with a jet of charged water from the Ambassadorial seltzer bottle.

"Here—that's my genuine Nehi you're wasting, sir!" the Ambassador objected. Retief handed him the ornate flask, at the same time directing a final jet at Whish's upturned face.

"Mr. Ambassador," Retief addressed his chief quietly. "I have a feeling that it would be a good idea to adjourn this meeting to another place—the sub-basement, perhaps."

"May I inquire," His Excellency responded in tones of Righteous Wrath Restrained by Innate Kindliness (721-h), "What prompts your curious proposal, Mr. Retief? Ah, you used to work for Herb Lunchwell, I believe, in GSO or whatever? Perhaps you'd best hurry along and assist him with the semi-annual. Can't afford late submission, of course. My stocks of blank Foreign Office Notes, for example, are perilously low."

"According to the Post Report, sir," Magnan spoke up, "this Booch Festival is dedicated to practical jokes designed to disguise other, more devious pranks. The more layers of deceit, the more points the japester acquires. As I was just commenting to Retief—or rather he was suggesting to me—we've only experienced about one and a half levels of Slubbese high spirits so far, so there's probably more and violenter to come."

" 'Violenter,' Ben?" Hairshirt echoed. " 'More violent' might, I venture to suggest, be a happier locution, though your—or Retief's—point is well taken." He shifted his gaze to Whish, now cowering behind a bookcase near the door. "What about it, Whish?" he boomed heartily. "Anything else up your figurative sleeve? By the way, Retief," he added offhandedly, "you'd best look into this business about Big Moon Ted is so upset about."

"Me, upset?" the colonel echoed. "It's to laugh, with respect, Mr. Ambassador. Like a cucumber, that's me. I merely did my duty in reporting a grave threat to Galactic Peace, with a copy to Sector, of course. What your Excellency decides to do about it, or not do about it, is entirely your own affair."

"Sector, eh, Ted?" Hairshirt mused. " 'Not do about it,' eh? Did I say anything whatsoever about not doing something about it? Have you gone mad, Ted? Do you wish never to exchange those rather tarnished eagles for bright, new stars?"

"Stars!" the colonel yelped. "Cripes, sir, I figgered coming up with the dope on a *faux pas* o' this size, ahead o' Sector, when we could be the first to report and all, would cinch the old promo!"

"To be sure, Ted, I'm getting off a despatch today with full details. I shall make it a point to mention you by name. Meanwhile. . . ." the Great Man turned to Retief. "Skip the semi-annual. Drop everything and look into the problem on Big Moon. I shall consider that my first priority. But as for Whish, here—any more surprises in store, major?"

"To wait and see!" the Groaci keened. "To soon discover, with no need of lengthy exposition on my part."

"Oh," Colonel Underknuckle put in. "So you admit it."

"To admit nothing, vile Soft One," Whish came back harshly. "To proclaim it!" Three of his eyes tilted toward the nearest open window, prompting Ted Underknuckle to hurry there precisely in time to be engulfed in an opaque cloud of yellow smoke jetting from an unseen source outside. Instantly, Whish darted around the Military Attaché and into the billowing fumes where he was lost to sight. Retief went to the door, found it solidly blocked from the outside; he went on to a window from which he could see the agile Groaci hastily descending a rope to the street below, where a crowd of curious Slubbese stood staring upward. Retief stepped out onto the ledge below the row of windows and, flat against the nubbly stuccoed wall, made his way across to the rope, which he promptly descended, to be accosted at once by a bigger than average (five-foot) Slubbese sub-humanoid in a baggy olive-drab uniform adorned with insignia indentifying him as a constable in the City Police. He appeared to be holding something behind his back.

"What's up, Terry?" the cop demanded.

"The Ambassador's blood pressure," Retief replied crisply. "It appears the Terran Chancery is under attack." He reached around the cop to grab Whish by one arm as the latter lunged to free himself from the officer's grasp.

"It won't be necessary to hold Whish, officer," Retief told the constable as he in turn grabbed for the Groaci and received a kick in the shin for his trouble.

"Hey, that's *my* pinch!" the baffled constable yelled, pausing to rub his lower limb while balefully eyeing Whish, now cowering behind Retief.

"Now, Retief, you wouldn't turn me over to this

vascular-juice-thirsty alien, would you?" the captive queried tonelessly.

"To be a good idea to save the invective for later, after your trial," Retief suggested in accent-free Groaci.

"To invoke diplomatic immunity!" Whish shrilled.

"To get off a stiff Note from His Terran Excellency to the Slubbese Foreign Office early next week," Retief promised.

"But this barbarian is poised to rend me asunder instanter!" Whish objected. "To crave the boon, Retief, of action more precipitate than normal bureaucratic process! In fact, to get the heck out of here before that mob . . ." he broke off to eye the growing circle of curious locals ". . . hears somebody say 'lynch.' "

" 'Lynch?' " a bystander picked up the term at once. "Who—the noisy little one, or the big one that's holding him?"

"Neither one, dopey—the cop," someone explained impatiently.

"Wow! Lynch a cop!" the phrase echoed quickly across the now definitely excited crowd.

"OK, you're unner arrest!" the beleaguered peace officer yelled.

"Who, me?" inquired the same echoic individual who had launched the lynch rumor. "What for, chief? I ain't done nothing, only that little caper last month at the Civic Club. . . ."

"That was *you* put the socks in the Cop Night stew?" the cop yelled, reaching. In a trice he had the cuffs on the unfortunate trickster. "And a full week before Booch Time, too," he added. "Yawtta be shamed."

"I am, chief, I am," the shackled Slubbese assured his captor.

"Clear the way, there," the cop shouted, thrusting his pinch ahead of him.

The crowd gave ground reluctantly. Retief waited until ranks had closed behind the constable, then said to Whish, "Let's find a quiet corner where we can have a heart-to-heart talk."

"Quiet corner, indeed!" Whish hissed. "This hick town was a disaster area even before their confounded Booch Festival turned disorder into chaos. How about the Pink Moon, just around the corner, back of the Yalcan Legation."

Retief agreed, and moments later they were occupying a booth in a shadowy corner of the seemingly moribund establishment. An elderly Slubbese waiter came shuffling over, sighing audibly. He was a pear-shaped being with pale, wrinkled lavender skin and a fringe of faded purple hair above his bleary pink eyes. He was dressed in a baggy puce and mauve coverall. He had short, bowed legs and shoulderless arms.

"Make that a hot fudge sundae and a stiff shot o' Bacchus brown," Whish ordered curtly. "And put some snap in it, pal. I got a tight schedule."

"You wanna sign this-year waiver?" the old fellow inquired in a once-gravelly voice now grown squeaky, offering a dog-eared paper.

"Nix," Whish snapped, thrusting aside the proffered document. He canted an eye at Retief.

"Prolly a perpetual lease on the joint in the fine print," he explained. "Especially during Booch, you know, these clowns will try anything."

"Speaking of trying things, Whish," Retief replied as the waiter went away, muttering. "Who sent you to the Embassy?"

"What, *me?*" the Groaci squawked, his throat sac vibrating in indication of Extreme Agitation Brought On by Baseless Accusation (417-c).

"Don't waste that 417 on me," Retief said. "I don't think you were in business for yourself."

"Do you not?" Whish hissed. "In the spirit of

joyous Booch, may not a humble worker in the vineyard get to bring a modicum of the season's spirit to his fellow bureaucrats?" He broke off to tilt an eye in the direction in which the elderly servitor had disappeared.

"All just boyish high spirits, eh?" Retief inquired casually. "Then tell me about the rope and the smoke-bomb to cover your departure."

"Why, as to that, the explanation is simplicity itself," Whish improvised. "A mate of mine, one Thilth, of the Econ Section as it happens, just happened to be gathering zitz-bugs on the roof, for his vermin collection, of course, and. . . ."

"Skip it," Retief suggested. "I already don't believe it and I haven't even heard it yet."

"Poor old Thilth would do well to reserve space in his specimen drawer for a small Terry," Whish whispered as if thinking aloud. Then, "Oh, surely one can simply overlook this morning's contretemps, Retief. As. . . ."

"Oh-oh," Retief cut him off. "Here comes the old 'fellow diplomat' pitch. Funny, you Groaci are overwhelmed with fraternal emotion only when you've been caught with your sticky fingers where they shouldn't be. I wonder why."

"That's simple enough, Retief," Whish replied, leaning forward earnestly. "You see, if I can shrewdly engender a bit of empathy in your assesment of my activities, you'll be inclined to take a more lenient line." The glib fellow leaned back with the air of one who had revealed an astonishing secret.

Retief nodded. "The question was rhetorical," he pointed out. "Now let's get back to who sent you, and why."

Whish spread his spatulate, suction-cup-tipped hands. "I already told you it was my own idea!" he keened. "Mere boyish high spirits, like you said," he amplified. "An impulse, nothing more."

"Too bad your impulses are so well rehearsed," Retief commented. "I might buy the jack-in-the-box bomb impulse, but impulsively preparing a rope for the getaway and a smoke-bomb to cover it are just a bit too studied to carry real conviction as boyish impulses."

"Drat!" Whish muttered. "I *told* that know-all. . . ."

"But you forgot to put it in writing," Retief pointed out. "Or did you?"

"Heavens, no!" Whish snapped, just as the weary waiter returned with Retief's musty ale and the Groaci's sundae and wine.

"Hey!" Whish objected as the overflowing plate was placed before him. "I wanted pickles, not bananas—Kosher dills," he added.

The waiter nodded glumly. "Maraschinos?" he inquired dubiously.

"Pickled onions," Whish corrected. "And just bring the chocolate sauce; I'll put it on myself."

The waiter shuffled away, still muttering querulously.

"What kind of ice cream is under the banana?" Retief asked. Whish replied that it was egg-and-olive. As if to prove it, he dug out a morsel of olive with the slender spoon provided and sniffed it dubiously, then subjected it to the scrutiny of his inconspicuous bloof-organ.

"Are you really going to eat that?" Retief asked.

Whish crossed two pairs of eyes, the dizzying Groaci equivalent of a wink. "Naw," he demurred. "Just another Booch item. Drives the old boy up the wall."

Retief watched as Whish transferred the sundae to a plastic container he produced from beneath his broken-ribbed hip-cloak.

"All right," Retief said when Whish had tucked the carton back out of sight. "That's enough Booch for now. Now we're going to talk business."

"Or?" Whish inquired archly.

"Or you're going to eat that mess," Retief informed him. "Start talking."

"Retief! You wouldn't," Whish gasped.

"Would I not?" Retief countered. "Tell me all about it."

"I am but an innocent go-between," Whish protested. "What do I know of great affairs?"

"Great affairs, eh?" Retief commented. "That big?"

"To read too much into a mere figure of speech," Whish protested. "To have merely overheard a comment in the conference room as I was emptying waste-paper baskets, as is my humble duty."

"Whish," Retief said reproachfully, "are you trying to tell me you're not a major in the State Security Establishment?"

"What would a mere Terry know of Stasestab?" Whish dismissed the query. "Stasestab is a Cosmic Top Private Agency. And besides that, it doesn't exist!"

"Sure," Retief said agreeably. "But if it existed it would be for the purpose of 'promoting the interests of the Groacian Destiny on alien worlds, especially at the expense of inferior life-forms which presume to impede that Destiny,' eh, Whish?"

"But that's a direct quotation from the CTP Stasestab Charter," Whish gasped. "Nonsense, that is," he corrected himself. "Never heard such yivshish in my life."

"How long do you think it would take to walk from here to the Outspace port?" Retief asked abruptly. "The Diplomatic Enclosure on the far side, I mean, where I noticed in the paper His

Groacian Excellency's packet boat is docked at the moment."

"Far too long for one to contemplate the stroll as a morning constitutional," Whish replied shortly. "Why?" he added suddenly, aligning all five eyes in an expression of concentration.

"If the streets weren't so crowded, that is," Retief amended. "Perhaps six or eight hours, if we hurry, assuming we aren't stopped for questioning by the cops, who, I noticed, are out in force this morning."

Whish brought his boney wrist up and carefully studied the oversized Gene Autry watch strapped to it. He jumped to his feet.

"We must off at once, Retief!" he hissed. "Or I, at least, must off. You're of course free to remain and enjoy your refreshments."

"What's the hurry?" Retief inquired. "Eight hours too long?"

"Certainly not!" Whish snapped. "Things are all set for five pee em—so we've scads of time. No wait—if that scamp Thilth has misled me, that could be cutting it a bit close. So one may as well provide a certain margin for error, eh, Retief?" As he finished his speech breathlessly, Whish scuttled suddenly sideways out of the booth, colliding with the top man just returning with Retief's ale, which slid from the tray to be caught in midair by Retief's deft grab.

"Settle down, Whish" he counseled. "Colonel Thilth wouldn't kid an old colleague like you, would he? Five, you said. Lots of time. Anyway, what's so interesting at the port?"

Before Whish could reply, there was a sudden flurry of activity from the direction of the door, and First Secretary of Embassy of Terra Magnan skidded to a halt beside the table, hurriedly smoothing his hair.

"Oh, there you are, Retief!" the slender diplomat blurted breathlessly. "His Excellency suggested I join you and caution you to do nothing precipitate! Got ropeburns in my descent, and had to give an officious flatfoot a tenner plus a piece of my mind! Then the mob turned on me. I fled barely in time. May I sit down?" He perched on the edge of Whish's bench seat and worked on his breathing, looking back over his shoulder anxiously.

" 'Catch that madman and see to it he doesn't set Slub-Terran relations back a decade, before teatime!' eh?" Retief reconstructed Magnan's instructions.

"Those weren't his *exact* words," Magnan panted. "But it's clear you grasp the intent of the Ambassadorial instructions."

"Whish here was just telling me everything's set to blow sky-high at five this afternoon," Retief told his senior officer. "He's in a hurry to get to the port before then."

"That," Whish stated indignantly, "is a misquotation, Ben." He pointed three eyes directly at Retief in Outraged Accusation (13-d), keeping the other two on Magnan.

"His casual way with a quotation rates your 't' at least, Whish," Magnan sniffed. "Now, shall we stroll back to Embassy Row, and have a nice chat just between ourselves?" He got to his feet and made Alphonse-and-Gaston ushering motions inviting the Groaci to follow suit.

"Oh, you think you're going to pump me, and maybe sneak inside the Embassy Compound for a look-see, do you, Ben? Tsk," Whish objected. "I gave you credit for more subtlety than that. Old Retief here squeezed a few hints out of me by illegal methods, but that's all you get! I'm clamming up now, so you can sweat out five pee em and see what happens."

"On behalf of His Excellency the Terran Ambassador Extraordinary and Minister Plenipotentiary," Magnan said hastily, "I apologize for Retief's methods, Whish, so don't be a spoilsport. What's this about five pee em? Why, that's after office hours— and on a Friday, too!"

"Oh, nothing much," Whish dismissed the subject. "Just a bit of sport in the spirit of Booch." He paused to entwine two eye-stalks in expression of Suppressed Hilarity (17-g).

"But," Magnan protested, "I must insist that sending His Terran Excellency a jack-in-the-box disguised as a bomb is hardly a jape calculated to merit the approval of the *Corps Diplomatique*! You owe me some explanation of all this, I insist!"

"Of all *what*?" Whish demanded. "I served my function as a humble messenger in extending his Groacian Ex's esteem to his Terran colleague—and Retief here chased me down and is attempting to force me to ingest pickles with chocolate sauce! Not only that, he doubted my plighted word! Aloud!"

Magnan gave Retief a shocked look. "Retief! You didn't! I mean, the protocols covering inhumane tactics. . . ."

" 'Inhumane'?" Whish echoed. "They're positively sub-Groaci! Now, I shall do the demanding: let Retief offer a suitable apology at once!"

"The esteemed gentlebeing says that I called him a liar," Retief said solemnly. "It's true, and I regret that."

Magnan plucked at Retief's sleeve, an anxious expression on his narrow face. "Perhaps a more elegant expression would be in order," he whispered. "Besides, what you said could be misinterpreted."

"I tell you, gentlemen," Whish cut in as sternly as his weak voice could manage, "His Excellency did not dispatch a jack-in-the-box disguised as a bomb. I defy anyone to give the lie to that."

"Why, what cheek!" Magnan gasped. "I was there myself, I saw it jump out and nearly frighten poor Ted back to the rank of corporal!"

Retief got to his feet abruptly. "I think this time he's being technically correct, Mr. Magnan," he said. "If it isn't a jack-in-the-box disguised as a bomb, then it must be a bomb disguised as a jack-in-the-box." He went across the dim-lit room to the public talker in a booth in the rear corner, quickly punched keys.

"Code Room. Jerry," a voice responded lazily.

"Jerry," Retief said. "Go to the Chancery at once, enter the Ambassador's office without waiting for an invitation, go to the desk, pick up the package there, and rush it to the sub-basement. Dunk it into a fire bucket, and then put it in the emergency vault and get out quick and close the door. Got it?"

"I got it, Mr. Retief," Jerry said dubiously. "But what *is* it? If I barge in on old Hairshirt, he'll have me boiled in oil, and maybe even fire me! What's it all about?"

"I'll tell you later, Jerry," Retief answered the young fellow. "Right now, do it—and fast!"

"OK, if you say so. But I know you'll back me up—not like most of the Embassy big shots. OK, Mr. Retief, I'll do it."

Back at the table, Retief soothed Magnan, then turned to Whish, whom Magnan had restrained by putting a foot on the elusive Groaci's knee under the table and exerting a pressure just short of that required to burst the fragile joint, a circumstance which the trapped alien related to Retief in an aggrieved tone.

"Nice work, Mr. Magnan," Retief congratulated his supervisor at the conclusion of the indictment.

"Let up now, and I'll just sit here beside him." He slid over on the seat to pin Whish against the wall, where he struggled for a moment, then relaxed, all five eyes adroop, miming Acceptance of Unjust Fate By Virtue of Superior Strength of Character (27-c).

"Better make that a z-plus, Whish," Retief suggested. "You know, the 'Gee, Fellows, This Time I Really Mean it' degree."

Whish adjusted his oculars accordingly. "I hope you're sport enough not to let Ambassador Shish find out I used my z," he offered submissively.

"Not unless you forget to mention just what it is your errand was intended to distract our attention from," Retief reassured the cowed Groaci.

"Oh, fie; back to that silly idea," Whish commented dismissingly.

Retief nodded. "That *was* egg-and-olive ice cream, wasn't it?" He queried, turning to catch the waiter's eye. Whish made a lunge for freedom under the table, fetching up in Magnan's lap.

"Ben!" the Groaci hissed. "You wouldn't let him! In all our past dealings—not ours personally, of course, since we've met only at receptions and cocktail parties, but in Groaci-Terran relations generally, I mean—the record has never been sullied by any such atrocity! I appeal to you as a representative of civilized *mores* to stop this madman before he carries out his fell intent!"

"Ah, to be sure, Whish," Magnan temporized, extricating himself from the Groaci's frantic embrace. "Do be calm. Just what fell intent is that to which you refer?"

"Ben," Whish shrilled, "this is no time for punctillious syntax! Call him off!" He broke off to tilt his triangular head alertly, all five oculars ranged across the top quivering erect.

"Mark!" he breathed. "The time for servile appeals to your good nature has passed, Ben!" he went on, more emphatically. "In moments the true status of Terry meddlers vis-à-vis Groacian Manifest Destiny will stand revealed!"

With a crash, the front door burst inward, and a full squad of Groaci Peace Keepers in flared helmets, gold-sequined greaves, dowdy greenish-black hip-cloaks and plain GI eye shields had crowded in, scatter-guns leveled at the occupied booth.

"To consort with dubious companions, Major Whish!" the non-commissioned officer in charge hissed. "To suggest you come out at once, my field of fire to clear!"

"The major wouldn't find that convenient," Retief told the sergeant. "He's just working out the details of how he can survive the lunch hour."

"To hold your tongue, impertinent Soft One," the NCO replied, adjusting the aim of his weapon to bear between Retief's eyes. Retief studied with interest the gun muzzle six inches from his face.

"A Groaci copy of a Japanese version of the Webley .59," he noted aloud. "By the way, Sarge, did you know your safety was on, in the locked position?" As the Groaci looked down, he rose, pushed the barrel of the crater gun aside, then jerked it toward him, snapping it from the grip of the squad leader with such vigor that the Groaci's helmet fell off with a noisy clatter. Retief took a grip on the non-com's neck and, reversing the weapon, instantly fired a round between two troopers to smash the front window.

"Tsk," he commented. "I must have been mistaken about that safety. Now, you boys may drop your guns and line up against the wall, right over there." He gestured toward the rustic brick partition beside the fireplace. Weapons clattered to the floor as the Groaci complied.

"Retief! No!" Whish keened. "To line up these

brave lads and shoot them down in cold vascular fluid would be an enormity on a par with the infamous massacre of the Saintly Valentine! Stay your hand, I beseech you! I—I'll tell you all you desire to know of our Booch Day surprise!"

Retief fired a second round, this one into the brick-work, to assist a laggard Groaci in assuming a symmetrical position in line.

"Really, Retief," Magnan quavered. "While, I acknowledge, it would be deeply satisfying, as well as amply justified, to slaughter these criminally misled fellows out of hand, it really wouldn't look at all well in my weekly Chumship Report. So perhaps you could limit your target practice to merely shattering their kneecaps, say, so a few would survive at least, to get their livelihood in the alleys of the city—those, I mean, who survive the fury of the Slubbese when they learn the part these cripples hoped to play in the destruction of the planet."

"Oh-oh," Whish muttered. "So somebody *did* blab. I mean, 'destroy the planet'? How absurd!"

"I didn't mean that literally," Magnan sniffed. "Even you Groaci would hardly sink so low as to wipe out an entire planet and its indigenous mentational species merely for petty political advantage."

"What's so petty about political advantage?" Whish demanded. And who say these Slubs are a mentational species? My pet moopah has got more savvy than these dullards!"

"Still, one can't exterminate them out of hand," Magnan pointed out.

"But it's OK to exterminate the second squad, third platoon, Company B, eh?" Whish challenged.

"I'll think it over," Retief conceded, putting a third shot half an inch from the hand of a larger-than-average corporal, which member had been inconspicuously creeping toward the reserve 2mm under his hip-cloak. The corporal jumped and slung his hand. "Them brick chips smarted some!" he wailed. "I'm putting this in my report, wise guy!"

"Silence, nest-fouling twin of a genetic deficiency!" the captive sergeant hissed at his subordinate. "To take note of the fact that both your advancement in the Service and my own would be severely inhibited by a .99 in the cranium! Goad not the Soft One, lest he vent his long-suppressed resentment of Groacian superiority in the form so vividly outlined but a moment agone!"

"Well, Sarge," the number two replied cheekily. "Saying about Groaci superiority and all ain't likely to sooth him none. Ten-HUT! you slobs," he added, casting a glance along the ragged rank beside him.

"Very well," Whish moaned. "Here it is, Retief—and I'm only telling him to save you boys from a dire fate, to no benefit to proud Groac," he added, addressing the sergeant, still struggling feebly in Retief's grip. "Better relax, Snish," he ordered. "A Terry's grip is stronger than a Groaci's neck any day, so take it easy. I'll get you out of this." He turned to Retief. "Later," he said, "I'm sure you'll be grateful that I prevailed upon you to stay your hand."

"Not really," Retief replied. "I had no intention of shooting anyone."

"But you said—you threatened . . ." Whish broke off, looking resentful, an expression he managed by squeezing his two outer pairs of eyes closely together, allowing the center one to droop.

"No, that was your idea entirely," Retief pointed out.

"Ask Ben," Whish proposed, turning to face the senior bureaucrat. "He said he'd shoot us all, didn't he, Ben?" the Groaci entreated. "You were a witness to the entire atrocity! Surely you won't deny it!"

"Actually," Magnan said thoughtfully, "all Retief said was, 'Drop your guns and line up,' then you started babbling about Interplanetary Law."

"Not once did I invoke the absurd fiction known as Interplanetary Law, Ben," Whish said reproachfully. "And it was you, yourself, who proposed to maim these splendid troops and send them out into hostile streets to beg."

"The options are still open, Major," Magnan said crisply. "You'd better start spilling the legumes, before you rouse my ire."

"I don't think we've quite convinced the major we mean business," Retief told Magnan. "If you'll stay here and keep an eye on them, I'm going over to the waterfront and check on a few items."

"Retief! I must demand. . . ." Whish started and lunged for freedom, rebounded from Retief's immobile fist and sank, whimpering, into his corner.

"Better keep a firm grip on him, Mr. Magnan," Retief suggested. He curtly ordered the sergeant and his squad to go outside and disperse; then he turned and left the saloon.

In the bustling street, an unusual number of uniformed Groaci were to be seen, officiously directing traffic, haranguing shopkeepers, and hustling outraged citizens toward paddy-wagons. Retief made his way through the crowd, to be abruptly confronted by a Groaci Peace Keeper wearing the elaborate shoulder-boards of a full colonel, a distinction rendered somewhat ludicrous in appearance by his lack of shoulders.

"Here, fellow!" the cop hissed. "Terry, aren't you, Big fellow? You wouldn't by any chance be the notorious wrecker and enemy of the Groacian state known as Retief, I suppose?"

"The odds are against it," Retief pointed out.

"At last census there were just over a hundred billion Terries registered, not counting hybrids, on five hundred and sixty-one worlds, so the chances that any specific one would be standing right here contemplating throwing you into the refuse bin at this moment are small indeed."

"To be logical," the colonel acknowledged. "But you being a Terry and all, you better watch it; I got my best three eyes on you, and my snarf-organ, too." He turned away.

"But as it happens," Retief continued, "this time the laws of probability seen to be in abeyance." He took a firm grip on the Groaci's thin neck and dragged the feebly struggling officer to the large, bilious-yellow hopper marked in angular Slubbese linear X, 'official use only—property of Slub City.' He thrust the colonel in, head first, and continued on his way. The passers-by ignored the incident with the exception of one fellow in dock-wallopers' traditional attire, with a visage coarse-featured even for a Slubbese, who stopped to watch, then applauded raucously, muttered "Nice going, Terry!" and fell in behind Retief.

"Say, pal," the stevedore said companionably to Retief's back. "I kind of like your style. I heard about how you Terries are nefarious or something, and all, always picking on the noble Groaci and all, but frankly, I ain't nuts about the noble Groaci myownself. Where you headed, big fella? By the way, the handle's Vug."

Retief paused and waited for the local to overtake him, then said, "It's a pleasure, Vug. I'm Retief." He shook manipulatory members with his new acquaintance and inquired, "Where'd you learn to speak Terran?"

"I got me one of them brain-tapes like you see in the ads," Vug replied. "That reminds me, the other day I seen in my comic book where a fellow can pick up a snappy necktie that glows in the dark and like that. Only three plunt, too, including shipping and handling. I don't know what that handling is, but I guess it'll be a useful item when it comes. Onny trouble is, I don't have no idear how to get what they call a interplanetary credit voucher like it says in the ad I gotta send. Maybe you could tip me off, hey, you being a foreigner and all."

"I'll make a note of it," Retief suggested.

"Geeze, I figgered you was a right guy as soon as I seen the way you taken time to tuck that copper's feet inside and all before you slammed the lid," Vug commented admiringly. "But I ast you, where we going? And what's the rush? This is Booch, remember, and I got the day off. Figgered I might mosey over to one of the joints in skunktown, where a fellow can get into a few fights, and get a nice plate o' food, and some whiz-water, and some nice dames, too. Whatta ya say? But I guess you'd prefer one o' them strange-looking Terry broads, no offense."

"Not today, Vug," Retief declined gracefully. "I've got a small job of planet-saving to do, at the harbor."

"I better go along," Vug suggested. "I know my way around out there, which there's some pretty tough characters hang out along the waterfront. And we can grab a bite at the Collapsed Lung, a what they call quaint old dump, but the eats is good. You can get a plank steak hand-cut from the choicest planks, like the menu says."

"Sure, glad to have some company," Retief agreed. "By the way, what do you know about a drill-rig called *Challenger?*"

"Old trawler conversion," Vug told Retief. "These here Groaci fitted her up with a derrick yeah high. Been out exploring the Voon Deep, I hear. That's the deepest part of the Big Trench, about half way to North. Don't know what they expect to find out there. Oil formations is all up on the shelf; they ain't looking for tendril-tonic, that's for sure. But I hear rumors," he added, "there's Something Up—onny they're drilling down. That's a little joke, Retief. You got to excuse me: I got this here sense of humor and all."

"It must be a sensitive faculty indeed," Retief observed.

"You bet," Vug confirmed. "Some guys wouldn't have saw the potential for a good jape in that there, about 'up' and 'down,' and all."

"Perhaps the CDT could find a position for you, Vug, if you're interested," Retief said, "advising Ambassadors when to laugh."

"Naw, I got no innerest in a fancy desk job," Vug declined. "Thanks anyways for the thought. But what's a post like that pay a feller?"

"Not much—only about fifteen hundred guck," Retief replied.

"A thou-five a year?" Vug echoed. "Not bad. Maybe I better give it some thought after all."

"Per week," Retief corrected. "Plus commissary privileges and a fat retirement plan."

"You're talking me inta it." Vug warned. "Plenty o' travel, too, I guess. And a crack at some o' that Terry whiz-water, which I hear it's got plenty vitamins."

"All that, and close association with His Excellency, too," Retief confirmed.

"Well, ya gotta take the bitter with the sweet," Vug philosophized. "Do I get to wear one of them fancy suits with the chrome-plated lapels, and a stripe on the pants and all?"

"It's obligatory," Retief said.

"Too bad I don't wear no pants," Vug pointed out. "Would it be OK if I just had the stripes?"

* * *

A few minutes later, comfortably ensconced in a corner booth in the Collapsed Lung, Retief scanned a pamphlet relating the circumstances surrounding the long-ago establishment of the house and the genesis of its name. The tranquility of the crowded premises was somewhat diminished by the four—no, make that five, Retief corrected—fist fights in progress, spurred on by the merry cries of the clientele, themselves bearing the marks of recent combat, and the monotonous chant of the proprietor, distinguishable from the other combatants by his vigorously-wielded bung-starter and his steady cry of "Break it up, you bums."

"See?" Vug said contentedly, over the din, supplemented by a jukebox exhorting all present to *Do the Hucklebuck*, one of Franky's lesser efforts. "I tole you it was a nice cheerful place," Vug asserted. "Now, Retief, if some of the boys try to come over and give you a hard time, you gotta excuse 'em, which they're onny tryna make ya feel welcome."

At that moment, a local citizen nearly as big as Vug lurched to a halt beside the table, his shadow falling across it.

"Hey, Vug, what's this you drug in here to the Lung?" he demanded, eyeing Retief distastefully. "Some kinda foreign bookworm, hey?" The stranger poked a blunt, sausage-like finger, lacking its first joint, at Retief's pamphlet.

"We don't cotton to no dudes around these here parts, stranger," he announced.

"That's good," Retief commented. "I can't stand 'em myself, and by the way, I'm not a stranger back in my home town."

"Yore home town is a dirty, low-down dump," Retief's new acquaintance announced. "Prolly full o' rats and frubs and cockroaches and cops."

"Right on almost all counts," Retief agreed. "We don't have many cops. Killed 'em all off."

"Don't come in here bragging about yer lousy home town, which it's prolly some kind o' slum," the Slubbese warned; then he drove a straight right jab at Retief's jaw. Retief moved his head slightly to avoid the blow and with one hand pinned his attacker's arm to the table, thus bringing the fellow's face to within an inch of the scarred table-top, his head twisted to stare up at Retief.

"You gotta excuse Gub, which he had a few," Vug commented. "He don't mean no harm."

"I was onny kidding around, pal," Gub explained, his voice a trifle strained by his awkward position and the overextension of the elbow joint. "I ain't gonna hurt you bad, feller."

"You sure aren't," Retief agreed. "On the other hand, you were standing in my light, and on top of that, nobody has a right to be as ugly as you are." He stood in a leisurely way, hauled Gub in, lifted him above his head, and threw him into the thick of the action.

"You ain't sore, Retief?" Vug inquired anxiously. "Old Gub ain't a bad guy, just got no judgment, is all, like the time he stuck his finger in the oil hole on the boat-hoist, just cause it was there, you know, like that mountain someplace. He yelled some when them gears chewed his fingernail fer him. He's what you call a slow learner."

"We have a few of those in the Corps," Retief commented. "They persist in offering an arm to a shark on the theory that will make him go away satisfied."

"Heck," Vug commented. "Any dummy oughta know that just gets them going, when they taste blood."

"A discovery," Retief said, "which so far has eluded our Underground Deep-Think Teams."

Retief and Vug lunched on snickberry-and-sardine salad and a tasty local beer. Then, without further incident, departed the Lung and took a broken-down ex-Dallas, Texas, cab to the waterfront. They alighted on a blighted corner in front of a former ship chandler's warehouse. At once, a pair of down-at-heels locals emerged and sauntered over. The first, a paunchy fellow wearing a tarnished green vest, halted before Retief and looked him up and down.

"You're lost, chum," he stated indifferently. "No easy pickings for capitalist imperialist blood-suckers around here," he amplified, planting himself squarely in Retief's path.

"Too bad," Retief commiserated. "Maybe you can find some over by the *Challenger*."

"Hah?" the paunchy Slubbese mimed confusion, an inept attempt at a 202—about a 'c' the fellow was trying for, Retief decided (Rightful Astonishment at Unwarranted Misinterpretation of Pure Motives). "It ain't *me's* looking to break the rice bowls o' the downtrod masses!" he protested. "But it might be an idear at that," he added confusedly.

"May I trouble you to step aside, sir?" Retief inquired mildly.

"Nix, Retief," Vug cautioned. "These kind of bums always interpret courtesy as weakness. Thinks you're scared of him." With that Vug jostled the fellow aside and started across the slimy cobbled street, pausing as a taxi even shabbier than the one which he and Retief had arrived shuddered to a stop at the curb just by the wharf where *Challenger* was tied up.

Retief caught a glimpse of the passenger inside the elderly vehicle, crossed over in time to see a short, knobly-kneed individual wrapped in an unseasonable cloak emerge, hand over a coin which elicited a yelp of protest from the driver, and go briskly to the gate barring access to the dock. The driver looked up in astonished delight as Retief came up and handed him another coin.

"Geeze, Terry—you *are* one o' them Terries, no offense. . . ." the startled chauffer began confusedly.

"It's an honor," Retief reassured the blunt-featured Slubbese. "Now, did Major Whish stop off anywhere on the way here?" he added smoothly.

"The other Terry," the cabbie remarked reminiscently, "boy, was he excited! Chased me a block and a half, and if my junction-box wouldn't of settled down, he'd of caught me. Kept yelling stuff about saving the world. Some kind o' religious nut, I guess."

"Mr. Magnan will be flattered at your assessment," Retief told the fellow. "But did Whish come directly here from the Pink Moon, or. . . ."

"Had me stop at a hair-goods boutique on Gutter Boulevard," the driver replied. "Had the old meter ticking for eleven minutes and some. Then the bum hands me a five-sprug piece—don't hardly cover the fare, let alone the tip. But o' course your tenner fixed that OK. What are you, his keeper, or what?"

"Almost," Retief acknowledged. "Technically, I'm Assistant Cultural Attaché for Disgraceful Affairs."

"Oh, sounds like a important post," the driver commented, just as Vug came up and tugged at Retief's sleeve.

"I guess you din't notice, Retief," he muttered in a conspiratorial tone. "But the bum got outta the hack is one o' them Groaci—I can tell 'em from you Terries by the skinny legs. Anyways, he acks kind of sneaky, over there looking the drilling rig over, got something in mind, I bet. And you was saying about the tub. So I figgered maybe. . . ."

"Precisely," Retief confirmed Vug's thinking. "Come on." He led the way across to where Whish was busy with a large ring of keys, working on the oversized padlock securing the gate. The Groaci whipped four of his five stalked eyes around in an astonished expression as the Big Terran came up beside him.

"To wonder at your presence here, during office hours," he exclaimed breathlessly. "But now I recall," he added. "Your flimsily built Embassy collapsed earlier today. Pity and all that."

"Not quite," Retief corrected. "It seems the bomb was a real one, all right, but it was accidentally stored in an old vault in the basement, so if and when it went off, no harm was done."

"But that's. . . !" Whish started, then broke off. "That's too bad," he amended awkwardly. "No wonder Pud and his chaps are a trifle late." He consulted his strap-watch and sighed. "One's entire reserve stock, destroyed by accident," he muttered. "To offer me commiserations, Retief." Just then the lock fell open and he ducked through the gate, instantly slamming it behind him, and resecuring the lock.

"To excuse me," he whispered, "but of course, as a fellow diplomat, you understand my zeal in maintaining the security of Groacian state property. Not that you'd dream of violating a high security area, prominently posted," he added through the wire mesh, before darting away along the pier.

"Tough bope-nodes, we can't follow him," Vug commented. "Looks like the little rascal made points that time. I betcha he's up to no good, too."

"I have the honor to decline that wager," Retief replied, at the same time examining the big padlock, a Groaci copy of a Japanese version of an early Yale model, he noted. Grasping it firmly, he twisted it to the left until the sheet-metal hasp began to bend, then yanked it hard, eliciting a sharp *ping!* as it came free. He tossed it into the oil-scummed water lapping at the ancient timbers of the wharf, opened the gate and Magnan passed through, while Vug watched, his small, deep-set eyes registering shock.

"Nix, Retief," he said hoarsely. "This here is a top-security area. We got no right—even if it *did* have a broke lock on it. Come on, let's do a fast fade before the little devil puts out a squeal and we get about six carloads of law down here to put the sneeze on us."

"You run along, Vug," Retief suggested. "I have business to transact with Major Whish." He turned and went along the narrow pier, lined with plank-hulled boats in various stages of terminal decay, their bilges awash in murky fluid dotted with floating fish heads.

There was the sharp *bzzzpp!* of a Groaci power gun and splinters flew from the weathered planks beside him, leaving a deep gouge from which arose a resinous odor. Not deviating from his course, Retief advanced steadily toward the bales stacked in the shadow of the drill-rig, from behind which the shot had come. As he reached the first bundle (of half-cured ice-worm hides, he noted) there was a sudden faint scraping sound from behind the smelly skins. Retief came around the bundle in time to grab the thin arm of Whish just as the latter snapped a new power cell into his handgun. Retief plucked the weapon from the major's grasp and dropped it into his pocket.

"Tsk," he chided his captive. "Naughty. That shot you fired was a considerable overreaction, for an innocent: diplomat just out to look over the state of selfless Groac's gift to the Slubbese people. What are you really here for, Whish?"

"As you well know, vile Terry meddler," Whish keened. "Our oceanographic studies can redound to the immeasurable benefit of the backward autocthones of this benighted world. I shouldn't like to be in the shoes of the luckless foreigner who sought to interfere therewith. Now, unhand me, and maybe I'll let you off with a formal apology."

"Not likely, Major," Retief demurred. "Let's go take a look belowdecks. You were in too big a hurry to get here."

"Baseless base canards!" Whish hissed, then switched to Groaci. "To defy you to violate sacred Groacian premises, especially the very precincts which embody and symbolize Groac's gift to Slub. Crowds of outraged locals will rend you limb from limb."

"I guess I'll have to take that chance," Retief told the excited fellow. "Lead on, Major." Vug trailed them at a distance.

"To have reminded you that I am but a humble Admin type," Whish reproved. "To wonder why you persist in your delusion that I am a field-grade Intelligence officer."

"I'm impressed by your modesty, Major," Retief said. "It must be a fairly big operation you're covering up, to inspire a rank-conscious Groaci field-grader to come on like a GS-3 clerk."

"Pah!" Whish spat. "To find it useless to reason with a miscreant of your stripe!"

"Sure," Retief agreed. "So let's get on with it."

He waved the Groaci ahead up the swaying gangplank. Pausing only to salute the quarterdeck, Whish scuttled across and darted toward the tumbledown deckhouse, halted abruptly and patted the baggy pockets stitched to his doublet in the manner of one searching for his wallet, and turned to announce to Retief, close behind him, "Ah, Fate intervenes! You are saved from further violation of Groacian sovereignty, scientific objectivity, and my own inviolate person by the curious circumstance that I appear to have forgotten my keys!"

"To this?" Retief asked, indicating the five-foot high, dark-green painted door set in the clapboard wall beside them. Without awaiting a reply, he snap-kicked the panel at latch level and it burst inward with only a mild splintering of the door jamb.

"After you, Major," he offered graciously, and thrust his host ahead of him into the cluttered cabin. Whish turned quickly to a chart table and began rummaging among the papers scattered thickly there. Retief came up silently and grabbed the Groaci's arm.

"I noticed you were in a hurry to cover up something over here," Retief explained. "So let's see what it is." Whish plunged and fluttered, screeching thinly.

"To pry no more into matters beyond the comprehension of a non-scientist!" he shrilled. "To stay your hand, Retief! Some matters were better left unbroached!"

"Perhaps he's right," Magnan's voice came from the open door. "It *is* a bit much, Retief, to invade the premises of the well-publicized Groaci Goodies for Undesirables project and Groaci-handle the Project Director. The media, I fear, will see this in a light perhaps even dimmer than that which will illume Ambassador Hairshirt's view of the matter."

Retief nodded as if agreeing, and invited his supervisor to enter, at the same time brushing aside the papers Whish had, apparently casually, spread across the chart displayed on the illuminated board.

"I was able to trace Whish's cab, luckily," Magnan explained. "I'm glad to see you've laid him by the heels. But shouldn't we be doing something about this Project Cancel, rather than sightseeing?"

"All in good time, Mr. Magnan," Retief soothed his senior.

"I was almost set upon when I alighted from my conveyance," Magnan told Retief aggrievedly. "The vehicle was something called a Reo, a '32,' the driver told me, whatever that is. But as I was saying, I stopped off in front of a most noisome dive with a sign bearing a crude painting of a pinkish cheese, it seemed, and the legend 'Ye Busted Lunge'. Anyway, these three, truly evil-looking locals rushed out, but I fixed them with a stern glance and they tugged at their forelocks and withdrew!"

"They seen he was a Terran, Retief," Vug's hoarse voice came from the entry. "And they wasn't messing with no more Terries today. Funny thing, Retief," he said. "Under them rotten deck-planks, there's new steelwork. This here tub is more than meets the snoof-organ, like they say."

"I was about to say it was a frightfully shabby vessel for a project of such celebrity," Magnan said, brushing aside scarlet cobwebs. He came over to peer over Retief's shoulder. "Gracious me!" he exclaimed. "If it weren't so fantastic, I'd think that was a compilation of stress-profiles from the Voon Deep area." He edged around Retief. "And this red X," he put a well-chewed forefinger on the symbol boldly inked on the chart. "The standard indication for EXTREME DANGER! What, may I ask, Whish, does it indicate in this context?"

"Mere caution on the part of the Chief Engineer," Whish dismissed the query. "One should dislike to have some simple fishing vessel venture into the work area, of course."

"Still," Magnan demurred, "according to the code of the Interworld Commission for Navigation, the designation is to be employed only for minefields, active volcanoes, and the like. It appears rather excessive."

"You think so, Ben?" Whish riposted smoothly. "Let us wait and see."

"I don't like it, Retief," Magnan confided behind his hand. "I think perhaps the scamp is still being devious."

"That's what the major was about to tell me," Retief told the older man. He turned to Whish. "Let's go below and look at the drill rig," he suggested. When Whish redoubled his expostulations, Retief added, "Unless you'd prefer that we remain here, and dig a bit deeper into the documentation."

"That was a little joke!" Vug cried delightedly. "I can tell."

"If I must conduct a sightseeing tour, then I suppose I must," the Groaci snapped, and dashed for the door. Magnan stepped back quickly, and Whish tripped over his foot.

Retief grabbed the screeching major by the ankle and hoisted him up, then shifted his hold to the Intelligence officer's neck and righted him. "I've changed my mind," he said. "You're too eager to go, by half."

"Look here, Retief," Magnan said excitedly from a desk by the bulkhead. "Specifications for 'Class P High Explosives (special underwater formulae).' What do you suppose . . ."

"In our researches," Whish keened, "it is sometimes necessary to clear overburden from points of interest, remove volcanic debris, et cetera—matters unqualified personnel cannot be expected to grasp. I renew my demand that you cease this lawless meddling and let go my neck, Retief!"

Retief complied, and Whish impacted the deck with a force that dislodged his medium-ornate eye-shields, for which he went scrambling under the chart table. Magnan stooped and retrieved him, clutching an overflowing wastebasket.

"What have we here?" Magnan inquired as he removed the receptacle from his captive's clutch.

"Mere rubbish, Ben," Whish dismissed the query off-handedly. "Trash I'd been meaning to burn—nothing more."

"I see," Magnan replied. "Still, I think we'd best have a look." He offered the container to Retief, who plucked from it a crumpled sheet which he opened flat, finding it to be covered with calculations in crabbed Groaci numerals.

"Your computers are out for repair?" Magnan asked Whish, now limp in his grasp.

"By no means," Whish snapped. "Actually, Ben," he added in a tone of candor, "I've been playing the local pools."

"I haven't heard of one called 'Cancel,' " Retief commented, "which seems to be the entry in the 'subject' column here."

"Botheration!" Whish hissed. "Burn the rubbish and let's forget the matter. If you care nothing for Interplanetary protocols, you might at least consider my career! Now, let us proceed to other matters: you were about to examine the cargo hold, as I recall, quite illegally, of course."

"No, it was the technical area I had in mind," Retief corrected.

"Speak up, Major," Magnan commanded sternly. "Before I forget I'm a gentlebeing."

"Don't rib me, Ben," Whish dismissed the demand. "I know you already Know All. I heard you threaten to tell the locals about the scheme to destroy, as you put it, the planet, even though that's an exaggeration. Clearly, some wretch has already blabbed!" He wagged his head dispiritedly. "An undetected security risk, probably in my own department," he mourned. "Operation

Cancel was our best-kept state secret. I dread to contemplate His Excellency's wrath when he finds out there's been a leak."

"I shall want full details of Cancel for my report, of course," Magnan sharply reminded the crestfallen Groaci.

"I suppose it hardly matters, now," Whish conceded. "Since you're aware that in less than four hours the minor world once known to its inferior inhabitants as Slub will be racked by tectonic activity which will release valuable unoccupied former sea-bottoms for Groaci colonization, you may as well know that the hell-bomb was placed less than a week ago by myself, as an unbilled embellishment to the spurious oil exploration expedition you were so kind as to sponsor, Ben. We smuggled in the components as office supplies meriting duty-free entry, of course, as is customary. The rest is mere yivshish."

"Major Whish!" Magnan cried, pale with shock, or with something which made him pale. "You didn't! You couldn't! A Class X-One explosive device placed among the black smokers in the Voon Deep, where *Challenger* carried out her reconnaissance, would initiate a new age of mountain building! West Continent would slide over against North and subduct, carrying with it into the magma all the major ports on the planet—and the rich farmlands of the entire coastal plain would be inundated! The very concept is too hellish to contemplate!"

"See, I said you know all about it, Ben," Whish snapped in a tone of Righteous Vindication (13-b). "So why don't we think about something pleasanter, eh?" He went on in a reasonable tone. "Like the fashion in which selfless Groacian emergency teams now luckily standing by off-planet, will rush in to restore order, salvage national treasures, and dole out hot soup to any unfortunate survivors; after which, quite naturally, Groac will stake legitimate claims to newly exposed and thus uninhabited coastal areas, now made available for productive colonization. And think of the dramatic scenes during the rearrangement phase: great new mountain ranges thrusting skyward along the present Old Fault on North; the boiling of the sea as volcanoes of released magma come welling up from the depths; the limitless vista of the vast expanses of newly exposed globigerinous ooooze drying in the sun, after ages of accumulation in the depths, as the sea drains away from the uplifted continental shelves! The yokels of the entire Arm will flock to view it all! The tapes alone will pay for the entire operation!"

"But, Whish," Magnan protested gamely. "Can't you foresee the reaction of the Galactic community to this enormity?"

"I foresee only sensational grosses," Whish replied complacently. "Plus *lebensraum* where Groacian ladies can rear their lovable grubs in peace, untroubled by the mutterings of displaced inferiors, or envious diplomats."

"The *Challenger* is sea-ready, I believe," Retief said. "With the drill strings still in place. Let's go for a ride," Retief suggested. "At worst, we'll get a ringside view of the catastrophe."

"Art mad, vile Terry?" Whish screeched. "Immolate yourself, if you desire a spectacular demise, but as for myself and my boys, we'll to the spaceport instanter, the Ambassador's transport to share, the better to view the spectacle from deep space."

Magnan rose. "Actually, Retief," he said, "the little wretch has a well-taken point. I believe that I myself would prefer to observe the phenomenon from orbit. Accordingly, I must waste no time getting back to the Embassy to warn His Ex; there'll

be time to evacuate in good order, voucher files
and all, if I start now. I'll see you after the show."

"It might be a good idea to wait, just in case the
star act fails to materialize," Retief suggested. "No
point in unduly upsetting His Excellency."

"Poor Clarence," Whish sighed. "The poor old
thing means so well—but he's simply not equipped
to face up to reality."

"Face up to Groaci double-dealing, you mean,
Whish," Magnan corrected.

"'Double-dealing,' my dear Ben," Whish explained, "is an epithet applied by losers to superior strategy. And in that connection, I suggest
you take note that the infamous Retief entices you
to share his fate!" Whish keened as soon as Retief
had left the cabin. "I have Told All, as I agreed, so
it is now your clear duty to guarantee my safe
passage to my Embassy!"

"Not so fast, Whish," Magnan temporized.
"Clearly, you have a point; but in view of Section
3, paragraphs A-1 and 2 of the Yalcan Protocols,
one might argue that your position remains equiv-
ocal."

"The Protocols you cite were never ratified by
proud Groac, Ben!" Whish shrilled triumphantly,
"and thus are not binding on me."

"Your cynicism does you scant credit, Major,"
Magnan reproved the now cocky alien.

"You can skip all that, Ben," Whish replied
indifferently. "Your lawless meddling avails you
naught. I have presented you with a *fait accompli*,
so you may as well accept it in a reasonable fashion, demonstrating at a minimum the qualities of
good losership, and hurry to abandon the continent before H hour."

"Perhaps I'd best accompany Retief, after all,"
Magnan decided and hurried off, leaving Whish in
Vug's care.

*   *   *

In the dim-lit and cavernous hold, where Retief noted new light-alloy trusswork and the smooth humming of modern mechanical equipment, contrasting sharply with the rust and caked dirt of the setting, a number of small cubicles had been partitioned off along the bulkhead. He went to the nearest, pushed firmly on the top of the locked door until it bent inward sufficiently to spring the latch, and stepped inside. He flipped the wall-switch and a battery of high-intensity glare-panels showed him the bulky forms of climatic units, Class Nine navigation computers, and a state of the art proton-flow power unit. Among these standard items (for a ship of the line, Retief reflected), he noted the less familiar shapes of a 'cosmic disaster'-sized impact absorption sink, a pair of half-sun beamers, various specialized imagers and holographic amplifiers, a bool-type generator of cryptic function, plus a number of other heavy items unfamiliar to him. At that mament, there was a distant *whump!* and Retief stepped through the open door and saw an ascending dust cloud above the town's rooftops.

"Good lord, Retief!" Magnan gasped as he came up. He glanced inside. "This looks more like a command center than a humble trawler, or even a deep-sea survey vessel. What was that noise?"

"More like launch control," Retief corrected. "Notice the polyphase inductor panel, and the hologram gear. The noise was Whish's reserve supplies he had stashed in our number two vault going up."

"To be sure," Magnan agreed judiciously as he stepped back inside the hold. "Retief, you were right! There *was* a bomb under the jack-in-the-box: there *is* more to the Groaci scheme than the rather elementary though large-scale disaster Whish

so graphically outlined—a bit too eagerly, as you
pointed out. Which leaves us," he went on, "with
the question: how can he top mountain-building
and subduction, and still hope to leave something
for Groac to salvage?"

"Does it not?" Whish's reedy voice came from
behind them.

"Sorry, Retief, and Mr. Magnan, too," Vug spoke
up from outside. "But the little runt faked me
outta position—said he just remembered about a
bomb and all. Just then something blew over Embassy Row. I hope it wasn't nothing important.
Sorry about that; nothin' I could do."

"It's all right, Vug," Retief soothed the agitated
dock-walloper. "It was merely a small distraction
from the main business."

"You mean about what these here Groaci sap-
suckers were up to out to Voon Deep?"

"Not quite," Retief corrected. "That was red
herring number two. I have a hunch I need to
check into a little more closely. Mr. Magnan, will
you take the recording rod from the big pressure
monitor over there?"

After receiving more explicit directions, Magnan
complied. "Goodness, Retief," he gobbled, as he
studied the bar-shaped magnetic stack he had extracted from the complex apparatus. "This is a
thousand-day rod, and it's nearly full! That would
be enough to chart the tidal pattern for the entire
planet through at least a full biennial cycle."

Retief accepted the proffered recording and nodded toward a storage cabinet. "Let's take a look in
the working files here," he suggested.

"Beware, rash Terry!" Whish shrilled, thrusting
forward. "You compound your folly by probing
into sealed records protected by the Yalcan Accord!"

"To which Groac does not subscribe, remember, Major," Magnan reminded him stiffly.

"Take a look at this, Mr. Magnan," Retief said, indicating a paper he had laid out on a table. Magnan went over, peered at it uncertainly.

"Why, whatever has a map of South Polar Continent to do with plate tectonics in the Voon area?" he asked his junior colleague, puzzled.

"Not much," Retief said. "But if that charge were planted a little further south along the mid-ocean ridge, say about here . . . ?" he indicated on the underlying map a point just off the coast of West Continent, near a chain of volcanic islands.

"Yes, yes, I see!" Magnan said excitedly. "That might well reactivate the vulcanism, with disastrous effects to the Beauteous Islands. But the Groaci would hardly be likely to destroy the idyllic Beauties, where their own aristocracy have established their villas as well as their diplomatic R & R facility." Magnan glanced at Whish, who was standing anxiously by, observing.

"Retief," Magnan said quickly, "I don't like that 402 of his. Too smug by half."

"That's not my 402, Ben," Whish corrected in his thin, but confident tone. "That's my 721 (Self-assurance Born of Superior Knowledge, Legitimately Gained)."

"Sometimes," Retief put in, "rendered, 'If You Think You're So Smart, Let's See You Figure This One Out.' "

"Only by envious non-diplomatic personnel not privy to the nuances of us professionals," Whish countered. "The very fact that you're aware of such crudities merely reveals your habit of hobnobbing with riff-raff."

"Speaking of riff-raff," Magnan said, "where's that Vug fellow?"

"Right here, Mr. Magnan," Vug called, from a locker next to the bool generator. "Looky what I found!" He emerged waving a half-unrolled chart.

"Happens I know these here waters," he commented, unrolling the map which, Magnan noticed, was of the icy southern seas. "Sailed them trackless wastes, Slub and boy, for thirty years!" he announced. "Look here," he went on, aiming a blunt finger at a series of red-printed contour lines at the north edge of the chart. "Old Morp Current, got slush in it's far as Bagbird Banks here—that's what makes the waters rich enough the Koomies never get far away."

"Well, what has your brutal Koom-innards industry to do with high-level matters of state?" Magnan demanded with some asperity.

"Plenty, which the Slubbese economy and all is based on Koomy-guts," Vug declared. " 'No Koomy-guts, no chow in the chow-bowls of the peasants,' is what the recruitment posters say."

Retief had cleared away the overburden of miscellaneous papers and was studying the big chart Vug had unrolled on the table. Magnan glanced at the map's complex pattern of swirling colored lines indicating depths and currents, and turned away.

"We'd best get back to the Embassy at once, Retief," he said wearily. "And report our interim findings, calmly, of course. If there's more to these schemes than we've yet unmasked, we may legitimately leave it to His Excellency to decide on a course of action."

"If he decides on a course of action, or inaction, more likely, without being in full possession of the facts," Retief pointed out, "it's unlikely he'll make a correct decision."

"Still," Magnan reposted, "the responsibility is his. That's one of the burdens of his high office. Happily, we are mere underlings who may safely leave these matters to our appointed superiors."

"Mr. Magnan," Retief replied. "I must take exception to your use of the word 'safely.' "

Magnan gave him a shocked look. "You mean?" he stuttered. "Is it possible that this wretch—" he waved an arm toward Whish, "has arranged matters in such a fashion as to menace diplomatic members of an Embassy staff?" He turned to face the Groaci. "Whish, how *could* you commit such a breach of protocol?"

"Suicide, you mean, Mr. Magnan," Retief corrected. "If we go, he goes, too. Along with Ambassador Shish and the entire Groaci Mission."

"Absurd!" Whish hissed. "You've taken leave of your senses, Retief! I assure you, I do not seek immolation on this benighted pest-world!"

"What you seek and what you find are sometimes not quite the same, Major," Retief reminded the excited alien. "Remember your big plans for Furthuron, for example? That was one of Groac's more egregious miscalculations—but my money is on the Slubbese Affair to beat it."

"There *is* no 'Slubbese Affair,' sir!" Whish stated coldly. "There is only selfless Groac uplifting the benighted. Like this rude chap here." He turned to confront Vug. "Do you, fellow, take exception to Groacian enterprise here on your backward planet?"

"I ain't no chap," Vug retorted stoutly. "And long's you don't mess up the Koomy grounds, I got no complaints. Except maybe too many five-eyed flat-feet around town lately."

"I assure you, sirrah," Whish replied, "that only the minimal complement of Peace Keepers has been posted here to maintain order during these stressful times of change. You'll note they're guarding the Slubbese Treasury around the clock, as well as private stocks of valuables."

"Lay off, you're gonna make me cry," Vug protested. "But whycome our valuables are gonna need guarding? I got a hunnert and thirty-one sprug and sixty-five blun in my retirement account myownself."

"Merely routine precautions," Whish dismissed the matter.

While the others chatted, Retief was studying one document after another, referring frequently to the master chart. He called Vug over, and indicated a point on the chart. "Anything unusual you know of in this general area?" he asked the old salt.

"Well, I guess!" Vug confirmed emphatically. "That's the Throat of Goolgi, big old whirlpool can swallow a ship whole. Most dreaded spot on the six seas. How'd you know?"

"I saw it marked DANGER on another chart up topside." Retief told him. "Apparently the warm Wunt Current passes close to the cold Morp Current there, and sets up a cyclonic motion in the air which carries the water along with it, assisted by the Coriolis force."

"Yeah, sumpin like that," Vug agreed carelessly. "Some of the old timers say the reep catch is phenomenal just north of the Throat. Tricky navigating, getting in close enough to find the reep without getting caught. Reason reep fillets bring such good prices."

Whish had ventured close to the chart table, and canted a long ocular toward it. "After the blast," he commented, "that phenomenon will vanish—yet another boon conferred on Slub by Groacian technology."

"What blast was that?" Vug inquired. "Did I miss sumpin?"

"Just a little fireworks display the major was instrumental in arranging," Retief explained. "But, major, I have a hunch you were stretching the facts a trifle when you said you'd planted the big one three hours ago. I suspect you're running a little behind schedule, and in fact, have yet to set the detonator, which is why you were so eager to Tell All, and con Mr. Magnan and me down here, so you could tag along and look for a chance to slip away and complete your assignment."

"Absurd!" Whish whispered. "You read sinister intentions into the most innocent acts. Clearly, it was you who lured *me* here!"

"Sure," Retief agreed readily. "But look at this chart for a moment." He pointed to a stretch of open sea labelled 'The Demon's Hexagon.' "What would happen if your firecracker went off over here, a few leagues to the east of the spot you planned?"

"Why, that would totally obviate the entire purpose of the blast," Whish dismissed the idea. "That's quite clear of the mid-ocean ridge, and the tectonic repercussions would be negligible. Of course, it would create an eddy which might well influence the Morp Stream, to no end whatever. Why do you trouble yourself with these feckless speculations?"

"Let's go aft and see what's to be seen," Retief suggested, ignoring Whish's querulous remarks.

"Nothing's to be seen aft!" Whish protested at once. "Why not try forward, eh? It's closer, and not quite so dirty."

"Really, Major Whish," Magnan sniffed. "Your tactics are transparent. Aft it is. Lead on, Retief."

"It's Booch Day, remember, Mr. Magnan?" Retief replied. "Double-deception day, so he's trying to mislead us into believing he's misleading us. So let's go forward."

Whish's eyes drooped dejectedly as he trailed the Terran diplomats back topside to the chart room, Vug bringing up the rear.

In the navigator's office, Retief, carrying papers selected from the files, went at once to the pipe

organ-like console of the big IBM 7000, punched
the STATUS-REVIEW key and watched the numbers flash past on the digital read-out screen, while
a strip of plastic clattered from the RECORD slot.
He examined the latter briefly, then adjusted controls, picked up a stout drafting rod and inserted it
under the edge of a closed cover marked in red in
the long-tailed Groaci script ABSOLUTELY NOT
TO BE TOUCHED UNDER LETHAL PENALTY
and forced it open, not without a small tinkle of
breaking metal. Whish screeched. Retief deftly
punched in a complex pattern on the multi-colored
needle-switch array thus revealed, then activated
the CURRENT EXTRAPOLATE display accessory.
A screen lit up, showing a computer-constructed
view of the planet Slub, as seen from synchronous
orbit above the equator, a greenish orb with promi-
nent white-glaring polar caps, the whole wreathed
in wisps of gray-white cloud cover.

"What in the world are you doing, Retief?"
Magnan demanded. "We're in rather a hurry to
report to the Ambassador, if you'll recall. Surely
this is no time to play arcade games!"

"Somebody's already done my work for me,"
Retief replied, pausing to make an adjustment to
the clock in the panel. "I intended to feed in the
numbers I found below, and see what came out,
but whoever was planning this little Booch Day
surprise was thoughtful enough to work up a complete program for us to look at. This is what would
happen if Whish's little blast went off on schedule."

"Confounded scientists-wallahs!" Whish hissed.
"I *told* the obstreperous fellow that everything was
to be locked-in under GUTS security!"

"He did as you ordered, Major," Retief reassured the agitated Security-Groaci. "But as it happens, I broke your codes some years ago."

"Vile treacher!" Whish screeched. "All this time

you've allowed the High Command to press on, elaborating large schemes for the greater glory of proud Groac, none of which was to eventuate, due to your insidious meddling! It won't do, Retief," he added in a more controlled tone. "Thwarting the odd ploy here and there is one thing—and I see now why your obnoxious person has so often been witness to moments of frustration of the orderly unfolding of Groacian Destiny. But making jackasses out of the highest lords of Groac, as they solemnly confer in their secret conclaves deep in the sacred precints of the High Command redoubt— in full view of Terran nosy parkers—to be altogether Too Much! Better look out, Retief," he concluded. "When the word gets back, you will become the object of a Category Ultimate Kill Order. You've sealed your own fate this time. Bit too clever, eh?"

"Quite possibly," Retief agreed mildly. "But then there is always the question of whether anyone will actually tip off the High Command, eh?"

"Surely you jest," Whish came back sharply. "Do you imagine that I intend to remain silent after your revelation?"

"Time will tell, Major," Retief reminded the Intelligence officer.

"Speaking of sealed fates, Whish," Magnan put in. "Since you're the only one outside Retief and myself who is aware that your security has been breached, I'd not give a perished Rockamorran head-bladder for your chances of surviving to blab."

Whish's eye-stalks sprang erect, quivering. "You don't mean. . . ." he whispered. "You're civilized diplomats! Surely you wouldn't. . . ."

"I wouldn't count on it, Bub," Vug counseled the Groaci as the later sprang for the exit, to meet Vug's large fist amidships. He rebounded and lay gasping on the deck.

"I've never seen a Groaci ocular display quite like that," Magnan remarked, watching the complex pattern of twitching of the fallen Groaci's stalked visual organs.

"I'm giving myself the last rites," Whish gasped.

Magnan's attention drifted from the excited alien to the screen, where a vivid yellow-orange spot had appeared against the dark gray of the ocean, at a point off the east coast of Southwest Continent. As he stared, concentric circles radiated from the glowing center, moving swiftly past the Beauteous Island chain, which failed to reappear afterward, and over the continental coast, moving well inland in a deep arc before breaking up and draining back, cutting new river channels in the newly deposited soil.

"Good lord!" Magnan yelped. "The blast sent a tsunami right across the Beauties, and flooded several hundred miles of farmland!"

"That was just the Phase One," Retief replied calmly. "Watch. I'll speed up the time-scale." He did so, and the single glowing point elaborated into a long chain of similar hot-spots, extending northwest and southeast. More giant waves assaulted the coast of South Continent, leaving extensive lakes and a modified shoreline in their wake.

"Why," Magnan squealed. "It's engulfed the entire Platinum Coast! And—and—what in the world!" He broke off to stare at the screen in astonishment as a new island, a long, narrow ridge, broached the sea, then was partially innundated to form a string of islands south and slightly west of the lost Beauties.

"That's right in the path of the Stream!" he managed at last. "It's diverting the warm waters east and south! North Continent will be exposed to the Polar currents: temperatures will drop far enough to re-glaciate the Temperate Zone! Agriculture will become impossible! The planet will starve!"

"No, Mr. Magnan," Retief corrected. "They won't have time to starve—they'll drown, when the South Polar cap melts. According to Groaci calculations, the warm Stream will split and flow around the ice on all sides. Watch the screen."

The deeper-blue area representing the Stream was already swirling away from its immemorial easterly course to flow southward toward the pole.

"That's one year," Magnan noted on the time-scale read-out. "In two, the ice will be melting at a stupendous rate. I read somewhere that if the whole two miles thick cap melted it would raise sea level three hundred feet all over the planet— drown every major city on Slub! What are we to do, Retief?" Magnan turned his stricken gaze to his colleague, appealingly.

"You've shown yourself to be resourceful in the past, Retief," he groaned. "So *do* something!"

Retief turned to Whish, who was calmly watching the screens with two eyes, while the other three kept tabs on the positions of Retief, Magnan and Vug.

"On the other hand," Retief commented, "I don't think anything's going to happen after all."

Magnan clutched at Retief's arm, and all five of Whish's eyes snapped around to bear on him.

"But, but. . . ." Magnan managed. Whish uttered a crackling purr which Retief recognized as the Groaci equivalent of an indulgent chuckle.

"Look at the clock," Retief suggested to Magnan. "Five till five. If the big one was actually going up at five, the major wouldn't be so calm."

"Nonsense, Retief," Whish remarked cooly. "I told you five pee em, and five pee em it is."

"You're not a good liar, Whish," Retief said. "Your throat sac turns bluish every time. Regular built-in polygraph. But why lie about something so easy to disprove? All we have to do is wait five more minutes."

"To what end, my Retief?" Whish retorted in a tone of Mild Puzzlement Occasioned by Egregious Intransigence (1037-c).

"No need to get into the four-digit work, Whish," Magnan rebuked sharply. "Your sarcasm does you little credit," he added, then turned to Retief. "But why *would* he lie?" he demanded, averting his eyes from the clock.

"Just to keep us occupied trying to guess his motives, I'd say," Retief replied. "By the way, I set the clock ahead an hour, so don't be disappointed if the big hand gets to twelve with no fireworks."

"I shall endeavor to surpress my regret, Retief," Magnan said resentfully. "You might have told me, you know. For the second time today I'd prepared myself for death."

"Don't worry, Mr. Magnan," Retief consoled his superior. "It won't go to waste. Actually," he went on, addressing Whish now, "the fact is you haven't actually placed the detonator yet, have you, major?"

"Why, wherever did you acquire that notion?" Whish came back in a crafty tone betrayed by the crossing of his middle pair of eyestalks.

"I noticed the special access hatch in the hold," Retief told him. "It still had the Department of Dirty Tricks seal on it."

"The Directorate of Diverse Tactics," Whish corrected sharply. "But what do you know of these matters, rash Terry?"

"Enough to read the code on the tag, tricky Groaci," Retief replied. "There's another matter that bears looking into, Mr. Magnan," he told the older man. "Did you notice the section cut out of all three charts we looked at? The same material is missing from the archives here. Do let's see what the computer has to say about it." He took a step toward the console, and Whish, with a shrill cry, hurled himself into the big Terran's path.

"Stop, I entreat you, Retief!" he keened. "In the name of Allah, Buddha, the Great Worm, Odin, and Yahveh!" He broke off to utter a broken sob. "Let be, vile Terry!" he resumed, "You have probed enough into matters no man was meant to wot of!"

"Not quite enough, Major," Retief contradicted, almost kindly, as he stepped over the now prostrate Groaci, who clutched desperately at his ankle, only to be shaken off.

"What in the world?" Magnan spoke up in a shocked tone. "We've uncovered the plot within the plot—within another plot if you want to include the bomb scare at the office this morning. Goodness, was that really only this morning? It seems days!"

"Booch Day, remember," Retief reminded him. "The kindly Groaci were planning a real *tour de force*, eh, Major?"

"We strive only to better the plight of the confounded scum," Whish declared righteously.

"What's 'confounded' mean?" Vug demanded, reappearing at that moment. "I know Groaci lingo pretty good, but not all them big words, you know. What kinda scum did he say we are?"

"It is a term synonymous with 'enlightened,' " Whish explained glibly. "It's the very best kind of scum."

"I don't like the sound o' that too good, neither," Vug told the cowering Groaci, smacking a ham-like fist into his palm. "How about it, Retief," he asked. "Is 'enlightened' good, or what?"

"It hardly matters, Vug," Retief told him. "All in all, you could say the major wasn't being complimentary."

"You think maybe I oughta cave in his mush for him, in defense o' the national honor and all?" the old Slubbese sailor asked concernedly.

"Certainly," Retief advised. "But later—I want him in talking condition for a few more minutes."

"Such ingratitude!" Whish hissed. "After all that proud Groac has done for this backward world!" He subsided when Vug prodded his chitinous thorax with a rough-shod foot, eliciting a sharp *bonk!*

"No need to act hastily now, Retief," Whish cautioned, while attempting unsuccessfully to straighten the bent ribs in his hip-cloak, at the same time as he interposed himself in the Terran's path.

"Be not alarmed, Major," Retief counseled, side-stepping him. "It's only a computer work-up, you know." At the console, he consulted a document he had brought from the technical area belowdecks, and punched new data into the machine.

"This is what would happen if the bomb happened to be placed just a little off target to the south," he explained.

"Unthinkable!" Whish shrilled. "To refrain from toying with such ideas, rash Terry!"

"Who said I'm toying?" Retief inquired mildly.

"Retief—Ben—I appeal to you. . . ." Whish turned his attention to the senior diplomat. "To cause this madman to stay his hand! No public relations campaign, no matter how shrewdly mounted, could conceal from Enlightened Galactic Opinion the enormity of the disaster such meddling would occasion—with Terra culpable, you may be sure! The Groacian Propaganda Ministry will see to it the facts are well publicized!"

"It's only a computer construct," Retief pointed

out as he punched in new instructions. "Why all
the excitement?"

"Aside from your own trivial fates," Whish hissed,
"to be pegged-out on the sulphur pits of Yan would
be a luxury cruise compared to my own! If—"

"Never mind, Major," Magnan cut in, "Retief's
only playing with your nervous system."

"Or he's playing with mine," Retief corrected.
"Take a look at this." He indicated the screen on
which changes were now taking place.

"It's speeded up to a year per second," he explained. Now on the cloud-swathed orb glowing
against the black of space with Big Moon a brilliant disc in the background, the color-coded oce-
anic currents swirled and shifted around new island
chains, and the glaring white of new ice formations
now crusted the southern half of West Continent,
while the acreage of desert spread deep into the
heart of East. Floods had obscured vast stretches
of coastline on both sides of the troubled sea.

"Chaos!" Magnan commented. "How could they
have contemplated such senseless vandalism?"

"They didn't," Retief corrected. "This one's
mine."

"All that," Magnan mused aloud, "just from the
detonation of a middle-sized nuke on the sea-
bottom."

"All that and more," Retief corrected as he
switched off the machine. "Now let's take that
cruise."

"Whatever for?" Magnan wailed. "We should be
rushing back to the Embassy to report Disaster
unalloyed!"

"Wouldn't it be better," Retief countered, "to
report Disaster averted?" He went past Magnan to
the entry.

"Of course, but. . . ." Magnan whimpered,
following.

"Vug," Retief called. "Let's get this tub to sea."

"Sure thing, boss," the former sailor agreed, and hurried belowdecks to see to the pre-castoff check-list, while Retief returned to the high-tech area.

Half an hour later, with the tubby vessel pitching sickeningly in the choppy waters as they ploughed out to sea through the bay-mouth, Whish keened in the background, while Vug looked over Retief's shoulder as he worked at the auxiliary hoist-control panel. "What you doing Retief?" he inquired. "That's a no-no, you know, messing with the special deep water sounding gear."

"Actually, this is the gadget which sets and activates the detonator, according to that manual Whish was so eager to throw overboard," Retief pointed out. "Next to it is the gadget that actually deposits the sonar gear, or, in this case, the bomb."

"I'll level wit you, pal," Vug said. "I don't feel too good putting to sea with a hell-bomb belowdecks."

"It won't be there long," Retief reminded his helper. "We'll have it in place in one of the Groaci's old test-holes in less than an hour. Meanwhile, you'd better get back topside and see if Mr. Magnan needs any help keeping Whish sedated."

"I clobbered him good last time up," Vug explained. "And Mr. Magnan's got him laid out on a bunk in the Captain's cabin, and the door's locked. He ain't going to cause no trouble. But I got to feed the nav them new coordinates you give me, now's we're clear o' the port and off automatics."

"Fine. I'll be through here in a few minutes, and then we'll try out the autochef," Retief replied. "This sea air certainly stimulates the appetite."

"My appetite's on permanent shore leave," Vug told his mentor. "Never put to sea yet I didn't get

the cobblies soon's she starts to buck thataway.
But I got to get back to the bridge." He broke off
to hurry away.

Retief went along to confirm that the vessel was
now at the precise location he had given Vug, then
went below again.

Belowdecks, he went directly to the Don't Even
Think About Touching This Classified hoist-control
panel and checked dials. As he watched, a red
light glowed suddenly, blinking DANGER!, and a
needle snapped over against its pin.

"Good enough," Retief said aloud to no one. He
activated a screen which glowed a murky green
with a cloudy view of swirling mud disturbed by
the probe—a spidery crane-arm supporting a glis-
tening ovoid with a red X on the side over the
mouth of a black funnel-shaped pit. He manipu-
lated a Waldo and the arm promptly dipped, lowering the ovoid into the opening. He released it
and backed off the arm. After forty seconds, a
green light lit up on the board. He checked the
chronometer on the panel, compared it with the
watch on his finger and hurried back topside.
Magnan greeted him with a wail, Vug following,
looking mournful.

"Retief! this time the moment has truly arrived!"
Magnan wailed, "It's going to blow . . ."

"It's not aboard any longer," Retief reassured
his colleague.

"You didn't simply jettison it!" Magnan yelped.
"A blast of that magnitude will create disastrous
effects! Why, we ourselves—this vessel, that is—
will be thrown clear out of the water! She'll break
up! Retief, you've doomed us all!"

"Take it easy, pal," Vug counseled. "I bet Retief
knows what he's doing."

"I took the precaution of dropping it down an
old hole," Retief explained casually.

"Even worse!" Magnan yelped. "Such irresponsibility! The consequences of a sub-crustal blast are totally unpredictable!"

"Not quite, Mr. Magnan," Retief countered. "The computer gave me a pretty good idea of what to expect. The first item will be a tsunami about a quarter-mile high, traveling outward from the blast area at two hundred mph. We'd better get our stern to it fast, Vug."

Even as the surface heaved upward off the port bow, Vug leapt to the controls and pivoted the seaworthy vessel sharply so that the boil of white water took her squarely astern, bubbling across the decks as the ship lurched and accelerated like a body surfer riding a big one. The air was wet with blowing spume; then a downpour struck as the water thrown skyward fell back torrentially. Vug held on and steered, and *Challenger* sped on, her bow-wave curling back to merge with the boiling foam of the immense wave she was riding. At full power, Vug managed to pull the ship out from under the overhanging lip of the immense breaker as it collapsed thunderously behind. Magnan was busy at the ship-to-shore, speaking urgently of earthquakes and typhoons.

"Yippee!" Vug yelled. "Bet old *Challenger* never knowed she could do two hunnert knots! We'll make what's left o' the port in half a hour!"

Amidst howling wind, parallel gusts of salty rain, and the crashing of surf and collapsing dockside structures, Vug steered the ship directly into her assigned approach-control area and relinquished control to the Port Authority, stubbornly functioning in the face of the devasting storm so suddenly evoked by the sub-oceanic blast. Five minutes later, the survey vessel lay snugly in her covered berth, battered but intact. Retief turned Whish over to Vug, who dumped him carelessly down an unused coal chute.

"Serves the little sneak right," Magnan sniffed, feeling himself to confirm that he was actually intact after the wild ride ashore.

"Keep in touch, Vug," Retief urged the old salt as the latter disembarked hurriedly, muttering of exotic intoxicants and the comforting presence of a nubile female named Ook.

For half an hour, Retief and Magnan picked their way through frond-and-rubble-littered streets, deserted by all but a few half-clad looters, before they found a taxi cruising aimlessly.

"Oh, hi, Terries!" the driver called. It was the same battered-looking chap who had earlier delivered Whish to the wharves.

"I guess I was right when I seen you fellers headed for the Groaci's mystery-ship. I tole my mates, 'There's something afoot, mark my words,' I tole em. And sure enough . . ." He looked happily about at the devastation. "A tidal wave and a typhoon hits within a half a hour. Figgered I might see you. Come on, let's get clear o' the waterfront before the next one hits."

His passengers safely inside, he sped away, swerving to avoid fallen timbers, collapsed billboards, uprooted trees and drifts of assorted rubbish left behind by the first shallow wave that had driven ashore ten minutes earlier, keeping an eye alert for the next inundation. He pulled up before the Terran Embassy with a squeal of brakes and turned to extend a hand.

"That'll be twenty-two fifty, gents," he announced, his voice almost lost in the howl of the gale. "You want me to wait, or what? Oh, boy, what a Booch Day! Ain't had so much fun since that Groaci cop got run over by a bus driver was busy saluting him!"

Retief and Magnan stepped out of the rocking vehicle into a Force Ten gale: Magnan uttered a yelp and almost fell; Retief grabbed him and hauled him across until he could get a grip on the ornamental iron railing. Inside the boarded-up glass doors, the Marine guard peered out dubiously, then opened up and let them into the comparative quiet of the shabby lobby.

"Hi Mr. Retief. Hi Mr. Magnan," the lad said. "What you doing out in that weather? His Nibs ordered everybody home three hours ago. He's due in any time now, I unnerstand. Left word he wants to see you two gents."

"Hello, Henry," Retief returned the greeting. "Glad to see you defied that 'go home' order."

"Naw, I just didn't get the word is all," Henry protested. "Anyways—'simplify,' or whatever the old saying is. Simplify."

"Sounds like a good suggestion," Retief commented as the lift doors closed between them.

"Grotesque!" Magnan snapped. "The proper form is 'Semper Fi,' of course. An abbreviation of the Latin *semper fideles*, meaning 'always faithful.' How could he mangle tradition so?"

"Beats me," Retief conceded. "Still, 'simplify' almost means something practical, which is more than can be said for 'semper fi.' "

The door to the Chancery wing being open, they entered and went to the Ambassador's spacious tump leather and heo wood upholstered office and sat down. Outside the picture window, the wind shrieked, and there was a constant rattling of small flying objects impacting the building, which shuddered but held firm.

"Heavens, Retief," Magnan said breathlessly af-

ter his brisk dash. "I *do* hope he'll understand—
the irregularities, I mean."

"It's the regularities you should be sweating,"
Retief pointed out easily. "Holding a diplomatic
member of a Most Favored Planet's Embassy hostage is, after all, a standard ploy. But sending your
Chief of Mission off on a wild moobie-bird chase is
another matter."

"To be sure," Magnan agreed, steepling his fingers as one about to Clarify All. "Perhaps I *was* a
trifle precipitate; still, it *did* seem expedient to tell
the old buzzard—ha ha—His Distinguished Excellency, that is to say—that the world was about to
suffer a bout of catastrophism."

"That part was all right, sir," Retief explained.
"It was where you made up the part about the
Groaci landing party, Peace Keepers and Legation
staff, plus assorted Groaci tourists all rushing to
the port and commandeering all transports, that
you went a bit too far. Still, you can always deny
it."

"Alas, it was directly to Miss Frumperts, his
toady, that I passed the warning," Magnan mourned.
"It's the next worse thing to having spoken directly to His Ex."

"You bet it was, Buster!" A harsh female voice
snapped directly behind Magnan's chair, causing
him to leap halfway to his feet and freeze in a
crouch, clutching his chest.

"I've told you and told you, Miss Frumperts,"
he gasped. "You mustn't subject me to sudden
shocks. My cardiac condition, you know. Although
I carry on stoutly through thick times and thin,
I'm not a well bureaucrat."

"Was that 'stoutly' some kind of crack, Ben?"
the Ambassador's private secretary demanded coldly
as she maneuvered her three hundred pounds of

basically unattractive protoplasm around behind the Great Man's desk.

"Now, I called you boys up here to tell you that as soon as His Excellency the Terran Ambassador Extraordinary and Minister Plenipotentiary gets back from his breakfast, he's got a few things to tell you about not making a jackass out of your boss."

"You mean, Miss Frumperts, that you passed that somewhat peremptory summons to Henry on your own initiative?" Magnan objected in a shocked tone. "Hardly appropriate, I think, for an administrative employee to take such a tone with senior diplomatic members of the Embassy staff."

"You can skip the whining, Ben," the portly stenographer dismissed his objection curtly. "What I really called you up here for was to give you a chance to work out a viable version of the case before old Hairy actually hits the office. So don't get too smart for your own good. OK, Ben? I'm tryna do you a favor, fer crudsake!"

"Forgive me, Euphronia," Magnan pled brokenly, dabbing at an eye with one of the Ambassador's gold embossed tissues. "Damn monogram scratched me!" he complained abruptly, casting the offending serviette from him. "It's just. . . ." he fixed his bleary eyes on the major domo, ". . . .that I wasn't expecting such kindness after so much suffering. One is quite unmanned." He sobbed openly and took another tissue in which to bark noisily.

"Sure, Ben, I got compassion for yer hardships," Euphronia grated in an attempt at a soothing tone. "Let's get our script straight, now: you scared the pants off His Ex and then all you come up with is a high wind, not even a little bitty earthquake. He gets a rocket from that creepy little Groaci *Chargé*, Thilth, and right while he's in the middle of denying everything, that little wimp Whish comes charging in here in full view of the local yellow press! Bad tactics, Ben. The strategy don't look too good, neither."

Miss Frumperts paused to extract a dope-stick from the Ambassadorial humidor, perfunctorily offering one to her guests. She lit up, blew anise-scented purplish smoke in Magnan's direction, and continued. "Quite a fix you got yerself in, Ben," she commented offhandedly. "But maybe we can salvage something. Anything to this 'grand theft scow' rap?"

"Actually," Magnan gobbled, "it was Retief—that is to say, I'm sure he had excellent reasons for any apparent illegalities—or at least some kind of alibi." He paused for breath, snorting at the violet fumes now wreathing his narrow head. He made ineffectual batting motions as if to dispel the smog-patch, at which Euphronia snarled and ostentatiously snubbed out her dope-stick.

"You want it all, don't you, Ben?" she said bitterly. "Can't even let a girl enjoy a little pick-up without you got to start pulling rank. Ha! And me tryna help you!"

"But," Magnan protested. "I only, I didn't mean—why, heavens, I *like* choking on poisonous fumes!"

" 'Sarcasm is the last resort of the failed bureaucrat,' " Miss Frumperts spat, turning her attention to patting her mummified coiffure, which made her plump face look like a plate of congealed lard set in a ragged ring of spongecake.

"Let's cut through the yackity-yak and get to the point," the secretary suggested in the peremptory manner she had acquired from long association with Himself. "Now," she went on relentlessly. "Number one: Retief here done nothing on his assignment to get the dope on the Groaci presence on the near moon, right?" Without awaiting a response she pressed on. "Then, youse broke up a local pot-house and humiliated a Groaci officer and his whole squad. Next, you violated Slub sovereighty by dumping a Groaci cop ranked light colonel in a dustbin, which he almost got compacted before a Groaci trooper pulled him out, scoring points for Groac. After that, lessee, you swiped the scow, and taken a Groaci diplomat hostage."

"Not hostage," Magnan cut in sharply. "He was an honored guest on the cruise."

"Then how come the Groaci Peace Keepers found him trussed up and dumped in a former coal bin?" Euphronia demanded. "Which they released him to come tearing over here making all kinds charges and all."

"Our local colleague, a patriot known as Vug, was perhaps a trifle overzealous," Magnan conceded. "But Whish made the mistake of trying to fake Vug into the coal bin first. That annoyed Vug and he retaliated."

"Sure, but this is all small tubers compared with the Big One, which a deputation of top Slub scholars says you boys set off a underwater blast that kind of rearranged the sea-bottom off West Continent. . . ." she broke off to turn a candid gaze on Magnan. "Fer my part, Ben," she confided. "I don't see what it matters what goes on two hundred fathoms down, except maybe to a bunch o' fish."

"Well, you see, Euphronia—you don't mind if I call you Euphronia?" Magnan began uncertainly.

"I usually go by 'Gertie,' " the corpulent typist corrected, coyly. "That 'Yufronya' handle is a downer my old man hung on me, which he wanted a boy."

"Very well, 'Gertie' it is, Gertie," Magnan gobbled. "Now, Gertie. . . ."

"Don't work it to death, Ben," Gertie cut in.

"Get to the point. You wanna plead insanity or what?"

"As for the preliminary atrocities," Magnan said crisply. "I can establish that I was elsewhere. As for my colleague, Retief, I'm sure he too can account for his activities."

"How about it, Retief?" Gertie turned a look like a slab of cold fat on the junior diplomat.

"As you suggested, Miss Frumperts," he replied, "it might be well to jump ahead to the Big One."

"OK, Gert, I'll take it from here," the irascible voice of Ambassador Hairshirt cut in sharply from his private entry behind the Terran flag. "You done a good job softening these boys up, Gert," he added, waiting with a clearly mimed impatience for her to abdicate his chair, which he then assumed, at once turning his gaze on Retief.

"Proceed, young fellow," he snapped. "You were just about to confess your complicity in an atrocity of truly breathtaking proportions." He leaned back expansively. "Indeed, I should imagine that the Inquiry accompanying the termination of your diplomatic career will be the sensation of the Twenty-Eighth Century."

"Mr. Ambassador," Magnan put in. "While pretending to carry out a deep-sea profiling mission to aid the Slubbish fisheries," he recited resentfully, "the Groaci in fact drilled a series of test holes, looking for precisely the right spot where crustal stresses were sufficiently delicately balanced that a few kilotons of ion-bomb would start things moving. The first plan was to accelerate the approach of North Continent to West from half an inch a year to a mile or so. In a few decades there'd be a collision that would pretty well clear things out and cloud the issues, thus leaving a power vacuum for the Groaci to move into. That had its drawbacks and was cancelled last week in favor of Plan Two: to melt the southern ice cap and shift the major currents, thereby also depopulating vast areas and making South Polar Continent available to Groaci pioneers. Just yesterday they realized they'd incidentally drown the Beauteous Isles where the Groaci run an R & R camp for burnt-out bureaucrats—so that was out. Then, it seems Major Whish, an undercover security man acting as advisor to the Groaci Seaquest Commission, on its Grand Scheme, got a hot idea of his own." As Magnan paused, Retief made an adjustment on the small monitor screen he had brought along, then took up the account:

"When I checked on things belowdecks, I discovered that Major Whish had been detailed to oversee the planting of the bomb by automatic apparatus, but he'd fallen behind schedule, which required that the device detonate at five pm on Booch Day, and had conned us into taking her to sea barely in time to do his dirty work. And a quarter to five pm was now his deadline for planting the bomb in time for a fast getaway to the spaceport."

"You admit that this bungling conspirator enlisted your assistance in his fell schemes?" Hairshirt whispered, slumping in his chair.

"We pretended to be taken in," Retief corrected, "so as to get the major and his secrets and the bomb-placing capabilities all together at the right spot."

Hairshirt glared at Magnan. "Ben, you went along with this excessively devious strategy?"

"Well, Mr. Ambassador," the slender diplomat replied, "it hardly seemed right to interfere under the circumstances."

"What circumstances?" Hairshirt demanded. "You were senior, You had but to say the word!"

"But he's bigger," Magnan pointed out. "I had very little choice, actually."

"Mr. Retief," Hairshirt said in an ominous tone, his 1204, about a 'c,' Retief estimated (Oh Boy, Are You Going to Get It Now, Buster). "Such tactics are hardly in consonance with hallowed *Corps* policy."

"Precisely, Mr. Ambassador," Retief agreed. "It seemed to me that it was time to do something more constructive than upholding tradition."

"Indeed?" His Excellency countered rhetorically. "Perhaps, Mr. Retief, you exaggerate the seriousness of the situation. It appears to me that Ben had matters well in hand before you, er, did whatever it was you did that upset Ambassador Shish sufficiently to call me via brown-line to cut short my visit to the Beauties."

"Actually, sir," Magnan put in quickly. "it's as well you returned when you did, since had Major Whish set in motion the Groaci scheme, the Beauties would have been engulfed by a tsunami of truly cosmic proportions—that's according to the Groaci's own 'most likely outcome' projection."

"Indeed?" Hairshirt smoothed his irregular features with a visible effort. "You mean that Minister of Stuff Goob and his entire staff are . . . ?"

"To be sure," Magnan confirmed. "Still, Your Excellency was spared. That is . . ."

"Mr. Magnan means that the Groaci would have sacrificed the Minister of Stuff and all other personnel on the islands, had their scheme proceeded beyond the projection stage."

"Inhuman!" the Ambassador blurted, gripping the arms of his hip-o-matic chair and thus inadvertantly causing the power swivel option to rotate the chair in a fast 720. "Ghastly!" the startled passenger yelled. "Stop this thing!" He clung, his eyes tight shut and his face mottled with fury as the chair spun him around and around and, still whirling, advanced to the wall behind the desk and rammed it hard, continuing the furious rotation in obedience to its victim's frantic grip on the control panel set in the arm. Magnan leapt forward, was rewarded by a solid kick in the knee by the Ambassador's outflung foot. Retief stepped in and forcibly pried the Ambassador's hand from its convulsive grip and stopped the chair.

"Treason! Sabotage!" Hairshirt yelled as he staggered from the treacherous seat. "Magnan! Find the malefactor responsible for this outrage and see to it he's shot!"

"You did it yourself, sir," Magnan pointed out diffidently. "That is, the chair did it, of course, but you were pressing the control." The unhappy Second Secretary went to the chair and righted it.

"I don't care!" Hairshirt yelled. "Shoot him anyway!"

"Mr. Ambassador," Magnan said solemnly. "I shall take the liberty of ignoring that order, as I'm sure you'd regret it in the morning."

"Only until sunrise," Retief pointed out.

"Sink the Beauties, you say," Hairshirt shouted, returning to official business like the seasoned professional he was. "Dastardly! Lacking a hill station, where would I go when the press of business became too great? Goob, too," he reflected more calmly. "Decent sort of chap, actually, for a Slubbese. So the question now confronting us is: what just and passionate revenge—ah, response— shall we choose to this atrocity?"

"Dispassionate, sir," Magnan corrected his chief.

"Who could be dispassionate?" Hairshirt demanded, "when the finest little gambling-hall-cum-steamroom, complete with the niftiest little masseuses west of Madam Cleo's, has just been washed away by a tidal wave—just when I had my system perfected, too! Little Peaches, Frou-Frou, and Hammer-hips, too—all gone, cut down in the flower of their nubility!"

"Not actually, sir," Magnan reminded his irate boss. "You'll recall, sir, that I—that is, Retief and I, actually—averted that disaster by substituting a completely different disaster of our own."

"To which action I presume I can ascribe the tornado now demolishing the city," the Ambassador snapped with a sour glance at the window beyond which the air was filled with wind-driven wastepaper, wooly-tree fronds and other movables.

"More of a hurricane, actually, sir," Magnan corrected. "Yes, I suppose it *is* a direct consequence of our prompt action in switching targets, but at least Your Excellency is alive to experience it."

"There is that," Hairshirt acknowleged shortly. "But of what avail to survive drowning only in order to be crushed in the rubble of a collapsing Embassy?"

"It probably won't come to that, Mr. Ambassador," Magnan hoped aloud. "The projection shows the eye moving east at nine miles per hour. The worst will soon be over."

"And what other phenomena, if any, may I anticipate due to your unauthorized activities?" the Chief of Mission demanded in a discouraging tone.

"There wasn't time," Magnan offered brokenly. "No time at all. The way it was, you see, sir, the hell-bomb was armed and on final countdown. We couldn't stop the detonation. The best we could manage was to relocate it. Had we simply allowed it to blow in its cradle aboard the survey vessel, not only would we have been vaporized, but the city itself would have been levelled, and the disturbance to the tides would have had repercussions involving the erosion of the peninsula on which the city is situated, and the cutting of a new tidal channel up north, across the fatlands."

"The fatlands, Ben," Hairshirt intoned, "are the chow-basket of Slub. How can you discuss so calmly the prospect of starvation on a planet-wide scale?"

"I'm not calm!" Magnan reposted heatedly. "And it wasn't me, er, I, who was planning to starve Slub. . . ."

"Oh, Retief, eh?" Hairshirt purred. "Might have known. . . ."

"Not him, either—er, he neither, I mean!" Magnan gobbled.

"Ben, Ben," Hairshirt chided. "This is no time for grammar. So, after you planned to subject the people of Slub to slow starvation, I presume you'd have proposed a massive aid program, rushing in supplies from Terra to forever win the hearts of the survivors. . . ."

"Not quite, Mr. Ambassador," Magnan protested. "No one planned to destroy the fatlands!"

"You mustn't try my indulgence too far, Ben," Hairshirt reproved gently. "I distinctly heard you refer to the cutting of a tidal channel which would have reduced the fatlands to a salt marsh."

"Sir," Magnan protested. "I didn't say a word about a salt marsh!"

"Never mind, Ben; the idea is not entirely without merit," Hairshirt said soothingly. "With most of the indigent, indigenous—get it?—anyway, with only a few grateful survivors around, Terran influence would become the dominant force in Slubbese affairs."

"So what?" Magnan demanded, still smarting from the Ambassadorial implication. "What do we want with this pest-hole anyway?"

"Ben, would you fly in the face of the most cherished tradition of the *Corps*? True, wisdom would seem to suggest that we saddle Groac with the burden of trying to bring order to this chaotic world. But then we'd lose points, don't you see, Ben? Like in Korea and Viet Nam, back in early historical times."

"Still . . ." Magnan protested and lapsed into silence.

"Don't brood, Ben," Hairshirt urged. "You're learning—albeit slowly, as shall be duly noted in the unlikely column of the Developmental Potential section of your next ER. Now, Retief," Hairshirt shifted his sights. "You may proceed to detail the disaster you claim to have precipitated in defiance of *Corps* policy and my own specific instructions, while you ignored the task I had set you, to secure intelligence regarding Groaci's fortifications of Big Moon."

"The bomb was ready in the delivery probe," Retief explained. "Armed and counting, ready to be placed. I took the liberty of redirecting it from the bore hole in which the explosion would have activated the Old Fault and closed up West Sea within a few decades, and instead put it in a test hole bored earlier in the program."

"And what, pray, did this accomplish?" Hairshirt demanded.

"It caused the rift in the Polar plate to open, dividing Polar Continent into two sections, one of which rotated in response to the Coriolis force, closing off the sea passage south of West Continent. As a result, the Tidal bulge is now unable freely to equalize itself, and a permanent standing wave exists in the south Western Sea."

"While the circumstances you detail seem mild enough," Hairshirt stated judiciously. "The fact remains that at the moment a typhoon is raging on a scale unprecedented in meteorological history. And the Groaci are still in full possession of Big Moon, and what they are doing there defies imagination. Am I to report to Sector that having detected the criminal activities of the Groaci anent the satellite, I then stood by inactive, and permitted their scheme to proceed to fruition?"

"I wouldn't if I were you, Mr. Ambassador," Retief counseled. "I respectfully submit that what the Groaci do on Big Moon will be of no importance whatever."

"That, sir, is for *me* to determine!" Hairshirt yelled. "You forget yourself, Retief! It is *I* who am Chief of Mission here, and I say . . ."

Retief held up a hand. "Permit me, if you will, Mr. Ambassador, to mention the computer projection before committing yourself," he interjected between Ambassadorial yells.

"I can imagine nothing your precious computer could divulge which would influence my stated policy regarding illegal Groacian adventures within my area of responsibility!" Hairshirt shouted after drawing a breath sufficient to power the lengthy period.

"How about this," Retief suggested. "The tidal bulge on Slub exercises an attraction on Big Moon equal to one percent of the total system interaction. With the standing wave proceeding two degrees in advance of the Slub-Moon center-to-center line, it exercises a tug in the direction of Big Moon's orbital travel. As a result, the satellite's orbital velocity was increased by about ninety-five miles per hour." As Retief paused, Hairshirt resumed:

"What the devil do I care about that? So now I'll have the nuisance of having the lunar calendar recomputed, as if I hadn't enough problems! It appears, Mr. Retief, that all this astronomical triple-speak is no more than a red herring to distract my attention from your abysmal failure to so much as attempt to carry out your assignment vis-à-vis the Groacian plans for military aggrandizement."

"The more aggrandized the better," Retief responded. "Terran policy should be to encourage the Groaci to continue pouring their cash and technology into the Big Moondoggle."

"You would pusillanimously give up and permit Terra's prime antagonist to take over?" Hairshirt yelled, his overstrained voice a high-pitched squeal now.

"May I point out, Mr. Ambassador," Retief offered quietly, "that as its orbital velocity increases, the orbit itself must accommodate by becoming larger. In other words, the moon is now spiraling outward, receding from Slub at a rate of over a mile a minute. In a few hundred years, about the time their Thousand Year Plan is entering its final phase, Slub will be no more than a medium bright point of light in the lunar sky. The impregnable fortress will be too far away to have any effect on affairs on Slub, or on the trade lanes. In Ten Thousand years or so, Big Moon will be firmly in orbit around the star."

"And the surface temperature . . ." Hairshirt paused to manipulate the calculator set in his desk top . . . "will be hot enough to melt copper. So much for sophisticated Groacian circuitry, eh, boys? Well," Hairshirt rubbed his palms together with a sound like a cicada grooming its wing cases. "It looks as if I've done it again, and all in the finest tradition of Booch! Thanks for your help, though of course it was no more than your duty thus to implement your Chief's policies. By the way, Magnan, don't worry about the trifling damages to Corps property. And you say the Beauties aren't really devastated? In that case, I shall resume my va—conference with the Slubbese authorities, at once. Ta, fellows, and don't get caught in the storm."

The Woomy

1

"Fellows," Ambassador Nipcheese said heavily, "the five-eyed little sticky-fingers have stolen a march on us this time, for fair! —That is to say, gentlemen," he corrected himself, mopping his pinched features with an oversized hanky bearing the logo of the Snotch Hilton, "our Groacian colleagues have demonstrated admirable zeal in initiating their totally superfluous planetwide survey of timber resources here on Hellhole Too—or Snotch, I should say."

"For a moment there, Retief," First Secretary Magnan, the bookish Budget and Fiscal officer whispered behind his hand, "when he started off 'fellows,' I thought perhaps old Nippy was in the upswing of his cycle. But no such luck: he's back to 'gentlemen' already, in that peculiarly abrasive tone he employs on Bad Days." As he noted the ambassadorial eye fixed on him, its rim even redder than usual, Magnan was seized by a sudden fit of coughing which brought him to his feet, flushed and wheezing.

"I say, Ben," His Excellency commented with a trace of a wintry smile, "I'd no idea you were a lunger, poor chap. You need maybe a couple days' bed rest, at a minimum, followed by a few weeks of light duty with the voucher files, perhaps."

Magnan touched Retief's arm and whispered, between hacks, "Such hypocrisy! He knows I hate those damned voucher files worse than the Hellholies hate Groaci nose-flutes!"

"Perhaps I should fly in a lung specialist from Hellhole Three," Nipcheese suggested solicitously.

"We all know perfectly well that the entire outer Hellhole system consists of ice-worlds, whose denizens, if any, live under the ice and breathe methane through gills," Magnan whispered brokenly. "They wouldn't know a tubercular lung from a strawberry pizza!"

"Very well, Ben," the Chief of Mission said heavily, "if you spurn medical aid, and seek an honorable, though unnecessary demise in the line of duty, I can but concur. Pity: and you hardly out of middle age."

"Middle age!" Magnan echoed, nettled. "I'm barely thirty-eight!"

"Too bad," Nipcheese commented mildly, ostentatiously drawing a line on the blank pad before him. "Underage for nomination as 'Counsellor,' " he muttered as if to himself.

"You mean I was in line . . . ?" Magnan stuttered. "That if I'd been, say forty-seven, I'd have . . . ?"

"Forty-seven, eh, Ben?" Nipcheese mused. "Bit over-age in grade, eh, Ben? Bit late in life to plan a new career, alas. But regulations are regulations. So there you are."

"Where, sir?" Magnan inquired brokenly. "Where at am I? I mean, you said 'there you are,' but whereat?"

"Ben, I am of course perfectly aware of what I said," the Chief of Mission pointed out in a kindly tone, "and I find it a great pity that you failed to follow the thread of my discourse. Where are you at, my dear fellow, is on the horns of a dilemma."

"Which one, sir?" Magnan blurted. "Sometimes

it seems to me that this Mission consists of nothing but dilemnae."

"I'm going to pretend I didn't hear that rather harsh assessment of my conduct of this Embassy," Nipcheese stated in a tone suggestive of a sovereign commuting a death sentence.

"Gee, sir, thanks a bunch," Magnan whimpered. "Which I didn't actually *say* that, sir," he added in an undertone.

"You wish to contradict your chief in public, Ben?" Nipcheese queried as if amazed, and jotted rapidly on his pad.

"Not exactly, Mr. Ambassador," Magnan protested gamely, "I only meant we all have more problems than usual on Hell—Snotch, I mean—because of the hostile climate and the unfriendly natives, er, autochthones, I mean, and the inadequate facilities, and these damp woods everywhere, and—"

"Don't go on, Magnan," Nipcheese cut him off. "I get the idea: Critical of Corps policy," he added, jotting. "Never realized you were a whiner, Ben."

"Not me, sir!" Magnan cried. "I *love* a challenge! Why, for example, when you ordered me to take that inventory of the old contractor's camp last winter, with all the leftover supplies, abandoned after the supply tents collapsed—why, I was delighted! Nothing like a few hours a day chipping surplus plumbing fittings out of the ice while ducking razor-edged ice-shards, to get the old circulation going! And getting the limousine out of the bog after you personally drove it out on the seemingly solid surface which treacherously sank under the weight—why, it was sheer exhilaration to erect the tent over it and get the Herman-Nelsons going to melt her free—and then, before the interior of the car could be ruined by leakage, to break the ice-block free of the bog with dozers

and drag it back uphill to the Embassy compound—
ah! those are the moments of triumph that make it
all worthwhile!"

"Umm," Nipcheese almost purred. "Pity you
didn't *quite* snake it out of there in time, after
some idiot suggested melting the ice first. My
solid tump-leather upholstery was a sodden ruin,
Ben! And it's all *your* fault! Yes, Ben," His Excellency went on after a thoughtful pause, "I think
quite possibly your best bet would be to request,
through channels, reassignment to Sector. A quiet
stint on the Quoppina Desk would do wonders for
your nerves, and never mind the carping of the
small-minded critics who would suggest that you'd
shirked your duty here on Snotch Too!" The Ambassador finished his stirring exhortation in the
ringing tones of a Napolean cheering on his troops
at Marengo.

"Oh, Mr. Ambassador," Hy Felix, the Press
Attaché spoke up in his irritatingly patronizing
tone, "You were saying something about a useless
timber survey, before you started in skinning poor
Ben alive."

"Hy," Nipcheese reproved in a tone of Kindly
Incredulity (131-w), "are you suggesting . . . ?"

"Heck, no," Felix came back sharply. "I'm coming right out with it: You're roasting our esteemed
B&F officer over a slow fire, which that's how you
get your kicks, and I for one—"

" 'And all the ranks of Tuscany could scarce
forbear to cheer,' " Ned Goodlark, a young fellow
newly assigned to the Information Service Library
quoted quite audibly, netting an ocular stab from
his chief which he returned calmly.

"Mr. Felix," the Chief of Mission cut in with
the chill dignity of an iceberg sliding into the polar
sea, "and you too, Mr. Goodlark, I'm sure Ben
understands that my remarks were purely didactic

in intent. How are we to learn from our mistakes, unless someone points them out?"

"Right on!" Hy returned the volley. "Now, speaking of blunders, when you let old Ambassador Whisp slip that task force of his in here to Snotch without a shot fired, you set Terry progress in Tip Space back a decade!"

"You're suggesting I should have fired on the 'Welcome Foreigners' parade laid on by the admittedly easily impressed local Ministry of Stuff?" Nipcheese inquired wonderingly.

"That's his 30, Retief," Magnan whispered to his colleague. "Remarkably subtle style."

"Don't wear out the 30-w, boss," Hy suggested. "Or maybe it was your '-x,'" he conceded. "Anyways, the Groaci have got us flat-footed this time. My contacts tell me they're setting up strongpoints practically in sight of the capital!"

"Mere staging areas for the processing of incoming supplies for the survey teams," Nipcheese corrected. "Actually, I've offered Ambassador Whisp my good offices in clearing the materials through Customs as expeditiously as possible."

"The Terran Ambassador Extraordinary and Minister Plenipotentiary is now handing Foreign Offices notes to the local Ministry of Monkey Business, requesting duty-free entry for office supplies, to sneak in guns for the Groaci? Instead of the usual illegal communication equipment for Terry use in spying?" Hy demanded, using his own 30.

"Your 30 needs work, Hy," Nipcheese told him in a kindly tone. "As for smuggling in artillery for the Groaci, I have His Excellency Ambassador Whisp's personal assurance that only normal survey supplies and equipment are included in the shipments, including, of course, a few low-kiloton handguns for protection against the Woomy and other ferocious wildlife likely to be encountered by the Groaci technicians. Actually, I'm rather glad it's they who are exploring those endless forest lands, rather than yourselves, gentlemen."

"Well, I guess you got me on that one, Chief," Hy acknowledged. " 'His Excellency wins on points,' " he chanted as if relaying late results to the City Room.

"Now, as for you, Ben," Nipcheese returned his attention to his hapless underling, "Suppose you take a run up into the foothills this afternoon just to lay to rest Hy's rumors of military activity?"

"Do—do I hafta, sir?" Magnan cried, using his 31-z.

"Unless you aspire to the Quoppina desk even sooner than I had contemplated, Ben," the Great Man replied unyieldingly.

"C-can I take Retief with me?" Magnan begged.

"He's your deputy, Ben," Nipcheese pointed out. "I suppose you can take him along if you wish, but don't be gone too long, lest some nosy parker infer that we have no actual need of a B&F officer."

"Gee, thanks a million, sir," Magnan breathed, then, to Retief: "I told you all along he was a grand guy, didn't I?"

"I'll take the fifth on that one," Retief responded. "Do you mind, Mr. Magnan, if I take along a couple of fractional megaton handguns of my own just in case *we* run into the Woomy?"

"Retief, your timidity amazes me," Magnan reproved. "Everybody knows the Woomy is a mere myth, a figment of the intoxicated imaginations of the early explorers here, a year ago."

"Well," Retief replied. "If I should happen to get intoxicated, I might see it too; so I'd better be prepared."

"This is hardly the time to jape, Retief," Magnan

scolded, rising. "Remember, Terra expects better of you."

"What's better than a handgun in the face of the unexpected?" Retief countered. "Anyway, Terra is too far away to do a whole lot of expecting of me."

"Still, she has a right to expect no disgraceful reports regarding your discharge of your duties," Magnan stated doggedly.

"Sometimes, Mr. Magnan, the discharge of my duties involves the discharge of a handgun," Retief reminded his supervisor as he held the door open for him.

In the corridor outside the conference room, Magnan resumed his complaints.

"This is a perfectly routine visit to our diplomatic colleagues, engaged in a peaceful project for the benefit of the backward people of Hellhole Too, Retief. It would hardly enhance the image of Terra as a kindly, peace-loving and benign power if we were to initiate hostilities with a party of forestry experts."

"I won't initiate anything that would be described as 'hostilities,' " Retief reassured Magnan. "But suppose we take the armored scout car instead of the staff car."

"But the seats are so *hard* in the gun-wagon," Magnan protested, "and there's no telly."

"Just in case some peace-loving Groaci scientist happens to be target-practicing in our direction," Retief suggested, "an inch of two of flint steel will be more comfy under your rear than an equal thickness of padding."

"Under protest," Magnan hedged, for the record, "I agree. Now let's be off before the old— that is, His Ex thinks up any more goofy errands for me to run."

*   *   *

2

"Take it easy off-road, gents," the Motor Pool Chief admonished. "Not over 150 on the flats or the suspension could go, and don't run into no shrubs more'n three foot thick at waist-height. She's a little sensitive to direct hits on her tracks, too, so better keep the fender-skirts down." He patted the low-slung weapon-system affectionately. "She's my baby," he told Magnan. "It was my own idear to make her look like a replica of a Cord L-29, just to kind of divert suspicion that she's a rolling dreadnaught."

"Good thinking," Chief," Retief said. "And don't worry. I hear they don't have anything heavier than six-inch hellbores up there."

"Geeze, Mr. Retief," the mechanic blurted. "You mean them latrine rumors is true?"

"Nonsense, Ralph," Magnan snapped. "Take care your irresponsible remarks don't give rise to more of the same."

"Whatever you say, Mr. Magnan," Ralph agreed as he slammed the door behind the diplomats with a vault-like *chunk!*

"I'm not at all sure it's a good idea to undertake to drive this rolling fortress ourselves," Magnan commented as Retief started up and drove out of the gloom of the Embassy garage into the gloom of the Hellholy afternoon. As always, a rumpled blanket of purplish-gray cloud hung low over the grubby town and the wooded hills beyond the end of the unpaved main street. Ahead, a shiny new vehicle with a cracked windshield pulled out of the garage under the Groaci Embassy and gunned off ahead of the Cord, throwing out a sheet of thin, yellowish mud on both sides, eliciting shrill cries of outrage, not unmixed with overripe frinkle-fruit, from the flat, bluish, manta ray-like citizens thus splattered. Retief followed it.

"Pay no attention," Magnan advised stiffly. "Serves the wretches right since they persist in their refusal to pave the avenue, even though *Corps* funds have been made available for the purpose."

"And they spend the cash on miniature golf courses instead," Retief agreed. "But at least they made Guinness, with 2.3 courses for every citizen on the planet."

"I've tried often enough," Magnan carped, "to make clear to the Minister of Spare Time the fallacy of the 'Taking-in-each-other's-washing' school of economics."

"What do they care?" Retief inquired, "as long as we and the Groaci keep on competing to see who can endow them with more free goodies?"

"A point well taken," Magnan acknowledged. "Look out!" he yelled and ducked as an entire bunch of decayed frinkle-fruit impacted the windscreen directly before his face. Retief swerved, sending the local artillerist rippling with amazing agility for shelter among heaped refuse containers.

"It's no use," Magnan mourned, "they're altogether too swift—and even when you do catch one and run him over, he merely gets up and uses his manipulatory fringes to cock snooks at your rear view mirror."

"So I've noticed," Retief commented. "But suppose I roll over that steel garbage drum this fellow hid in? At least that would keep him out of circulation, stuck in there with the frinkle-fruit supply until somebody comes along to cut him free. That might be worth trying."

"Retief! You wouldn't!" Magnan cried in horror. "Think of the headlines! 'Terran Brutality in Broad Daylight.' "

"You're right," Retief agreed. "After dark would be better."

Moments later, the crude street ended as dank forest growth closed in on both sides, and the ruts cut by the carts of the locals overwhelmed the feeble attempt that had been made to level the surface. The Groaci vehicle had already disappeared into the dark, cave-like opening in the undergrowth, and Retief followed. A foot above the muck, the heavy car rode smoothly, spattering green foliage with ochre mud. The rude trail wound on like a green tunnel into the deep woods. Magnan peered out nervously into the green-black gloom, shying as they passed close between giant boles and ducking when curtains of hanging moss brushed the top of the car. He looked back.

"Goodness, Retief!" he blurted. "The town is already lost to sight. What did they say that mythical spook is called?"

"The Woomy," Retief answered.

The road had by now deteriorated to no more than an occasionally visible path worn by the feet and cartwheels of the infrequent itinerant traders who ventured here, overlaid by the tracks of the car ahead, whose tail-lights were visible in glimpses.

"He's gaining!" Magnan yelped.

"I didn't know we were chasing him," Retief replied, accelerating.

"We're not!" Magnan came back. "What right have we—uh, just don't lose sight of the scamp completely!"

The darkness was almost complete now, as the dense foliage closed in overhead, allowing only a few shafts of dusty light to penetrate to the damp humus covering the ground. Small animals darted from the intrusive beams of the headlights. A red rag tied to a slender sapling caught Retief's eye. He stopped the car, which sank down with a glutinous *squish!* to the muddy forest floor. Just past it, the track of the preceeding car veered sharply off-trail.

As the hum of the engine slowed to an idle, a vast *crunch!*ing sound became audible, accompanied by a bellowing roar.

Abruptly, the wan shafts of light penetrating to the forest floor were cut off completely. A dust storm struck, hurling loose soil and vegetable debris up in a whirling cloud, pelting the Cord, rocking it violently. Something huge and jet-black was moving slowly overhead, shattering forest giants in its passing. Great trees disintegrated into splinters. A wild scream penetrated the howling; then as suddenly as it had come, the noise faded and was gone. But where dense forest had stood, there was now only a desolate expanse of trampled debris, shattered tree-trunks tossed about like jackstraws among heaped splinters.

Abruptly, the hovering shape uttered a shrill screech and shot upward, allowing daylight to return to the scene of devastation.

"Retief! Look!" Magnan groaned, pointing upward. Retief nodded. "I noticed it," he commented.

"But—it's so big—and so black," Magnan quavered. "Retief! It's devastated hundreds of acres! It almost came down right on top of us! We'd have been crushed!"

"It wasn't after us," Retief corrected. "But I'll just ease off-side for a better view." He pulled the car in behind a large, bushy shrub.

"It was the Woomy!" Magnan yelped. "I can still hear it roaring! It's going to get us! Do something, quickly!"

Retief switched on a spotlight, played it over splintered tree stumps, heaped fragments, and, already distant, on the curve of a vast black shape, moving off above the shattered timber.

"It appears, Mr. Magnan," he said calmly, "that there's something to the legend of the Woomy after all."

"Retief!" Magnan gasped. "What—?"

"Look over there," Retief suggested, pointing.

Magnan leaned forward and stared in the indicated direction. "Well?" he queried impatiently. "Just what am I supposed to see?"

"Nothing much," Retief conceded. "Just that brand-new model J Groaci scout car, squashed flat."

"Mercy!" Magnan demanded. "I think I see something now, yes, there's twisted metal—torn like paper! It's ghastly. No one could have survived!"

"Let's go take a look," Retief suggested. Before he could proceed, Magnan grabbed his arm in a panicky clutch.

"Good Lord, Retief! Drive on at once! Why should we become involved?"

Retief shook off Magnan's grip gently. "Curiosity, Mr. Magnan," he explained. "This isn't the Trans-Borf Interchange, after all," he reminded his supervisor. He opened the canopy and stepped out into cool, damp air with a powerful pine-mint odor. Magnan scrambled after him, but halted at the sound of a low moan from the direction of the wreckage. Retief paused, then continued. A moment later he called: "Come on, Mr. Magnan. It's only a survivor. Seems he's pinned in the driver's seat."

Magnan came up cautiously, parting the underbrush to peer tentatively toward the source of the sound, prepared to avert his eyes at once if the sight were excessively gruesome. Then he stepped forward boldly. "Why, it's only Thitch, Ambassador Whisp's cheeky driver! What in the world do you suppose he came out here for?"

Thitch groaned again, raising two of his five

stalked eyes to peer, bloodshot, at the Terrans.

"To spare me, Terries!" he whispered. "To have suffered quite enough to satisfy the accounts-keeper of Hell! In any event, it hardly matters: I'm a goner! I'm heading west, fellows! Get me out of here so I can at least expire in comfort, OK?" His voice had risen to a breathy wheedling as he warmed to his subject.

"I assure you, Thitch," Magnan said stiffly, "that harming you is far from one's intentions. Civilized Terries would never dream of assaulting an injured fellow-being, even a low-ranking Groaci scoundrel! Now, why are you here, in this dismal place? What are you up to?" He paused to sneeze heartily.

"OK already, Ben," the trapped Groaci replied defensively. "Excuse the implication. Just pry this here dash panel off my lap where I can climb outa here."

"I told you he was cheeky," Magnan remarked to Retief. "Ordering me about, and he's only a GS-4."

Retief went over to the trapped Groaci. "Where's your passenger, Thitch?" he asked.

"What passenger?" Thitch hissed. "Have I said aught of a passenger? You leap prematurely to invalid conclusions!"

" 'Methinks he doth protest too much'," Magnan quoted, then, to Thitch: "Be reasonable, Thitch. You'd hardly be out here exploring this wasteland on your own. Ambassador Whisp would never permit it."

"As is well known, Ben," the driver retorted, "we Groaci are, regardless of rank, lovers of Nature in all her manifestations. Why I love nothing so much as a halcyon tour through these unspoiled scenes. Naturally, the ambassador, himself a child of Nature, indulges my innocent pleasure."

"Candidly, Thitch," Magnan sniffed, "I doubt a

martinet like Whisp would so much as dream of countenancing the use of an official vehicle for personal amusement. So where *is* he?"

"The aft hatch seems to have popped when the car came to grief," Retief pointed out.

"Any passenger you might have, despite your protestations, had," Magnan scolded the trapped Groaci, "could easily have extricated himself. Let's just have a look . . ." As if casually, Magnan picked his way through the underbrush to examine the area near the rear of the crushed vehicle.

"Aha!" he cried, stooping to bring up a fragment of an imperial-sized floral-patterned tissue bearing the gold-embossed arms of the Groacian Department of Alien Inferiors. He sniffed it. "Cinnamon-mint, his Excellency's favorite scent!" he announced. "So your ambassador *is* poking about here, in person! 'Fess up, Thitch," Magnan urged. "What's going on in this remote corner of a trifling world that requires the personal attention of the ambassador of a major power?"

"You read much into little," Thitch said tonelessly. "Doubtless the artifact you flourish so triumphantly was left behind on an earlier trip, and blew out but now when—when . . ." he broke off with a whimper.

"When what?" Magnan almost yelled. "What happened?"

"You wouldn't understand, Ben," the crestfallen Groaci temporized. "It was too terrible! First the eerie burbling, then the crashing of great trees—" He paused to point. "It came from that direction; there was no room to maneuver, and I simply resigned myself, and next moment it stepped on me."

"*What* stepped on you?" Magnan demanded in a tone almost as shrill as the Groaci's. "What in the worlds are you talking about?"

"It was the dreaded Woomy, of course; it's too terrible," Thitch moaned, two pairs of eyes now staring fixedly into each other, while the fifth undulated dizzyingly. "I simply *can't*—" the stricken chauffeur whimpered. Just then Retief, who had been examining the wreck, gripped the edge of the sprung-forward canopy and lifted it. There was a load *crack!* and it came free.

Thitch seemed hardly to notice. He sagged against the pink and yellow imitation blurb-beast hide upholstery and moaned. Retief gripped him gently by one arm and lifted him out, depositing him on a grassy tussock.

"Very dramatic," he commented. "But if you think I'm going to pack you over to the car and rush you back home, you're dreaming. Quit stalling, Thitch," he urged. "Tell Mr. Magnan why it was that the Woomy came burbling out of the woods and stepped on you."

"Sheer ferocity, what else?" Thitch managed in a breathy croak. "I never would have believed it could break down tall timber in its passing, and crush nine-point duralloy like a paper box!"

"It was tough, all right," Retief conceded. "So on that note we'll leave you—and His Groacian Excellency. Where's he hiding, by the way?"

"To imply," the driver demanded haughtily, "that His Excellency would stoop to some low subterfuge?" He paused as if the question rang a little hollow, even to his own auditory organs. "To suggest," he went on more mildly, "that the Groacian AE & MP is perhaps hiding back of that big frond over there, monitoring your reaction to the disaster? Preposterous!"

"Well," Magnan said in a stage whisper to Retief, "since His Ex has apparently set off on his own, and there's little likelihood that we could find him in this Pud-forsaken wilderness, there's no point in our hanging about in hope of offering him a fast and comfortable ride back to his Embassy." He started back toward the Cord.

"Bye, now, Thitch," he called over his shoulder in a cheerful tone to the disheveled Groaci survivor. "Pity we couldn't be of help."

"I say!" Thitch hissed. "To do nothing precipitate! As it happens, I just might be able to overtake his Excellency, as I know the direction in which he went, after abandoning me to my fate—er, valiantly deciding to go for help, that is." He scuttled away and was instantly lost to sight in the underbrush.

"Here he comes!" Magnan blurted, turning in the direction opposite to that in which Thitch had disappeared. The sounds of crashing underbrush and snapping twigs were clearly audible, and growing louder. Suddenly, a broad blue Snotchman with white zebra-stripes painted across his torso appeared, his aspect rendered doubly barbaric by a length of greenish bone thrust through the cartilege separating the recessed nostrils.

"Hey!" the newcomer barked, emerging into full view to expose an indigo physique innocent of apparal.

"It's a Hellholer savage," Magnan yelped, "not Ambassador Whisp after all."

"Either that," Retief replied judiciously, "or he's in costume already for next year's Outrage Day Masquerade."

"Whattaya mean, 'savage'?" the native tribesman demanded, advancing on Magnan as his tribesfellows crowded up behind him, all jabbering at once and staring at the Terrans.

"You must be them foreign Amblusters we were supposed to reassure," the first arrival stated. "Grunks, or something like that. OK, we're here; you feel reassured, boys?"

"Naw, Zib," the fellow behind him contradicted. "Our foreigners got more eyes: five or eleven or something. These babies got only three—maybe two."

"I was never too hot on the mathamatical stuff, Bus," Zib conceded. "So OK, they ain't the Grunk. So who are they, hah, you're so smart?"

"Ast 'em," Bus spat. "Me, I'm tired o' tearing around in the swamp looking fer some foreign hotshots supposed to pull off some kind o' swifty that'll pay Chief Gub good. Whatta we get outa the deal, hah, except flunkfly bites?" Bus pushed forward, jostling Zib, who decked him with a violent sweep of his muscular fringe.

"Ain't I got troubles enough?" he demanded, "Without some insubordinate slob bugging me? Get back in ranks, Bus," he concluded sadly. "And don't give me no more static, OK?"

Bus responded with a lunge toward his superior, locking his large sky-blue teeth on the latter's ambulatory fringes. Zib yelled and with a convulsive ripple flung Bus from him.

"OK, this here horseplay has got to come to a focus!" he shouted, kicking the prostrate Bus. "You know the penalty for tryna bite your NCOIC, Bus," he reminded his chastened subordinate. "String him up, boys!" he commanded the remainder of the detail. "Left fringe this time. We done the right last time he fouled up, right?"

"Dear me," Magnan said, plucking at Retief's sleeve. "I do hope we're not to be involved in another of those dreary power struggles among the powerless. Do something, Retief, before that poor fellow is torn asunder before our eyes!" He averted the latter organs from the spectacle as the native troops attached a stout length of vine to the lower fringes of their former comrade and proceeded to hoist him to a level at which his inverted eyeballs were at a level with their own.

"Hey, foreigner," Zib addressed Magnan. "Notice how I ain't doing no excessive brutality nor nothing: we done the other side last time, so we're giving it a rest this time out, see. Talk about giving a break to a bum which he don't deserve none!"

"The only break you're giving me, Zib-baby," Bus yelled, "is a broke hide, which you're gonna hafta carry me after, so maybe you oughta cut me down fast!"

"Retief!" Magnan gasped. "It's too horrible! And it's all my fault for calling this barbarian a savage. *Our* fault, that is, for being here in the first place!"

"OK, OK, don't rub it in, Mister Ambluster," Zib urged wearily. "I know I shunta let the boys sneak up like they done and throw a scare into youse that way, but, what the heck, they don't get much fun—except for old Bus, here," he amended. "He ain't bored none, eh, Bus?" The boss native prodded his dangling victim. "Speak up, Bus, tell the Ambluster you're a sport which yer onney getting a few kicks so the rest of us can have a few laffs, OK?"

As Zib poked the helpless Bus again, Magnan turned away with a wail. "I can't look," he moaned.

"His eyeballs!" he gasped. "They're bugging out— and they're turning blue!" Magnan fell to his knees, babbling.

"They're always blue," Retief pointed out.

"Whites and all?" Magnan countered.

"Especially the wites," Retief reassured his supervisor as he assisted him to his feet. "Still, you have a point." Then, with a quick motion, he drew a switchblade from his sock, flicked it open, and started toward the glowering Zib and his inverted prey.

"Hey!" the non-com objected, eyeing the glittering six-inch blade. "We're pals with you Gurcks or whatever. You don't wanna like louse up interspecies amity with no rash words!"

"Right," Retief confirmed, as he jostled Zib aside and, with a deft stroke, cut Bus down. The latter collapsed in a heap, uttering sharp cries.

"You've broken his neck!" Magnan accused.

"Not likely," Zib contradicted. "These here deepwoods recruits has got necks like yikky-tree roots. Come on, get up, Bus, and quit clowning." He gripped the noisy fellow by the fringe and hauled him upright protestingly.

"My orders was," Zib cut through the other's complaints, "to make contact with these here Amblusters or Grucks or whatever and get started on the salvage job! So if you got no more objections, Bus, we'll get on with it, and I'll try to fergit you done bit me." He kicked his crouching underling with his tooth-scarred fringe, now oozing indigo fluid, and turned away.

"They ain't the Grucks," Bus offered from his supine position. "Already tole you, Grucks has got seven eyes or thereabouts."

Zib turned back long enough to administer a resounding *whack!* to his fallen subordinate's sense organ cluster with his unwounded ambulatory fringe. "That's enough outa you, Bus," he chided. "I don't guess it matters a whole lot. Foreigners is foreigners."

"But what if they turn out to be Tezzies or whatever Cap'n said?" Bus objected. "Then we'd be like trafficking with the enemy and all. Shooting offense."

"Not broody likely," Zib returned contemptuously. "Cap'n said Tezzies was nine gurp high and had big white horns like a blunderbull."

"Did not," Bus persisted. "Said their feathers was green and they got their bones on the outside."

"Nonsense!" Magnan interrupted. "We Terries are a benign, featherless, hornless, internally-skeletoned, non-green people, peace-loving, though terrible in war. I suggest you avoid starting the latter."

"What ladder?" Zib and Bus demanded in unison.

"To pay no attention," a breathy Groaci voice spoke up from the concealment of a large priggfruit bush. "Those are Terries you have there, Sergeant, right enough. Hold them! As for the noble Groaci, in myself you see a prime exmaple!" With that, a disheveled figure in a sprung hip-cloak emerged from concealment, scratching absently at his sensitive throat sac. He advanced truculently, passing up Zib to confront Magnan.

"Well, Ben, what's the big idea, posing as a Groaci? That could get you shot as a spy, you know."

"Why, hello, Mr. Ambassador!" Magnan gushed. "Whatever brings you here to this remote spot? And we definitely were *not*, with respect, posing as Groaci!"

"One item at a time, Ben, OK?" the Groaci Chief of Mission admonished sharply. "Dear me," he went on, "I'm afraid you've put your foot in it for fair this time, Ben, snooping here where you've no business at all."

"I hate to contradict you, Mr. Ambassador," Magnan began hesitantly.

"Then don't do it," Whisp snapped, turning briskly to Zib. "I fear, Sergeant, that your briefing was inadequate. Allow me to orient you a trifle: I am, as I said, a Groacian national, and like all of that noble breed, I possess, as you will note, the ideal ocular endowment of five such organs; in addition, my person is protected by a chitinous cuticula, to wit." He rapped sharply on his forearm with a bony finger, eliciting a dull *bonk-bonk!*

"As you have no doubt detected," he went on, "these unfortunate Terries must make do with only two viewing organs, which afford them no trinocular and higher orders of perception. Also, they are detestably soft to the touch." He tapped Magnan's chest in an offhand way as the latter, startled, attempted to dodge. As a result the Groaci's impertinent digit impacted the St. Ignatz medal Magnan always wore next to his skin. Whisp jerked his head back at the resultant *Click! Click!* and muttered: ". . . most unusual . . . never before encountered . . . but of course—he's attempting to pass as a Groacian, and it's a part of his disguise. Sorry, Ben," he whispered. "Your cover's blown."

"Wait a minute, pal," Zib spoke up. "You said Tezzies was soft—"

"You fooled me on that one, Ben," Whisp hissed. "But let's see you produce three more eyes, all handsomely stalked!" He turned to Zib. "As I was telling you, Sarge, you were dispatched here to meet me and conduct me to your General Cug, for a Summit regarding the southern limits of the Reserved Areas."

Ignoring him, Zib tore a sapling from the ground, snapped off the top and stripped the yellow leaves from the five-foot-long, two-inch-diameter trunk. Then, without warning, he swung the stout staff at Retief, who put up an arm, intercepted the blow, gripped the shaft and jerked Zib close to him. Shifting his grip to the sergeant's thick neck, he held him immobile, used his left hand to knock aside the Hellholer's attempted blows, then lifted him with a two-handed neck-and-fringe grip and threw him back among his gaping troops.

"That one ain't so soft," Zib commented, getting

to his feet. He lunged suddenly at Bus, who had been snickering at his superior's discomfiture. Bus retreated behind Retief, who thrust Zib aside.

"Nonetheless," Whisp interrupted in a strained voice, "He has only the two curiously flat eyes. He is, clearly, a Terry, not a 'Tezzy,' Sergeant, as you persist in saying. Let him produce five eyes, I say!"

"Don't tempt me, Mr. Ambluster," Retief cautioned, faking a grab toward the official's five erect oculars, which promptly wilted, as he jumped back.

"Restrain the brute, Magnan!" Whisp keened. "I call upon you, Sergeant, for protection! If I should suffer disfigurement at the hands of the Terry monster, when General Cug hears of it, he'll roast you alive!"

"Take it easy, chum," Zib counseled the Groaci. "I guess you're a Gruck all right; the secret briefing folder said you were nervous Nellies."

"No nervous Nelly I!" Whisp screeched. "If, Sergeant, you have never seen a Groacian aristocrat of the First Ascendancy in a towering pet, you have no concept of what 'wrath' can mean. Don't provoke me," he added more calmly. "In the name of Groaci-Snotch relations I shall overlook both your failures to interpose your person in my defense, and your slurs on the exalted Groacian people!"

"OK, let's cut the yivshish and get down to cases," Zib suggested. "We come out here to meet you, like you said, and now we got to take you to Headquarters. It's a five-hour hike, mostly through boglands, except where it's froze. So let's get going." He turned to Bus. "Think we oughta truss him up, or what?" he inquired indifferently.

"Naw, he ain't under arrest, Sarge. He's a, like, guest. Besides, we got no rope. S'pose to give him VIP treatment," Bus reminded his supervisor.

"I forgot," Zib admitted. "So you give him a piggy-back, Bus. I'll leave one of the boys relieve you in a hour or two."

Grumbling, Bus went to Whisp and hoisted the protesting alien dignitary to his back. His lack of clearly defined shoulders made it necessary for the Groaci to clutch Bus's generous auditory fringe to retain his position, dangling from the Hellholer's neck.

Magnan nudged Retief. "Heavens, Retief!" he said quietly. "Are we just going to let them walk off with no accounting?"

"It seems like the best way to find out where HQ is located," Retief pointed out. "But maybe we'd better interrogate the sergeant a little, first."

"My idea precisely," Magnan agreed. "Now you seize the horrid great brute and I shall conduct the interview."

While the two Terrans were conferring, Zib had deployed his squad in a ragged circle, ringing the squashed war-car. One fellow, beating the brush off to the left, yelled suddenly:

"Oh, Sarge; here's another one! Not one of ours, and not squashed, so it don't look like a part of the Plan!"

"Drunk again, Pive?" Zib called, wearily. "I got enough on my plate already, without some wise guy starts throwing in more," he explained to Divine Providence, plodding reluctantly over to inspect Pive's find.

"Oh, dear," Magnan whimpered. "They've found our—or, rather—Ralph's car!"

A moment later, summoned by Zib's yell, the local troops noisily took up new stations near the Terran war-car.

"They mustn't so much as touch it!" Magnan declared. "If they even smudge the wax job, Ralph will be furious, and every time I call for a car for the next six months, he'll send over that horrid minivan!" Then he leapt aside as, with a bellow, the subject vehicle came roaring out of the jungle edge, dozing aside a sizable whufftree which fell with a *crash!* that lingered in the air after the car had come to a halt beside the Terrans.

"Hey, not too dusty," Zib shouted from the driver's seat behind the now-cracked windshield, which he struck with his fist, widening the crack. "Except the windscreen's kinda flimsy," he amended.

"That glass is proof against a forty-calibre hardshot!" Magnan yelled back, jumping in as if to restrain the fragmented substance from falling from its frame entirely.

"Soon's I hit, whuff, she went," Zib explained, defensively—no, Magnan decided, the fellow was complaining, not explaining.

"That's fastglass," Retief reminded his chief. "Designed to resist impacts above one hundred feet per second, but non-load-bearing under that, as an emergency escape route."

"Yes, I recall," Magnan replied, not crying. "But will Ralph?"

"Who's this Ralph?" Zib demanded, descending from the scratched car. "If he don't like what I done to his play-toy, tell him to see me!"

"That's hardly practical, Sergeant Zib," Magnan pointed out, "inasmuch as Ralph never leaves the Motor Pool, and you yourself appear to limit your operations to the Deep Woods."

"Yeah?" Zib challenged. "Wait and see, pal, just gimme a few days, and I'll dive into that pool and take him on his own figurative turf!"

Magnan turned to Retief. "That has an ominous ring," he declared gloomily. "I doubt he means to pay a courtesy call."

"Still, it's better'n hiking," Zib conceded as he

resumed his seat, after a brief inspection of the car's handsome radiator shell and bowl headlights, which had taken the brunt of the punishment. Without further ado, he gunned the car forward a few feet, skidded to a halt and yelled an order to Bus, who skittered forward eagerly.

"I'm making you acting corpuscle in my absence on hazardous duty," Zib shouted into the broad blue face of his subordinate, in the tone of one making a dire accusation. "Get 'em back to field camp by Second Moonrise, or I'll have yer tripes for slingshots!" With that he accelerated across the splinter-heaps that were all that remained of the dense forest, dodging giant stumps left and right.

"I suppose the concept of turning on the headlights, so as to avoid some of those collisions, is outside his naive world-view," Magnan mourned.

"Naw, Zib wouldn't use no headlights, even if he knew what they were," Corporal Bus dismissed the idea. "He'd figger they was for weak sisters. What he is, he's *machisimo* like they say. And that reminds me, Mr. Ambluster," he went on, addressing Retief, "I fergot to say 'Thanks a bunch' fer cutting me down. Old Zib'da left me dangle till tea-time." He turned away to bellow to the scattered troops, then added, "And that ain't often, out here in the sticks."

"He means he'd likely have had to wait a considerable time for tea-time to come along," Magnan explained superfluously. Then, to Bus, "I say, Acting Sergeant, are you sufficiently grateful to undertake to overtake—that is, try to catch up with Zib and repossess our possession, that is, recover the car?"

"Naw." Bus dismissed the idea out of hand. "Even if we was to catch the bum, he'd as lief burn us down as if we was savages. Bye now, Tezzies—and if anybody asts me, which ain't all that likely, I'll tell 'em *some* Tezzies, anyways, ain't such bad guys. Ta." With that he and his troops melted into the remaining underbrush and were gone. Magnan looked back at the wall of the remaining forest, great boles, crusted with verdant epiphytes, dangling vines and massed thorn bushes clearly visible by the wan light of the rising First Moon. The silence was unbroken except for the sibilance of the whispering pines.

"Alone," Magnan mourned aloud. "Lost and abandoned in this devastated wilderness."

"Not quite alone," Retief corrected. "There's the Woomy, remember."

"Retief, don't be cruel," Magnan begged. "You know I'm not at my best when confronted by the supernatural."

"I don't know, Mr. Magnan," Retief countered. "You did pretty well on Hoog when they were feeding me to the brass god."

"Ye . . . ss, there was that," Magnan conceded, preening a trifle. "One has one's code," he reminded his junior.

"And what does the code have to say about the present situation?" Retief inquired.

"Hark!" Magnan said abruptly, holding up a hand. "For a moment there it sounded almost as if the jabber trees were actually saying something. . . ."

He cocked his head like a dog listening to His Master's Voice. "Listen!" he urged.

"Please, Ben, to have a heart," Retief heard in a breathy whisper. "Leave a fellow foreigner join you to seek a way out of this horrid jungle."

"That's not the wind in the willows," Retief told Magnan. "That's Thitch." Then he called, "Come on out, Thitch, we'll talk it over."

The crestfallen Groaci chauffeur emerged from beneath the sheltering fronds of a Gong bush, eliciting a faint *bong!-bong!*ing as the broad, stiff, semi-metallic leaves brushed together.

"Hi, there, fellas," he began, only to be cut short by Magnan's authoritive bark: "Mind your protocol, Thitch! 'Fella' is hardly an appropriate mode of address for a sweeper-caste driver when greeting diplomatic officers, even under maximum infernal—ah, informal, that is—conditions!"

"Very well, Mr. Magnan, and Mr. Retief," Thitch assented sorrowfully. "If you feel that way about it, you prolly wouldn't be interested in the way I figger to be back in my trundle bed by oh-three-hundred hours." He nodded, then turned and with a discordant *bong!*ing eased back into the shadows.

"Wait!" Magnan yelled after him. "I didn't mean—I only meant—"

"A most eloquent plea, Ben," Thitch's reedy voice came from the darkness. "But you'd better keep it quiet; you'll attract the Woomy."

"Good lord!" Magnan whispered to Retief. "See? Thitch believes in it, too!"

"Perhaps he's merely trying to unnerve you," Retief suggested.

"What?" Magnan yelled. "Unnerve a scion of a line known down through the centuries for steely courage in the face of doom? That's ridiculous," he summed up, lowering his voice.

"Did you say 'doom,' Ben?" Thitch's jeering inquiry came back from the dark. "No need to be overly pessimistic. Perhaps you'll escape merely maimed for life. After all, a creature so huge would hardly bother with so insignificant an object as yourself; he'd only step on you by accident, the way he done me, if at all. Ta."

"Come, Retief," Magnan said more calmly, Rising Above the taunts of the low-caste Groaci. "I don't wish to remain here to be insulted by trash."

Retief motioned Magnan to conspiratorial silence

with a finger across his lips; at the same time he moved quietly around to the far side of the gong bush and waited. A moment later, Thitch disengaged himself from his place of concealment, not without a few faint *bong*'s, and, turning to flee, dashed directly into Retief's embrace.

"Drat the confounded noisy shrub!" Thitch hissed, struggling in vain to break away from the Terran's grip. "To unhand me, Retief!" he demanded breathily. "To be on a very tight schedule indeed! To have no time to waste here!"

Retief shook the Groaci almost gently until his plain GI eye-shields fell, and retained a hold on the drivers' dowdy, ribless, issue hip-cloak as its owner groped among leaf-litter for them.

"Look here, Retief," Thitch proposed earnestly, once his eyeshields were back in place. "You're a reasonable fellow, unlike your feckless associate, Second Secretary and Consul Ben Magnan. So suppose you and I strike up a deal that will put us quickly back amid the comforts of civilization, leaving poor Ben to his own limited devices."

"On the other hand," Retief countered, "suppose you tell me all about how you plan to get back to town in such a hurry, and I'll consider— only consider, mind you—not tying you up to a tree for the Woomy to find."

"It is to laugh," Thitch came back cheekily. "You don't imagine that I, a sophisticated Groacian grease-monkey, actually subscribe to that silly superstition?" As he fell silent, the moonlight dimmed abruptly as something vast loomed over them, blotting out half the satellite.

"If you don't subscribe to it, this must be a free sample," Retief observed, looking up at the huge, opaque silhouette as it drifted past.

From the other side of the bush, Magnan's screech startled both Retief and his captive.

"Retief! Where did you go? It's back! Come here! I told you you'd attract it!" He broke off as the moonlight returned suddenly.

"Calmly, Mr. Magnan," Retief called softly. "It's a good distance off and going away; and Thitch was just about to tell me all about it." He lowered the latter until his running feet nearly touched the ground.

"To flee instanter, rash Terry!" the Groaci hissed. "To tell you nothing: to have offered a clean deal. To have been rudely rejected! But leave me go now and I'll give you one more chance!"

Retief dropped the noisy fellow, at the same time extending a foot to trip him up in mid-leap. Now the bloated apparition was tiny in the distance.

"Don't rush off, Thitch," Retief urged. "We still have lots to talk about."

"Never, vile Terry!" the driver screeched, rummaging in the bushy grass for another lost eyeshield. "Never will you force me to divulge Groacian State Secrets!"

"That big, eh?" Retief mused aloud. "Thanks for the tip; I'd assumed it was just some local-level skulduggery you were mixed up in."

"It is you, Terry miscreant, who are mixed up!" Thitch hissed. "What would I, a humble GS-3, know of great affairs?"

"As much as you could manage to overhear from the front seat, I'd say," Retief answered.

"What? I, eavesdrip on His Excellency's Top GUTS conferences with Snottish dignitaries?"

"Eaves*drop*," Magnan corrected from shelter. "And you forgot to mention just which dignitaries are involved in the conspiracy."

"No conspiracy, Ben," Thitch corrected. "Merely finalizing arrangements for the Opening."

"Of . . . ?" Magnan prompted.

"The Groacilaw, what else, Ben? That half of

the planet where the Groacian writ will run unchallenged by you slugabed Terries! Legal, too," he added complacently.

"Heavens!" Magnan exclaimed. "Well, Retief, it appears the noisome sticky-fingers have one-upped Ambassador Nipcheese with a vengance this time, just as he said."

"When did stealing half a planet become legal?" Retief asked the now-cocky driver.

"When lawyers first wrote laws in doubletalk," Thitch explained promptly. "Have you ever browsed through the Galactic Code? Fascinating reading:

" 'Whensoever it shall be manifest to a normally functioning neural system of whatever sentient species, the latter term to include all those life-forms deemed eligible under GC 112-13 (as amended) that a *de facto* state of depopulation as defined in GC 111-3 and pertinent sections of the Manual, shall exist for a period exceeding one zoof cycle (see Liverwell 2367) it shall be deemed available, under the terms of the Accord of July, 2636, for immediate effective occupancy, the Occupying power being obligated (see Groac versus Goldberg 2030) to carry out such improvement, to exclude exploitation in excess of the values set forth by law as shall most expeditiously render such territory suitable (ref. GM 221-3 a and b) for classification under GM in any of the categories therein specified.' Well?" Thitch demanded triumphantly, "What do you have to say to that, Terries?"

"Heavens!" Magnan cried. "The wretch is right! We've been aced out of half a world! The Ambassador will be furious!"

"Since Groac has the legal angles covered, that leaves the illegal approach for us," Retief pointed out.

"To be sure," Magnan agreed, steepling his fingers.

"You wouldn't *dare!*" Thitch declared, folding two eyestalks together in a dizzying expression.

"Would I not?" Magnan came back spiritedly. "And don't imagine you can intimidate me with that rather awkward 421 of yours! Why, at the disarmament talks at Yoon, but last fortnight, I withstood the consummate 421-2 of Broodmaster Yith for a full hour, without so much as blanching! You underestimate the moral fibre of a Terry diplomatic officer of Class Three, fellow-me-lad!"

"OK, OK, you got a hide like a beachmaster fellseal," Thitch sneered. "If you would of had any finer feelings, you'd of known when you weren't wanted in the vicinity, and tooken off. But that's a Terry for you. No subtlety."

"You speak to me of subtlety?" Magnan challenged. "You, who callously boast of the theft of half a planet from under the aggregate olfactory sensors of the rightful owners!"

"Sour snick-berries, eh, Ben?" Thitch dismissed the charge. "What about that time out at Yudore when you fellows violated the most sacred traditions of the autochones all over the place under the pretext of preventing some kind invasion you prolly dreamed up back at Sector?"

"That doesn't count," Magnan sniffed.

"We're wasting time, Mr. Magnan," Retief put in.

"Wasting?" Magnan challenged. "To what better use could we put an idle hour than in correcting the misapprehensions of this misguided representative of the laboring classes?"

"I guess my union'd have something to say about that crack, Ben," Thitch warned. "Better watch it, pal; you don't want I should file a beef with the Board."

"File and be damned!" Magnan retorted stoutly.

"I am *not* your 'pal'! No jury in the Arm—" he began to warm to his thesis.

"Let's get going," Retief suggested. "The sooner we catch up with Zib the better."

"Catch up!" Magnan echoed in tones of amazement, pointing toward the wasteland of chipped timber across which the stolen war-car had sped out of sight. "Even at minimum velocity, he's miles away by now; we'd never catch him!"

"He won't get far without the energy cell," Retief pointed out, holding up a small metallic-green cylinder. "The charge on the plates will take him about a mile, I estimate. So let's go."

As he spoke, Thitch had edged around until he stood beside Retief, facing Magnan.

"To make haste: We must press on at once," he urged in his feeble whisper.

"You presume to include yourself?" Magnan inquired. "Why should we trust you not to betray our approach?"

"Parallel interests, Ben," Thitch explained smugly. "The brigands have your car; they have *my* chief!"

"Nonsense!" Magnan dismissed the idea. "He's their honored escortee."

"He's right, Mr. Magnan," Retief commented. "When you consider that Ambassador Whisp is riding pig-aback on Private Pive, and that Mother Nature has equipped the Groaci with a set of sharp projections in the area of the ankle, it's a good bet that Snotch-Groaci relations are in a fragile state."

"Yes," Magnan agreed. "I suppose the honeymoon will endure but briefly, once the irascible Groaci martinet sets spurs to his mount. Very well, Thitch, you may tag along," he added graciously. "Suppose you take the point, just in case of ambush. Off you go." He shooed the Groaci ahead and gamely mounted the first drift of debris.

Following Zib's trail in the stolen car was a bit like following the bed of the Suez Canal: the powerful machine's air-jets had gouged a three-foot trench through the shattered stumps, uprooted vegetation, and limb fragments which lay in heaps, vine-festooned, under the settling dust. Though out of sight, the sound of the vehicle's passage was a continuous *crunch!*ing of dozed-aside rubbish, accompanied by faint yells in guttural Snottish. Moments later they spied the car itself, almost buried in rudely harvested vegetation, but boring on like a demented haystack. Since Zib's progress had been less spectacular than anticipated, half a dozen troopers were in view on the flanks, or rippling along in the wake of the blunderbus, churning along in the midst of a cloud of woody debris thrown up by the air-jets.

"It's stopping!" Magnan exclaimed, and indeed the car had halted, its path blocked by the stump of a forest patriarch, a gug-fruit tree three yards in diameter.

"He'll discover the haser controls in a minute or two," Retief predicted. Even as he spoke a harsh sound started up, accompanied by a boiling cloud of dark brown smoke.

"He can't keep that up for more than a few seconds," Magnan pointed out. "He'll drain his plates! We've got him!" he broke off with a yelp, then whirled to see a tall, flat local militiaman who had risen from concealment behind a heap of trash to prod him with his long wooden pike.

"Wrong, Tezzy," the fellow corrected. "It is *we* who got *you*." He jabbed symbolically with his weapon, causing Magnan to jump back.

"I fear, my man," Magnan said haughtily, "your cyphertape has imparted a false impression of verbal conjugation. 'We *have* you' would be the appropriate locution. Now put down that sticker and let's talk sensibly."

"Start with *you*," the Hellholer suggested. "Not sensible expect alert sentry put down sticker. Or talk grammar, either," he added.

"I don't know what sort of swindle the Groaci are working on you Hellholers," Magnan said. "But since it seems to involve war with Terra, it's clearly not going to work out to your advantage. So you'd do well to put down that absurd assegai and comport yourself in a more decorous fashion."

"That one went over like a moobie-bird, pal," the spearman said. "Plenty too many big word, not in bargain cut-rate talk-tape."

"I'll show you what he means," Retief offered, at the same time stepping in past the spear-point to grasp the bark-covered shaft and wrench it from the grip of the soldier's muscular manipulatory fringe. He rammed the flat butt of the weapon against the Hellholer's mid-section, causing him to curl into a rude cylinder. A second hearty prod knocked him backward to the humus-covered ground, where he at once snapped out flat and rippled swiftly away into the underbrush.

Magnan dusted his hands as one who has just completed a distasteful chore. "I think we'll hear no more from *that* fellow," he predicted. "Take due notice how effective my remarks were, once you explained them. A pity that all diplomacy can't be as effective."

Retief glanced toward the stalled car which had now sunk to half its height into the forest litter under the pounding of the lift jets. Zib had given up revving the engines and now the car was threshing aimlessly, unable to extricate itself from the pit of its own devising.

"You'd better wait here, Mr. Magnan," Retief suggested. "I'll go up and take a look."

"Good notion, Retief," Magnan agreed readily; and paused to sneeze. "I'm at my best conducting verbal combat, as you've just seen. In case another of these nasty sticker-fellows tries to sneak up behind you, I shall be here to deal with him." Retief nodded and left the trail to move up alongside the car in the shelter of the ridge of fallen timber edging the furrow it had left in its wake. The cloud of dust and leaf fragments was settling rapidly now that Zib had given up trying to power his way through, and the car sat, nearly invisible under its burden of new-fallen foliage and dusty debris, its engine idling dispiritedly. A trooper ventured forth across the springy moss, poking gingerly into it with his spear, probing for the car, but when he scored with a solid *thunk!*, he dodged back and skittered away to concealment. A moment later Zib's upper end emerged from the heaped trash, uttering harsh expletives in the local patois. He was attempting to massage his sense-organ cluster with his left manipulatory fringe, an effort rendered nugatory by his close-coupled anatomy. Then one bleary deep-blue eye fell on Retief, who had come forward to confront the alien car-thief.

"Oh, it's you, Tezzy criminal," the non-com exclaimed. "Good show. I plan to have you up before all kinds interplanetary tribunal and stuff, for attempting to interfere with a official operation of the Hellhole Armed Forces, and all."

"What do you mean, 'trying'?" Retief asked indifferently, as he closed in and delivered a straight right to the sergeant's mid-section, causing the latter to roll up like a taco, compacting a considerable mass of debris which he apparently found uncomfortable, since he at once snapped his flat form open again, dislodging the cylinder of vegetable matter.

"Dirty pool, Retief, using a feller's reflexes against him," Zib complained. "See, our remote ancestors, maybe a couple million years ago, used to be bottom-feeders, and their number-one enemy was what you call a jabberup. Flat and hard, like a sand-dollar, and they had a big, sharp, spring-loaded spike on their topside, and when one of the boys came along and started feeling acrost him, looking for eats, old Jabber'd cock that spike and *zong!* he speared him an ancestral Hellholer. Onney when he cocked it, that jabbed the butt end up first, and so our guys developed this here reflex to roll up when jabbed in the midriff. That put the vital organs and all out of reach o' the spike, and also usually flipped over the jabber, so great-granpa had a feed after all. Anyways, that's what our perfessors say, and they oughta know. So you found out about our weakness and rolled me up like a rug before I could get the old shredding hooks into ya. No fair."

"Very interesting," Retief acknowledged. "But I have an ancestral hang-up of my own: I inherited a dislike of being shredded."

"Fair enough," Zib agreed. "So I'll leave the hooks retracted, and you won't jab me no more, OK?"

"It seems you did a fair job of digging yourself in here," Retief observed, noting that the car was now buried in detritus to the roofline, and the leaf litter was dribbling down inside through the open escape hatch from which Zib had emerged.

"Ain't built like a Groaci war-car," Zib complained mildly. "Them suckers has got tracks, which you can climb straight up outa here."

"Maybe *I* better get it out," Retief suggested. "Before it sinks out of sight."

"Would you?" Zib inquired eagerly. "That's real blue of you, pal. Wait a minute and I'll get outa your way." He emerged and withdrew a few feet and Retief dropped down inside the car, brushed trash from the bucket seat and took the controls. He set the air-cushion on wide aperture and reversed the motor. The car shuddered and lurched upward. Quickly, Retief shifted to high tractor and, by using full left thrust, mounted the crumbling wall of the excavation, edged past the buttressed root of the gug-fruit tree and surged up and out. He caught a glimpse of Zib making motions as of one hailing a cab, returned a cheery wave, and headed for the deep woods, pausing after half a mile to replace the energy cell.

It was a brisk five-minute drive back along the trench until he encountered Magnan, disheveled but moving right along. The senior diplomat darted for cover at the sight of the dirty but only slightly battered Cord, but Retief played the opening bars of *Diplomatik Ober Alles*, commonly called *Rotten to the Corps*, on the car's air horns, an arrangement usually employed for official salutes to specially favored dignitaries. Magnan skidded to a halt at the familiar sound and re-emerged from behind a wide-spreading busybush, the pollen of which, he recalled belatedly, made an excellent itching-powder. Scratching absently, Magnan came cautiously over to the car, stooping to peer through the window.

"Oh, it's you, Retief," he cried as the latter stepped out.

"Wasn't that a busybush you were hiding under?" Retief inquired. "And where's young Thitch?"

"Lordy, I hope not!" Magnan replied, still raking at his ribs. "As for Thitch, far from lending me assistance over the rough spots, the pest seems to have wandered off. We must get back to town at once, Retief!" he added, urgently. "Perhaps I *did* brush against one."

Retief handed Magnan the first-aid kit as the now agitated diplomat settled in his seat. "Try a little compound 297 on that, sir," he suggested, indicating a small vial.

"But that's a controlled substance!" Magnan demurred. "Known to the demi-monde as Cloud Nine. I can't possibly violate CDT regs, Interstellar Law, and common decency so casually!" By now Magnan was struggling frantically to insert both arms inside his early late afternoon hemisemi-demi-informal dickey to scratch at a dozen places simultaneously.

"I wasn't proposing that you should embark on a life of dissipation," Retief pointed out. "Just take a drop on the tip of the tongue."

"Damned dickey's stiff as sheet insulon!" Magnan carped, yanking at the offending garment.

"It *is* sheet insulon," Retief pointed out. "Better take it off."

"And appear half-naked before these savages?" Magnan protested, yanking off the offending garment. "There," he gasped, "that's better. At least now I can get at it!" He bent his neck to stare glumly down at the angry rash already spreading on his chest. He began to writh as if attempting to escape himself, then accepted the vial of Compound 297, and after eyeing the oily pale-green contents through the transparent tube for a moment, pulled the stopper and touched it to his tongue.

"Ummm, tastes like ambrosia," he murmured as he hastily recorked the vial and restored it to its loop in the medical kit. "Retief," he added earnestly. "You won't tell . . . ?"

"Not if you give me another week to finish up

the *Report of Redundant Reports*," Retief countered.

"No problem, my boy," Magnan acceded easily, as he reassumed his discarded attire. "After all, we *are* lost out here in the immensity of the Great North Thicket, eh? Can't expect a chap to do more than two things at once."

"You'd better not let Ambassador Nipcheese hear you say that," Retief suggested.

"Of course, of course," Magnan agreed readily. "Now, shall we drive back and face the wrath of Ralph?"

"While we're here, why not look into just what Ambassador Whisp is up to?" Retief suggested. "And the good sergeant's plans, too."

"Gracious, we mustn't be nosy," Magnan countered. "Doubtless his Groacian Ex is bound on legitimate diplomatic business; as for the native levies, I suppose they can do as they like, in their own savage milieu."

"Including commandeering Ralph's—and the Ambassador's—favorite L-29 replica, and scratching the finish?"

"Retief! He didn't!" Magnan darted forward to examine the gracefully curved spoon fenders. "Good Lord!" he yelped. "There's a dent in the radiator shell, too! And I think the bumper is somewhat askew! I'd no idea the vehicle was so fragile," he grumped, reassuming his seat. Then looking back toward the flattened Groaci car still lying canted at the side of the trail, he added:

"Imagine what the Woomy would have done to this foolish L-29 conceit of Ambassador Nipcheese." He shuddered.

"Just a minute," Retief said, and went to take another look at the crushed vehicle. Magnan hurriedly followed to peer over his shoulder.

"Just look at that sturdy everlon twelve-gauge,"

he muttered. "The Woomy collapsed it like a gribble-grub bag."

"Strange," Retief commented, as he lifted a warped plastron seat-squib. "This looks a lot like the work of a little specialty shop in the Reef that has a knack for building plausible-looking wrecks that really aren't damaged."

"Not damaged?" Magnan yelped. "Why, the Groacian arms on the side are folded double! Ambassador Whisp would never countenance such deliberate defacing of his planetary symbol."

Retief reached down to pluck away the appliqued disc bearing the device, which at once sprang back to perfect smoothness.

"Oh," Magnan commented. "Why, I believe you may be right, Retief! But *why*? It's too devious for a mere First Secretary and Consul to figure out!"

"It's supposed to make us Believers in the Woomy," Retief theorized. "Concrete evidence that it's not only real, but hostile to the Groaci."

"But—it *is* real!" Magnan protested. "We saw it!"

"Still, Mr. Magnan," Retief demurred, "don't you think it was a little too much like a set-piece?"

"Lordy," Magnan moaned. "Whatever it was, it worked! I believe! Let's go home."

"Not quite yet," Retief suggested. "There must be a reason they didn't want us to go any farther."

"I'm sure," Magnan stated, "that the problem will soon yield to analysis by a Deep-think team back at Sector. Surely they didn't pay those exorbitant camouflage fees merely to abandon the thing here in the depths of the forest where no one will ever see it to be deluded!"

"We see it," Retief pointed out.

"But we mustn't get carried away by logic," Magnan cautioned. "After all, we *saw* the Woomy, too, and that's quite impossible!"

Retief nodded. "Oddly shaped feet, the Woomy must have," he pointed out, "to flatten the cargo deck and leave the driver's seat and his Ex's perch intact."

"Doubtless mere chance," Magnan suggested. "Unless the kindly Powers that watch over diplomats took a hand."

"Funny," Retief mused. "The car is squashed, but it's not pressed down into the soft loam."

"Perhaps the monster plucked it up and cracked it in its hands," Magnan offered. "Then placed it here."

"I hadn't heard the Woomy had hands," Retief replied. "And Thitch didn't say anything about being picked up, just crushed."

"No doubt these matters will all be cleared up at the inquiry," Magnan reassured his junior. "Meantime, let's gather a nosegay to present to Ralph." He began picking his way into the underbrush toward an extravagantly showy orchid-like blossom. He sniffed the flower with a blissful expression, then attempted to pluck it, but found the stem as tough as braided polyon. He abandoned the effort reluctantly, then sprang with a glad cry on a cluster of slightly smaller blooms, pale blue and dusted with yellow. Again he sniffed, paused to give Retief an amazed look and yelled.

"Look out, Retief! They're coming—oh, no! It's *too* dreadful!" He broke off his plaint to duck behind the shelter of a giant root-buttress, then stole another peek toward where Retief stood, studying a bumbumber bush.

"But—wherever did it—he—come from?" he gasped, and clambered over the concealing ridge of rock-hard wood to rush to Retief's side.

"No, I'm quite all right, Mr. Magnan," Retief said quietly. "What did you think had happened?"

"I didn't think!" Magnan protested. "I *saw* a

great big blue native jump out from behind that bumbumber brush and attack you with a spear with yellow feathers on it—the spear, not the native: *he* had green feathers!"

Retief returned to the dense-growing bumbumber bush and circled it carefully, then pounced and came up holding a larger-than-average local citizen by his barf-nodes, a thumb in each yik orifice. A string of draggled green bim-bird feathers was strung around the unhappy alien's broad ventral surface. He was holding a short spear with a barbed stone head, decorated with large, bile-yellow feathers.

"You got it right, Mr. Magnan," Retief said. "Except that he hadn't actually done it yet."

"Well, I thought . . ." Magnan started, then subsided.

"—As he no doubt intends to do," Retief pointed out. "Very perceptive of you, Mr. Magnan."

"I *saw* him!" Magnan repeated. "But . . . how—if he hadn't actually done it yet?"

"It looks like a clear case of clairvoyance," Retief commented. "Are you accustomed to seeing visions, Mr. Magnan?"

"Never—until now!" Magnan assured him. "But of course my great-aunt Matilda used to know all about our neighbors' affairs. Perhaps it's hereditary."

"I suppose," Retief agreed, "that if you can inherit magical powers you might as well inherit them from your maiden aunt."

"You jape," Magnan charged sorrowfully. "But I saw him, clear as day: he popped out from just next to that great ugly bush and—and—but it's too horrible: that spear was aimed for your chest, right between your show hanky and your longevity lapel-pin."

"Easy, Mr. Magnan," Retief soothed, conducting his distraught supervisor to a seat on a convenient log.

"It was just as I was savoring the heavenly aroma of the nosegay I'd plucked," Magnan moaned. He looked at his hand, then along the ground. "Where is it?" he yelped, jumping up. "I've lost it, my beautiful bloom!"

"We all lose our beautiful bloom after a while," Retief comforted his colleague.

2

"But, this was different," Magnan insisted. "I have a sort of feeling about that particular blossom. It was special. "But," he brightened abruptly, "of course you'll find it for me. Or *have* found it," he amended. "Don't keep me in suspense, Jim," he pled. "Be a sport: hand it over, there's a good fellow."

As Retief turned to reply, the flower Magnan had picked and sniffed at fell from the twig on which it had lodged when Magnan had foreseen the Hellholer's attack, directly into Retief's hand. He at once handed it over, a saucer-sized blue blossom with yellow dusting only slightly bruised by the rough handling it had received. Retief caught a whiff of its gardenias-in-the-moonlight perfume. Magnan leapt at it and took another great healing lungful of its aroma, then dropped it and came to his feet abruptly.

"Let's get going, Jim," he said briskly, though with a half-suppressed smile brightening his usually dour features. "If we get a wiggle on, we can surprise the scamps at their feeding time. Interesting to know what old Wispy's doing out here, too." He broke off to begin humming a tune from a recent hit musical and took a number of almost dancing steps toward the car.

"You surprise me, Mr. Magnan," Retief said as he climbed inside the vehicle.

"Call me 'Ben,' Jim," Magnan said airily.

"Are you sure you're all right, Ben?" Retief inquired, studying his companion's face, now beaming a broad smile. Magnan giggled.

"Never better, Jim," he gasped between chuckles. "Now let's off to the wars." He scrambled to his seat and sat beaming at Retief.

"They have spears," Retief reminded him. Magnan nodded complacently.

Retief steered the car to the edge of the cleared expanse, avoiding collision with major stumps.

"Why so cautious?" Magnan demanded merrily. "If Sergeant Zib can mow 'em down, so can we!"

"I thought it better to be inconspicuous," Retief explained. "And I think Ralph would prefer that we exercise a modicum of caution," he added.

"Ralph, smalph," Magnan came back happily. "Slip him ten and he'll be as happy as a clam."

"Ten guck wouldn't go very far toward replacing his light o' love," Retief countered.

"Who said anything about ten guck?" Magnan came back, "Ten thousand is more like it. Hardworking fellow, Ralph, but on the make just like everybody else."

Retief steered the car in behind a particularly dense clump of snarfweed and shut it down. As he got out, Magnan looked at him in surprise, still stifling laughter, then jumped down beside Retief, and, laughing merrily, tripped and fell, hopping up at once.

"From here on we go in on foot," Retief explained.

"To be sure," Magnan replied airily, executing a number of surprisingly graceful dance steps, concluding with an impressive *jeté* and fetching up in a tangle of fimble-weed, from which he emerged sneezing.

"Dratted pollen!" he wheezed. "I'll declare, Jim, it seems like every kind of flora on this hellhole is worse than the next!"

"You may be right, Ben," Retief replied without emphasis. He leaned into the car, rummaged for a moment in the glove-box, and brought out a flat leather case filled with the ambassadorial four-ounce medicine vials, which he emptied on the ground, one by one. Magnan watched approvingly.

"It will do the old hypochondriac good," he commented. Retief nodded and began taking pollen specimens from each of the nearby plants, starting with the snarfweed and concluding with the coarse yellow spores from a foom tree, carefully labelling each one.

"I'll try one of those," Magnan declared contentedly, reaching for the foom-pollen bottle. "After the sneezing phase is over, one feels rather good," he amplified. Retief fended off Magnan's grab and returned the vial to the case beside its fellows, each now containing a sample of powdery dust, no two the same color.

"Better not, Mr. Magnan," Retief cautioned. "There's no telling what mixing your doses might do."

"True," Magnan agreed, snickering. "Listen, Jim," he went on, "I've got a feeling I could . . . Just a minute, I need to concentrate . . ." with that, he leaned forward to a perilous angle and lifted his feet until he was floating horizontally, a foot and a half from the ground. "Lovely," he commented, still smiling broadly. "You know, Jim, I've always suspected I could do this, if I just thought about it the right way." He drifted forward a few feet and levelled off. "It's so *easy*," he called down. "You really ought to try it, Jim. It's just a matter of marshalling the Higher Mental Powers."

"It must be a bit like whiffling, that I learned to do a little back on Grote. Remember poor D'ong?"

"Charming lady," Magnan agreed, proffering a vial, which Retief waved away.

"I don't think that combination of uppers and downers and sidewarpers would agree with me," Retief demurred. "Even if I could duplicate it," he added.

"Fear not, Jimmy," Magnan called down cheerfully from some twenty feet above the forest floor. "It was the farfweed on top of the Compound 297 that did the trick. I can do it again any time. Might be useful the next time I'm running late for a reception in the Residence gardens. I can just float in over the hedge and mingle inobtrusively; old Nippy will never know."

"That sounds like a shrewd scheme, Ben," Retief conceded, "provided," he went on, "that you wait an hour or two, until everyone's blind."

"Nothing simpler," Magnan dismissed the suggestion, then uttered a sharp cry, as a heavy spear *thunk!*ed into the trunk of the giggy-puzzle-tree beside him. He made frantic swimming motions to no avail. "Retief!" he yelled. "*Do* something, quick! They're killing me!"

"To descend instanter, vile Terry!" a breathy Groaci voice yelled from concealment, at maximum volume. "To seek no more to spy out the legitimate activities of your betters as we seek peacefully to better the lot of the benighted savages!"

"It's Ambassador Whisp!" Magnan yelped.

"For once His Excellency has the right idea, Mr. Magnan," Retief called to his supervisor. "Drop down a few feet and they won't be able to see you."

"I . . . I . . . can't!" Magnan bleated. He had given up trying to scull and was clinging with desperation to a leafy bough. Another weapon went *whack!*ing through the foliage a foot from his head. He screeched.

"Climb down," Retief suggested. "Hand over hand."

"I'll try," Magnan quavered. There was a noisy threshing in the brush.

"Look out!" Magnan called. "They're coming!"

Retief nodded. "Their Red Engine technique needs work," he commented. "Grab some altitude and follow me." With that he resumed the driver's seat and pulled the car even deeper into the dense brush, hung a hard left and skirted the big giggy-puzzle-tree, then swung a wide turn to the right, through sparser brush, until he saw Whisp scuttling toward a gaily-colored tent with a granfalon bearing the Groaci colors flying from the top. Retief edged in closer, parked in deep shadow, and switched on the external auditory repeater, sweeping the directional pick-up cone to pinpoint a muffled conversation coming from the direction of the pavilion:

"To be outraged!" Ambassador Whisp's faint voice came in clearly, though nothing was visible beyond the deep black of the open tent-fly. "To recommend to you, General, that you have a care! Do you think I'm some kind grub-in-arms, don't know what's what?"

"It's not that, Mr. Ambluster," the unfamiliar voice of General Cug replied placatingly, in badly accented Groaci. "But you got to see my side. OK, Zib and his boys were set upon by a small army o' these here like Tezzy commandos, and had to fall back here to field HQ after heavy losses, to regroup, and just when I'm ready for the old counterpunch, you hafta go and charge me wit' cowardice in the sense-organ cluster o' the enemy. To be a gross injustice! Lemme tell you what I got in mind:"

"To skip lightly over what you have in your alleged mind—" Whisp cut in curtly.

"Whattaya mean 'alleged'?" Cug challenged at once.

"Oh, those are the very finest kind," the Groaci Ambassador assured his co-conspirator. "Most ambassadors have them."

"OK," Cug replied. "Now you better concentrate *your* alleged mind on what I got to say—"

"To mind your tone, my man," the Groaci cut in. "You mustn't let all this democratic twaddle go to your head."

"I ain't yours, and I ain't no man," Cug objected. "Anyways, it was you Grucks come around telling us simple hunter-gatherer types all this democratic twaddle in the first place!"

"To be sure," Whisp conceded. "But certain concepts, while valid at the theoretical level, or at least useful as bargaining chips, are not to be taken as substitutes for long-established realities."

"Sure not," Cug agreed in a thoughtful tone. "Otherwise I'd have half my army hanging out by the fringes like some kind of big wash."

"Precisely, General," Whisp confirmed. "Now, as to your plan . . . ?"

"Oh, yeah; well, I and my boys have got maybe six ton o' prime farf-weed stacked ready to load."

"Very well, Field-Marshall," the Groaci replied. "I expect my haulers to be in place by tomorrow at the latest, and you may commence loading at once."

"First, the payoff," Cug demurred. "And we decided a couple thousand guck a ton is more like it than the lousy couple hunnert you offered."

"Outrageous," Whisp hissed. "Prior to my generous offer, the stuff was valueless. You'd been feeding it to your domestic herds from time immemorial!"

"Sure, I know all that stuff." Cug countered. "But if you won't deal, the Tezzies will."

"Not a word to the Terries!" Whisp snapped. "The blue-noses would clap us all in irons in a trice!"

"Well, I don't wanna be clapped up in no trice," Cug acknowledged. "So let's get down to business, OK?"

"The terms of our arrangement," Whisp stated coldly, "have already been settled at a level higher than our own. So let us restrict our discussion to matters of delivery dates and modes."

"Ain't got none o' them modes," Cug protested. "Like I said, I got plenty prime weed ready, back in the deep sticks, OK? So let's you just pay up and I tell you where to send your haulers."

"I can agree to no deviation from the agreed arrangements," Whisp reiterated in a dull tone. "Unless first approved by one so authorized."

"I'm authorized, ain't I?" Cug countered. "That's what I come out here for, and you, too, so let's stop pussyfooting and start counting the take."

"The 'take,' as you so grossly call it," Whisp countered, "will be counted when the weed is safely packed, inventoried, and stored in Groacian godowns at Hell City. Not before."

"Gimme a break," Cug groaned. "My boys got enough on their plates already, collecting the stuff and toting it bareback to the sub-depots for your guys to haul out. They got to eat, too! So pay up now—"

"I see," Whisp cut in coldly, "that the future of Groac-Hellhole commercial relations is to be less halcyon than I had hoped, and indeed than I have already assured my Minister it would be. Enough of this yivshish! To get back to work and await your payment in patience!"

"So I and my boys don't eat until you Grucks got the stuff bagged and counted and stacked in a warehouse," Cug mourned. "What if your union men decide to strike, hah?"

"Look here, Sergeant," Whisp said earnestly. "I don't conceal from you the fact that this transaction is of great importance to Groacian policy in the Arm. Happily, only the inferior metabolisms of the loathsome Terries are subject to the curious effects of your native alkaloids, both your own sturdy race and noble Groacians being quite immune—a benign dispensation of Divine Providence, no doubt, to assure Groacian ascendency over the vile Soft Ones, with faithful Hellhole assured of an honored position in the New Order. Thus, the plan to establish plantations for large-scale intensive cultivation of farf-weed and googly-blooms and the rest."

"Nix, Mr. Ambluster," Cug returned flatly. "Us simple folk don't know nothing about the subtleties o' agriculture and agronomy, and all. We're strictly hunters and gatherers."

"But all that could be changed," Whisp protested, "if I should arrange for the loan of appropriately skilled expert personnel!"

"To forget it," Cug dismissed the idea. "To be off your rocker if you think we're going to invite a bunch of Gruck overseers in here to work our butts even harder'n what we been working!"

"To reconsider that position, General," Whisp suggested silkily, "inasmuch as the referenced personnel are at this moment alighting only a few miles north of here, ready to direct the preparation of the newly cleared plantation areas. To simply cooperate in the inevitable, and your own career development is assured."

"You expect me to connive in the enslavement of my own kind?" Cug demanded loudly. "How much will my annual retainer be?" he continued in a more businesslike tone.

A moment later, crashing sounds endued, and Retief saw the ornate tent shake violently, then collapse on struggling figures trapped under the fabric. Suddenly Groaci shock troops in flaring helmets appeared, streaming in from the concealing jungle, converging on the fallen tent in time to form up around the slight form of Ambassador Whisp as he struggled clear of the entangling fabric, still expostulating breathily: "Four-flusher! Renegado! To think you can back out now, after Groac's immense investment in site preparation?"

Retief silently backed the car away and took up a course which would skirt the recently denuded area, visible in glimpses through the still standing trees screening its eastern edge. After half a mile, the devastated swatch came to an end and dense forest resumed. Retief drew close and halted to observe activity in the final clear patch at the extremity of the open area, where something immense, black, and limp, shaped like a hundred-yard-wide beret, lay draped over the tree stumps, partially supported by spindly tripods not unlike oversized copies of the Groaci three-toed feet. Under and around the big blimp, Groaci technicians worked busily. Barely visible in the gloom under the sagging bulk of the apparatus were a number of massive, short-bladed air-impeller blades.

"The Woomy," Retief noted in the tape-log: "An adaption of a standard Groaci Mark VII ground-effect cargo carrier, with exposed and beefed-up fans. I'm going to take a look." He climbed down from the car, pulled a number of bushy cut branches over the vehicle and went forward, pausing to look up as a faint "yoo-hoo!" sounded from above. The tiny shape drifting downwind at some fifteen hundred feet was barely recognizable as First Secretary Magnan, waving excitedly and pointing toward the collapsed blimp. Retief stepped into a clear patch and waved him down, placing on the ground as an aiming point the white silk show-handerchief which was a *de rigeur* part of the chartreuse early late afternoon informal coverall he was wearing. Magnan immediately began a steep descent, maneuvered smartly around the obstructing foliage-mass, rotated to a feet-down posture, and landed lightly a foot from the silk which he picked up, shook free of leaf-litter, folded neatly and handed to Retief. He staggered a little, and commented:

"One *does* get a big giddy, and it's quite exhausting; remembering to breathe is a chore, and keeping the old sphincters cinched up tight is taxing after a time."

"Very impressive, Mr. Magnan," Retief commented, replacing the handkerchief in his breast pocket.

"To be sure," Magnan replied coolly, "I found I had little directional control, but soon got the knack of altitude, and as you saw, can ascend and descend quite handily. Pitch, roll, and yaw are neutral. I was drifting with a light breeze when I noticed the activity yonder, which of course has also attracted your attention. What are they about?" He peered through the screening foliage.

Retief nodded. "The Woomy is a device the Groaci are using to clear land for systematic planting of dope."

"Small wonder the natives panicked at sight of it," Magnan suggested.

"And of course Ambassador Whisp was quick to make use of the advantage," Retief commented. "Now it's time to put the advantage to *our* use."

"Just how," Magnan inquired uneasily, "do you

propose to do that? Clearly, the correct action at this time would be to notify the Ambassador and leave the rest to the Navy."

"That sounds remarkably like war," Retief pointed out. "What I have in mind is on a smaller scale."

"Well, of course, one doesn't wish to precipitate war," Magnan conceded. "So we'd best just sneak back to town and allow matters to eventuate."

By then, Retief had advanced to the edge of the stump-studded, splinter-strewn clearing.

"I'm going in low, off-side," he told Magnan. "I want to get in under that thing where it bulges over this way. I'd be obliged, Mr. Magnan, if you'd drift around and come in up-wind in the shelter of the bulk of the thing, and utter a loud noise at the right moment, and then drop on it like a stone."

"Well, I suppose one could . . ." Magnan nodded hesitantly. "But what if—never mind," he stammered. "Just tell Mother I died game." He assumed a forty-five degree tilt forward and lifted off, rising swiftly to an altitude of fifty feet. He hovered while the insistent breeze swept him slowly out over the devastated former forest land. Retief watched the Groaci, saw no signs of alarm: then he moved rapidly forward, keeping in the lee of heaped debris, moving up swiftly into the deep shadow of the half-deflated gasbag, while Magnan swung off in a wide curve around the bulk of the grounded Woomy.

As Retief reached the dark gondola the sounds of the busy Groaci at work only a few yards away on the other side of the control car continued undisturbed. He entered the cramped compartment with difficulty, squeezing between taut fabric and metal frame members. Inside, he at once identified the standard-model controls, plus a special panel devoted to operation of the special, beefed-up rotors. He waited, listening, and after a few moments heard an unearthly screech from above, followed at once by an excited rise in volume of the conversation of the Groaci technicians; another instant and a hearty *whump!* sent ripples through the sagging fabric overhead. He stepped back into the shelter of a protruding chart locker as the small personnel door at the other end of the gondola banged open and a Groaci in an oversized nautical-type peaked cap and a brass-buttoned tunic with the name SHIST lettered above the three rows of service ribbons burst in, darted at once to the factory-installed console, and began slamming home the heavy knife-switches. Retief heard the brief clatter of a compressor, followed at once by the sigh of released gasses; the fabric bag began to tighten and lift away, letting daylight into the cramped chamber. There were creaking sounds as the bag swelled out among the concealing trees, snapping sounds as stout branches yielded to the pressure, yells from the technicians, silenced by a harsh command from the officer aboard.

"To be assured," he shrilled at his crew, "that your chief has all under tight control, as usual—" he broke off with a yelp as Retief stepped out silently behind him and poked a finger into the alien's sensitive zot-patch, located where ribs would have been in a vertebrate.

"Woe unto you, rash Terry!" the captain hissed. "When my loyal minions fall upon you, I doubt I shall be able to restrain them from rending you limb from limb!"

"Probably not," Retief agreed calmly, "considering you can't control them even under normal conditions. But never mind the analysis of the weaknesses of the Groaci system of command."

"To rave, vile Terry!" the officer declared indignantly. "What foolish fancy is this: that I cannot command my own troops?"

"Surely, Captain Shist," Retief offered matter-of-factly, "you aren't going to claim they were acting on your orders when they used this blimp to destroy valuable stands of timber and terrorize the local autochtones?"

"Of course not!" the Groaci confirmed vehemently. "The scamps chose a moment to steal away and commit their pranks when I was closeted for my daily meditation."

"You can meditate now on the dim view Terra will take of your schemes for mass-producing a full line of psychoactive drugs to saturate the galactic market," Retief told the cowering fellow.

"Surely," the latter gasped, "you'd not bruit about any such irresponsible rumor? That would be too gross an abuse of civilized *mores* even for the infamous Retief, were he here!"

"I have some bad news for you," Retief said. "Against all odds—"

"And I, for you!" the Groaci hissed, turning suddenly to bring to bear a small but deadly-looking 1-mm needler. He jabbed it at Retief, who feinted a grab to the right, then knocked the weapon spinning with a quick movement of his left hand. Shist uttered a yelp and leapt for the opening by which he had entered, only to collide with Magnan, just easing inside. The Terran recovered in time to seize the Groaci by the collar as he sought to dart past.

"Captain Shist, Naval Attaché to the Embassy of Groac, I believe," Magnan commented, unruffled. "What in the world are *you* doing here?"

"Why, Ben," Shist temporized, "I was but carrying out routine maintainance to my command when this ruffian—" he indicated Retief with a flick of a stemmed ocular "—was so presumptuous as to board the vessel uninvited and offer indignities to my person! Good job you're here, Ben! You can restrain this madman!"

"Actually, Shist," Magnan replied coolly, "I rather doubt that. After all, he still has the weapon with which he immobilized you—"

"That's OK, Ben," Shist whispered urgently. "I got me a belly gun, just dropped it, over there. . . ." he peered into the gloom of the dark corner. "You could retrieve it, and disarm your reckless colleague!"

"Perhaps I could," Magnan said dreamily, "but *would* I? That seems to be the question."

"Listen, Ben," Shist said in a desperate whisper, "I'll cut you in for a full tenth! I got the connection all set, and the first load is already at the forward collection points, ready for pickup!"

"Why, you scoundrel!" Magnan burst out. "Openly trafficking in drugs under cover of a benign timber survey! It's a bit much, even for a Groaci!"

"Envious, eh, Terry?" Shist hissed, advancing a step, causing Magnan to back away. "True, you Soft Ones missed your great opportunity as first-comers here on Snotch, but even so, I've graciously offered you a share ample to set you up for life in a luxury villa on any of the pleasure-worlds of the Arm, so why not be a sport and—" Shist broke off abruptly to spring for an inconspicuous hatch, which snapped open at his touch and through which he leapt to freedom as Magnan lunged after him in vain.

"Never mind, Mr. Magnan," Retief comforted his supervisor. "It saves us the trouble of tying him up. Let's get airborne." With that he flipped switches and at once the *buzz!* and *zing!* of the particle engines started up: the gondola was jerked violently, then stabilized as the swelling gas-bag took its weight. A heavy vibration shook the deck underfoot, and a moment later there was a terrific crashing, accompanied by heavy shocks as the gondola swept through the tree-tops.

"Good lord!" Magnan gasped. "What in the world! Retief, we're floating away!"

"I've got her under control," Retief reassured him. "We'll level off above treetop level and head out north by west."

"What, may one ask, is to be found there, in the opposite direction to the city?"

"A newly arrived crew of agronomists," Retief explained. "All set to convert the newly-made wasteland into the biggest weed plantation in history."

"The rogues!" Magnan commented. "I suppose we should hurry back to the Embassy and prevail upon His Excellency to issue a stern Note."

"What I have in mind will be a lot more fun," Retief pointed out, "as well as quicker, and incidentally, far more effective."

"Oh, I see," Magnan commented. "A stern protest, delivered in person in the name of Ambassador Nipcheese."

"More like a Halloween prank," Retief explained, "but in a good cause."

"Really, Retief," Magnan said stiffly, "I can hardly countenance any action prejudicial to the dignity of diplomatic process! More fun, did you say?"

By this time, the gas-bag had floated to the far edge of the cleared area. Looking over the side of the gondola, Magnan could see a grounded air-car, and around it a swarm of tiny figures, busy unloading. He grabbed up a collapsible telescope, clamped it to the bulkhead beside him, and focused on the scene, first espying a Groaci noble in scarlet and brass, then moving on to the crew of workers in mud-colored labor harness, without so much as a rusty greave to their name.

"Coolie-caste Groaci and an overseer!" he burst

out. "And they have tools: hoes, rakes, shovels and so on. And over there—yes! A parked tractor, a modified Yavac Class One, with a soil-moving blade. And they're heaping up wood, and, good lord, Retief—they're setting it ablaze! They'll start a forest fire that will rage unchecked across the continent! We'd best hurry back and get that Note off at once, after all!"

"Let's see what a few passes by the Woomy will do," Retief suggested.

"The W-woomy?" Magnan repeated uncertainly. "Where? We *must* be off, Retief! No one would blame us for retreating in the face of supernatural horror!"

"Easy, Mr. Magnan," Retief said. "We're the Woomy."

"Oh, you intend to impersonate the monster? Ingenious, but do you suppose they'll be so gullible?"

"We're not impersonators, Mr. Magnan," Retief pointed out. "We're the real thing."

"You mean—? You don't mean—?" Magnan leaned out the openwork side to gaze skyward at the vast bulk of the now fully inflated gasbag above. "But it's only a primitive dirigible balloon! Who would . . . ?"

"You, for one," Retief suggested quietly. "Let's see if we've got any Believers down there." He adjusted controls, and the roar of the burners decreased in volume. In Magnan's glass the scene swelled rapidly. The scarlet-clad taskmaster looked up, executed a double-take which nearly dislodged his ceremonial headpiece, then waved excitedly, his vocal orifice working busily. Magnan shifted his view to the laborers, who paused, turned to look toward the excited boss, then glanced upward— staring, Magnan felt, directly at him. An instant later they were in headlong retreat, first scattering, then converging on the cargo-boat, while their crimson-draped leader pelted behind them, ignored.

Retief pulled up after the low pass, circled widely, and started back, but the clearing was already deserted. The air-car had lifted and was making time to the south.

"So much for diplomatic process," Magnan mourned. "I doubt I shall be able to report the facts of this matter to His Excellency. Best we seal our lips and never let the outrages—neither theirs or ours—enter the annals of Galactic diplomacy."

"Suits me," Retief agreed readily. "But we ought to go back and tip off Ambluster Nipcheese before he cedes the entire planet to Ambluster Whisp."

3

In the gloom of the Embassy garage, nestled under the Chancery wing, Ralph mournfully surveyed the car.

"Top bumper bar's bent," he muttered. "Radiator shell, too: got a dent right under the Cord badge. Grass stains on the upholstery; can't figure what you fellers been doing to this-year machine."

"Don't fret, Ralphie," Magnan urged cheerfully. "I'll sign a voucher for you to order all the parts you need from the Big W. Wish Book."

"No kidding, Mr. Magnan?" Ralph gulped. "That's blue of you, like these year locals say. I'll work up a order right away, before old Nippy—par me, I mean in preparation for inspection by His Ex."

"We'll make a diplomat of you yet, Ralphie," Magnan assured the uncouth fellow.

Ralph edged over to touch Retief's sleeve. "Say, Mr. Retief," he muttered. "What's with Ben? All this 'Ralphie' stuff, and not bitching about the parts bill, and all."

"Don't found any long-range plans on it, Ralph,"

Retief advised him. "He's just coming down off a high."

"Shall we ride the lift up?" Magnan inquired airily of his assistant. "Or, tell you what: you ride and I'll race you."

"I suggest you keep your feet on the ground, Mr. Magnan," Retief said firmly. "There is a certain orthodox element here in the embassy which might not understand any open manifestation of the Higher Mental Powers."

"Right," Magnan agreed readily. "And what if the stimulus wore off while I was cruising at five hundred feet?"

"It's clear that your discovery will have to be managed very carefully," Retief pointed out as they entered the lift. During the slow ride up to the Chancery, Magnan expermented with rising vertically a few inches, then settling in again soundlessly. "I can foresee," he commented, "a number of ways in which one might relieve the tedium of Staff Meeting, and at the same time alleviate the discomfort of sitting on those hard chairs. Oh, boy, just wait till I show Nat Sitzfleisch; he's always carping about getting bunions on his bum.

"It's going to take some time," he went on, "to work out the precise mixture and proportion to selectively stimulate telekinesis, clairvoyance, lightning calculating, fortune-telling, and so on. First, we'll have to find an excuse—ah, formulate policy, that is—to make another expedition into the forest and secure additional samples. Why, I wouldn't be surprised if every species of plant on Snotch produced a distinct psychoactive pollen."

The car *whoosh!*ed to a stop, and they stepped out into the ambassadorial anteroom, where Euphegenia, the Great Man's personal secretary, crouched as usual behind her desk, interminably filing her nails. She glanced up at their arrival.

"His Ex is closeted on urgent matters," she snapped. "Why can't I get it across to you fellows that you got to have an appointment?"

"Those are His Excellency's specific instructions?" Magnan inquired diffidently.

"Heck, no," Eupheginia snapped. "He's as easy to see as the Pope; but *I* got personal matters to attend to, too, you know!" she grumped. "Like my hair-do," she added, patting the spongy orangish mass surmounting her meaty features.

"Going to have, or already had?" Magnan asked in the tone of One Innocently Seeking Clarification of an Obscure Point (497-c).

"Don't use that second-rate 497 of yours on *me*, Ben Magnan," the lady snarled, "or I'll tell Nippy you been brutalizing the help again."

"Tell him again, or brutalizing again?" Magnan wanted to know, this time using his -z.

Eupheginia's slab-like cheeks turned a mottled pinkish-gray. "OK, rub it in!" she wailed. "I said 'help,' but that don't mean I got to take crap off every First Secretary—"

"*And* Consul," Magnan amended. "And I proffered no 'crap' as you so bluntly put it, my dear."

"I ain't yer dear!" she came back, and reached for a steno pad on which she made hasty notes. "Anything else?" she demanded, pen poised. A blue light blinked on her console. "OK, yez can go in now," she snapped. "He's outa the john."

"One wonders," Magnan mused aloud as he advanced to the inner portal, "where the Department finds such exemplary personnel to fill the difficult slot of Ambassadorial Secretary . . ."

"Easy," Miss Glumpert responded. "They give me six off a twenty-to-life bum rap if I'd sign on."

"Oh, and for what alleged lapse were you incarcerated, Yewfy?"

"Only his Ex gets to call me 'Yewfy,' " the lady

pointed out alertly. "Lousy third-degree manslaughter," she explained.

"And just whom did you slaughter?" Magnan pressed the point. "It's so important to take an interest in the help," he explained to Retief.

"Some bum said he was a inspector, come nosing around the job where I was splitting a little rock to build a new outhouse back of the barn," Miss Glumpert told Magnan.

He at once turned back to clasp her hand warmly. "Congratulations, my child!" he said fervently. "What weapon did you employ?"

"Who needs 'em?" the secretary demanded, extricating her hand from Magnan's clutch and flexing both it and its fellow like a cat shredding draperies. "Reminded me a lot of you," she added, keeping a beady eye fixed on Magnan's until his gaze fell and he hurried back to escape into the Ambassadorial Inner Sanctum.

"Good lord, Retief!" he muttered, avoiding the red eye glaring at him from behind the nine-foot solid rhodium desk. "Lucky she hadn't a meat cleaver to hand."

"What, gentlemen, is the meaning of this intrusion?" Ambassador Nipcheese attempted a growl which came off as an uncertain falsetto. "I'm in my hutch pondering the great problems besetting the Mission, and you two clowns come busting in like I was just an ordinary clod or something!"

"We—that is, Retief—will explain later," Magnan stalled. "Right now I have the honor, Mr. Ambassador" (he shot an accusatory look at Retief) "to report that the Woomy has been laid to rest forever, and you have nipped in the bud, literally, the most nefarious scheme since the Groaci attempted to flog plastic weenies to the Low Fulese!"

"I did, hey?" Nipcheese purred. "Tell me about it, Ben. Now, you boys sit down and take a cigar, you look tired. I thought you were just out for a spin in the countryside."

"If Your Excellency will recall," Magnan ventured, "I'm sure you will confirm that I was dispatched to look into certain apparent irregularities in the Groaci timber-survey project."

"To be sure," Nipcheese nodded. "A matter of no great moment, Ben; don't be anxious about admitting you failed to find any evidence of chicanery."

"Ah, but I *did*," Magnan intoned. As he spoke, he sidled toward the desk and inobtrusively deposited a pinch of pale pink dust on the tip of the next-up cigar in the ambassadorial dispenser, which article His Excellency picked up a moment later, puffing it alight. He smiled beatifically, exhaled lingeringly, and said,

"It occurs to me, Ben, that you and Retief have been working rather hard; need a vacation, eh? Just speak up—no nonsense about my colleague Ambassador Whisp being up to something, mind you. Where would you like to go? I can arrange transport on a Corps courier vessel due in next week.

"Actually," he went on, "I've been thinking of a bit of a sabbatical myself. You fellows wouldn't mind if I came along?"

"Gosh, sir," Magnan gobbled. "We'd be honored! By the way, Mr. Ambassador," he continued, making use of his verbal momentum, "about the Cord—"

"I know, I know," Nipcheese cut him off with an upraised palm. "She's getting a bit shabby, rather embarrassing to you to be seen in her, I suppose, but I've been thinking for some time I should send her in to Frank's Former Fashions in the Belt and have her re-restored."

"Capital notion, sir!" Magnan cried. "Not that she isn't an elegant equipage as she is, of course."

"Picture it, boys," Nipcheese urged, his expression rapt: "All new leather inside, fifteen coats of lacquer, and all new triple-plated chrome. And now, at least I'll search out those obscure parts that I never succeeded in finding for the original job: bud vase, dash clock with key wind, original floor mats, radiator mascot, trunk rack and maybe even a welled fender for a sidemount!"

"Entrancing!" Magnan agreed. "And the special equipment to make the fusion cell sound like the original Continental eight-cylinder internal combustion engine, too!"

"The original 231V was absolutely silent, Ben," Nipcheese reproved gently. "Still, your principle was sound, if you'll forgive a pun. Sound: sound, get it?" Nipcheese cackled as he rose from his hip-u-matic chair and came around the desk to clap a hand each to the nearest shoulder of Magnan and Retief, still puffing at his cigar, which he now laid in an ashtray.

"Damn fine smoke," he commented. "Makes a man feel twenty years younger. Let's go find a quaint little place where a man can have a few beers and relax. We've *all* been working too hard!"

"What did you put in that mixture?" Retief asked Magnan quietly.

"I call it my Number One, Jimmy," Magnan explained. "Farf-weed base, laced with a few drops of Compound 297 and just a pinch of google-berry pollen. I hope I didn't overdo it."

"Not at all, Ben," Retief reassured his colleague, "In fact, I foresee the dawning of a new day in bureaucratic life."

Humming a little tune, Howard Nipcheese led the way to the Sturdy Rogue, one of the more raffish dives on Happy Street, where he at once went to the phone booth. Returning to the corner table, he reported:

"Old Whisp is out, attending a convention of Do-gooders as Guest of Honor. But never mind, I'll see him tomorrow at the Inter-Being Chumship meeting: meantime you fellas can brief me on what the five-eyed little wretch has been getting his sticky fingers in this time. If I can't parlay this coup into a Career Ambassadorship I don't know Mrs. Nipcheese's boy Howie."

WE'RE LOOKING FOR
TROUBLE

Well, feedback, anyway. Baen Books endeavors to publish only the best in science fiction and fantasy—but we need you to tell us whether we're doing it right. Why not let us know? We'll award a Baen Books gift certificate worth $100 (plus a copy of our catalog) to the reader who best tells us what he or she likes about Baen Books—and where we could do better. We reserve the right to quote any or all of you. Contest closes December 31, 1987. All letters should be addressed to Baen Books, 260 Fifth Avenue, New York, N.Y. 10001.

At the same time, ask about the Baen Book Club—buy five books, get another five free! For information, send a self-addressed, stamped envelope. For a copy of our catalog, enclose one dollar as well.